From *The Lions of Lucerne* to *Full Black*, Brad Thor delivers "high-voltage entertainment reminiscent of Robert Ludlum" (*Library Journal*). While keeping readers riveted with heart-pounding suspense, the #1 *New York Times* bestselling author is also "changing the scope of the espionage novel in today's world" (*Tampa Tribune*).

Praise for Brad Thor's explosive new Delta Force series

THE ATHENA PROJECT

"Think 007 in stilettos. . . . The thriller genre just got shaken and stirred."
—Sandra Brown, #1 *New York Times* bestselling author of *Tough Customer*

"Riveting and addicting prose on every page. . . ."
—Bookreporter.com

"There's no wasted motion in a Brad Thor novel, just a cool, commanding professionalism that delivers . . . in spades." —Breitbart.com

"Fun, fast, and will suck you into the sequels."
—Blackfive.net

"Pulse-pounding." —*New York Post*

"Thor nails it. A thriller both men and women will love."
—James Rollins, *New York Times* bestselling author of *The Devil Colony*

This title is also available from Simon & Schuster Audio and as an eBook

TAKEDOWN

"High-octane . . . crisp and cinematic, with . . . gun-blazing, gut-busting action." —*The Tennessean*

"Exciting . . . frightening. . . . [A] masterpiece."
—*Midwest Book Review*

BLOWBACK

One of NPR's top 100 "Killer Thrillers" of all time!

"Haunting, high-voltage. . . . One of the best thriller writers in the business." —*Ottawa Citizen*

"An incredible international thriller. . . . Riveting and superior." —Brunei Press Syndicate

STATE OF THE UNION

"Frighteningly real." —*Ottawa Citizen*

"[A] blistering, testosterone-fueled espionage thriller."
—*Publishers Weekly*

PATH OF THE ASSASSIN

"The action is relentless, the pacing sublime."
—*Ottawa Citizen*

THE LIONS OF LUCERNE

"Fast-paced, scarily authentic—I just couldn't put it down." —Vince Flynn

"A hot read for a winter night. . . . Bottom line: *Lions* roars." —*People*

ALSO BY BRAD THOR

BRAD THOR

THE ATHENA PROJECT

A THRILLER

POCKET STAR BOOKS

New York   London   Toronto   Sydney   New Delhi

Pocket Star Books
A Division of Simon & Schuster, Inc.
1230 Avenue of the Americas
New York, NY 10020

This book is a work of fiction. Names, characters, places, and incidents either are products of the author's imagination or are used fictitiously. Any resemblance to actual events or locales or persons, living or dead, is entirely coincidental.

First Pocket Star Books paperback edition November 2011

POCKET STAR BOOKS and colophon are registered trademarks of Simon & Schuster, Inc.

For information about special discounts for bulk purchases, please contact Simon & Schuster Special Sales at 1-866-506-1949 or business@simonandschuster.com.

The Simon & Schuster Speakers Bureau can bring authors to your live event. For more information or to book an event, contact the Simon & Schuster Speakers Bureau at 1-866-248-3049 or visit our website at www.simonspeakers.com.

Cover design by Jae Song

Manufactured in the United States of America

10   9   8   7   6   5   4   3   2   1

ISBN 978-1-4391-9297-9
ISBN 978-1-4391-9305-1 (ebook)

"We make war so that we may live in peace."

—*Aristotle*

All of the science in this novel is
based on reality.

THE
ATHENA
PROJECT

PROLOGUE

The sound of suppressed gunfire in the narrow fuselage was drowned out by the roar of the slipstream coupled with the plane's engines. The soldiers accompanying the crates of documents back to Berlin lay dead and dying, their uniforms soaked with blood. Twenty-two-year-old Jacqueline Marceau ejected the spent magazine from her MP40 and inserted a fresh one.

Keeping an eye trained on the cockpit door, she shackled her prisoner, then retrieved her parachute and struggled into it.

She pulled a cap over her head and tucked her long blond hair inside so it wouldn't whip her face on the way down. Next came goggles and a pair of leather gloves. It might have been summertime on the ground, but at this altitude it was bitterly cold.

She gave her gear one final check and then helped her prisoner to his feet. "Time to move, Herr Stiegler."

The SS officer tried to fight back, but Marceau was ready for him. She slammed her weapon into his groin and as he doubled over, wrapped a webbing harness around his torso.

Stepping behind him, Marceau grabbed his chin and yanked his head back, causing him to stand up straighter. As he did, she ran the two final straps between his legs and clipped them in to the back of the harness.

"I hope you're not afraid of heights," she quipped, shoving the man toward the Arado's rear loading ramp.

Displeased with his pace, Marceau jabbed him in the kidney with the MP40 and told him, *"Mach schnell!"*

Stiegler tried to call out to the cockpit for help, but it was no use. Marceau gave him another punch with her weapon and drove him to the edge of the ramp.

The Arado 232 might have been the Luftwaffe's general-purpose transport aircraft, but this one was armed like a Messerschmitt. The navigator operated a 13 mm machine gun in the nose, the radio operator a 20 mm gun in a rotating turret on the roof, and the loadmaster—now deceased—another 13 mm gun from above the cargo bay at the rear ramp. They'd be floating ducks until they hit the ground and were able to take cover. The best thing they could do was get out before anyone knew they were gone.

At the ramp, Marceau looked for the wiring that led to the cockpit and the indicator lamp that would light up as soon as she opened the hydraulically powered clamshell doors. She fished a diagram from her pocket and tried to zero in on the right wire to cut. That's when Stiegler tried to overpower her once more.

Using his shoulder as a ram, he charged right into her, toppling her over backward. Marceau lost her grip on her weapon and threw her hands out, looking for something to grab as she fell. What she found was the cargo door release.

A red light began flashing as the doors started to open. Marceau was about to let a curse fly when the red light was obscured by something else—Stiegler's head snapping forward right toward the bridge of her nose.

Marceau moved, but not fast enough. Stiegler's head glanced off the side of hers, sending a searing bolt of pain through her skull. What was worse was that he was on top of her now. Nearly seven inches taller and almost twice her weight, he definitely had the advantage, even in manacles.

She tried to bring her knee up to get him in the groin again, but he had her legs and arms pinned. He knew he had won, and his lips began to curl into a smile. Marceau relaxed her body and turned her head away. The message could not have been any clearer. *I give up.*

Stiegler bent down, his mouth hovering inches away from her face, and she could smell the red wine he had been consuming before they took off from Paris. With the thick parachute between her and the floor, she felt like a turtle that had been flipped onto its back.

"You have been a very bad girl," he began to whisper to her. That's when she struck.

Whipping her head to the side, she grabbed as much of Stiegler's right ear in her mouth as she could, bit down, and tore.

The SS officer screamed in pain and scrambled to get off the twenty-two-year-old.

Blood gushed from the side of his head, down his neck, and onto his coat. Marceau spat a portion of Stiegler's ear out and leaped to her feet. As she did, she was greeted with a hail of bullets.

Hitting the deck, she rolled and recovered her weapon. Raising it to engage the threat, she saw that the copilot had emerged from the cockpit, most likely in response to the cargo doors having been engaged. He had emptied the magazine of his Luger and was hastily trying to insert a new one when Marceau put a tight group of rounds into his chest and he fell to the floor.

The navigator would be out next, followed by the radio operator. It was past time to bail out.

Rushing over to Stiegler, she clipped herself to the back of his harness and began dragging him toward the rear of the plane. When he tried to swing his head backward and connect with her face, she slammed her MP40 into what remained of his right ear.

The pain must have been intense. She felt the man's knees buckle, and she almost lost her balance trying to keep him upright.

Dragging Stiegler back to the cargo doors, Marceau activated the ramp and watched as it slowly began to lower.

One of the dead soldiers at the rear of the plane had two stick grenades tucked inside his belt. With Stiegler still woozy from the blow, Marceau planted her feet, then carefully reached down and withdrew both grenades.

Hobbling back to the ramp with her captive, she could now see daylight behind the plane. It was maddening how long the ramp lowering process took. She couldn't afford to wait any longer. Pushing Stiegler forward, she began walking him out onto it.

Once there, she gave the briefcase a final tug to make sure it was still firmly attached to his wrist. Ten seconds more and the ramp would be down far enough for them to jump. After that, all that mattered was that her primary chute open. With the auxiliary chute, or Belly Wart as it was known, sandwiched between them, there was no way it would deploy if she needed it. She'd have to cut him loose and let him fall to his death, which wasn't an option.

As far as she knew, a "tandem" jump, as she had termed it, had never been done before, but her mission was to bring back both Stiegler *and* the briefcase he had chained to his wrist. It had been considered suicidal. In fact, no one in her organization actually believed it could be done. That had only made Marceau more determined to succeed.

With less than five seconds left, she inched Stiegler forward. It was then that she suddenly heard a shout from behind.

"Halt!"

Marceau spun her captive around just in time to see the navigator, armed with an MP40 like hers, bring his weapon up and fire.

Bullets ricocheted and punched holes along the fuselage. They also punched holes in Josef Stiegler.

Marceau felt him begin to slump forward. As strong as she was, there was no way she could hold him up and return fire.

The navigator advanced. He was using shorter, more controlled bursts. Almost all of the rounds were now hitting Stiegler. Marceau dragged him backward, only feet from the edge of the ramp.

Stiegler's body went limp and the dead weight caused her to stumble. When she did, she caught not one, but two rounds through her right shoulder, and her weapon clattered to the deck. There was no time to pick it up.

Ignoring the pain, she wrapped her arm around Stiegler's midsection and continued to drag him. *How was she not at the end of the ramp already? How much farther could it be?*

Stiegler's legs finally gave out and his body folded in half. The only thing keeping him up was Marceau's remaining strength, coupled with her intense force of will.

The navigator looked at Marceau and smiled. It was the same smile Stiegler had given her. Marceau smiled back as the man leveled his weapon, steadied his aim, and pulled the trigger.

Whether it was a lack of training, the noise from the engines, or the heat of combat, the navigator had failed to notice that his weapon was empty.

Raising the stick grenades, their base caps already unscrewed, Marceau put the priming cords between her teeth. The navigator's smile instantly disappeared and the color drained from his face.

Jacqueline Marceau yanked both cords at once and tossed the navigator a wink as she threw the grenades over his head into the interior of the plane. She then stepped backward with Stiegler and leaped off the ramp.

As the Luftwaffe plane erupted into a billowing fireball, Marceau deployed her chute and steered herself and her captive toward a long, green valley dotted with a handful of cows and a small chalet.

CHAPTER 1

The heat was unbearable. Ryan Naylor was drenched with sweat and the butt of his Glock pistol chafed against the small of his back. Some might have said it served him right. Doctors shouldn't be carrying weapons; even here. But Ryan Naylor wasn't just a doctor.

As the thirty-two-year-old surgeon slapped another mosquito trying to drain the blood from his neck, he wondered if he was being led into a trap.

"How much farther?" he asked in Spanish.

"Not much," said one of the men in front of him. It was the same answer he'd been given repeatedly since they'd gotten out of their Land Cruisers to push deeper into the jungle on foot.

In the canopy of trees above, multiple species of birds and monkeys called down, upset at the alien presence.

Half of Naylor's Camelback was already empty, but he'd yet to see any of the Guaranis he was traveling with raise their canteens.

The men marched in small-unit fashion, keeping five yards between each other in case of ambush. They carried rifles that looked like relics from the Gran Chaco War of the 1930s. How they managed to keep them from rusting in the oppressive humidity was beyond him. But as he had learned early on, the Guaranis had a much different way of doing just about everything.

Naylor had been sent to Paraguay by the U.S. military to gather intelligence. He was based out of Ciudad del Este, Spanish for City of the East and capital of the Alto Paraná region.

Begun as a small village originally named after a Paraguayan dictator, it had grown to a bustling city of over 250,000 and was an illicit paradise, with trafficking in everything from pirated software and DVDs to drugs, weapons, and money laundering. But there was something else that had attracted the U.S. military's interest. It was also home to a large Middle Eastern community.

Upward of twenty thousand of the city's inhabitants were either themselves from or descendants of people from places like Syria, Lebanon, the West Bank, and Gaza. The city even boasted two Arabic-language television stations.

Set against the backdrop of Paraguay's corrupt government, Ciudad del Este's Middle Eastern community provided the perfect human camouflage for transient Arab men involved in Islamic terrorism.

Organizations such as al Qaeda, Hamas, Hezbollah, Islamic Jihad, Al Gamaat, and Al Islamiyya had all set up shop there. The Hezbollah operation alone was believed to have sent more than fifty million dollars back to the Middle East. In the remote deserts and jungles of the shared border area of Paraguay, Argentina, and Brazil were multiple terror training camps, more extensive and professional than anything ever seen in Afghanistan or Sudan.

Techniques for building IEDs and explosively formed projectiles were taught and perfected daily with instructors from the Iranian Revolutionary Guard, Syrian secret service, and Libyan intelligence service whose operatives rotated in and out as "visiting professors."

As if that wasn't enough to worry American authorities, Sunni and Shia extremist groups had joined forces to work and train together in the region.

A team of over forty FBI agents had been permanently encamped in Ciudad del Este to map out and dismantle the business dealings of the terrorist organizations, but it was the U.S. military, in particular Army intelligence, that had been charged with locating the terrorist training camps and gathering as much information about them as possible. That's where Ryan Naylor came in.

Born and raised in New Haven, Connecticut, Naylor had served in the National Guard and attended college on the GI Bill. The Army then paid for him to attend medical school where he trained as a trauma surgeon. Like most surgeons, Naylor had a healthy ego, but it had never blossomed into arrogance. He was actually a very well-grounded doctor.

He stood a little over six feet tall, had brown hair, green eyes, and a handsome face. His mother had been of Dutch descent. He never knew his father.

After completing his residency, he'd pursued a fellowship in plastic surgery. He wanted to do more than simply repair damage, he wanted to make people normal, make them whole again. During his fellowship, he'd found himself drawn to facial surgery, in particular fixing cleft lips and cleft palates. Whether or not the Army felt this was a waste of his time and their money, they never said. All they cared about was that he complete his training and report for duty.

Having done tours in Iraq and Afghanistan, he fully expected to be sent back to a field hospital, but the Army had other plans for him. They wanted Naylor to become a missionary.

He spent the next year in what he euphemistically referred to as "Spy School." His high-school Spanish was taken to a level he never would have thought himself capable of, he learned to pilot a variety of light aircraft, the ins and outs of tradecraft, how to conduct deep reconnaissance assignments, radio and satellite communications, and at night, he attended church and Bible study classes.

When his training was complete and he was activated, Naylor volunteered for a Christian medical organization with missions scattered throughout South America. One of their locations was in Ciudad del Este.

There were very few ways an American could get far enough into the Paraguayan sticks to gather effective intelligence. Posing as a doctor was one of the best. By delivering medical care to remote communities, Naylor was in a position to build effective relationships with the people most likely to hear and know about terrorist activities. And that was exactly what he had been doing. He had quickly developed an exceptional human network throughout most of the villages he served.

Out of the handful of operatives the United States had working in Paraguay, Naylor produced the best reports. Not only did he bring back grade A material from the field every time, but his sources continued to feed high-quality intelligence back to him when he was in Ciudad del Este.

When the man walking in front of him suddenly stopped, Naylor, whose mind had been wandering, chastised himself for not staying focused. Even though the jungle was monotonous and the heat stifling, it was no excuse to get lazy and let his guard down. He knew better.

Two men at the head of their column were having a discussion. In the distance, Naylor thought he could hear a river. Breaking ranks, he walked up to them. "What's going on?" he asked in Spanish.

"The others don't want to go any farther," said one of the men. "I will take you the rest of the way myself."

"Wait a second. Why?"

"Because they're afraid."

"Afraid of what? Sickness? Whatever the people there died from?"

The older man shook his head. "From what we were told, the people there did not die from sickness."

Naylor had no idea what the people had died from. All he knew was that a villager had stumbled across several dead bodies in a remote part of the jungle, a place no one lived in. The bodies belonged to foreigners, the man had said. Shortly after recounting his tale he had stopped talking. It was almost as if he had slipped into shock, though some sort of catatonic state was more likely. Naylor wasn't a psychiatrist, but whatever the man had seen had deeply disturbed him.

The area they were now in was rumored to have housed an al Qaeda training camp at one point, though no one could ever say exactly where. Add to that a report of "dead foreigners," and that was all Naylor had needed to hear. He had no idea what had so spooked the villager who had stumbled upon the bodies, but his interest had been piqued, and once his mind was set on something, it was impossible to dissuade him from it.

The other men of their party made camp, while Ryan and the old man trudged deeper into the jungle.

Forty-five minutes later, the soft earth beneath their feet turned to what Naylor at first thought were rocks and then realized were actually pavers. Though choked with weeds, it appeared that they were on some sort of long-abandoned road.

They followed the path as it wound down into a wide gulley. There were enormous stones, some twenty feet high and fifteen feet across in places. Some appeared to have been worked with tools. Despite their having been eroded by time and the elements, Naylor could make out letters or strange symbols of some sort on them.

Ryan reached out to touch one of the monoliths, but the old man caught his wrist and pulled his hand back. "The stones are evil," he said. "Don't touch them."

"Where are we?" Ryan asked.

"We are close," replied the old man as he let go of Naylor and continued. "Close to the dead."

The gulley was unusually cool. Naylor hadn't

noticed it at first, but the temperature had to be at least fifteen to twenty degrees cooler. The trees on the ridges above them were full enough that the thick jungle canopy remained intact. Even if somebody in an airplane knew what he was looking for, this little valley would be impossible to spot.

Wildly overgrown, it stretched on for a hundred yards before leveling out and being swallowed back up again by the jungle. Naylor kept his eyes peeled for any sign of recent human habitation, but there were no remains of campfires, no shelters, no refuse, nothing. It was also eerily quiet. He'd been so focused on the road and then the tall stones that he hadn't noticed that the jungle around them was now completely silent. The screaming birds and monkeys had completely disappeared.

"This way," the old man said, pointing off to the right, into the jungle.

Naylor didn't bother responding, he simply nodded and followed behind.

They walked until the pavers ended and kept going. Ryan wondered if this had once been the site of some ancient civilization. He had his digital camera with him and he made a mental note to snap some pictures of the monoliths on their way back. They would add color to his next report.

As Naylor swung his pack over to one shoulder to fish out his camera, the old man stopped and held up his hand. This time, Ryan was paying attention and he came to an immediate stop. He knew better than to speak.

The old man peered into the distance and then said, "Do you see it?"

Naylor moved up alongside him and looked. He

could see shapes, but he wasn't exactly sure what he was looking at. "Is that a jeep?"

The old man nodded. "And something else. Something bigger."

All of the Muslims were known by a single term among the Guaranis. "Arabs?" asked Naylor.

The old man shrugged and moved slowly forward. Though the gun had been rubbing his skin raw for hours, Ryan reached back anyway to make sure it was still there.

The closer they got to the objects, the slower the old man moved. They appeared to have been camouflaged. The hairs on the back of Ryan's neck were starting to stand up.

The first shape turned out to be a truck. The old man raised his index finger to his lips and motioned for Naylor to remain quiet. Ryan didn't need to be reminded.

As they neared, Naylor could see that the vehicle hadn't been intentionally camouflaged at all. It had been consumed by the jungle.

It was old. At least fifty years. Maybe more. It looked military. As Naylor studied the truck, the old man moved off to the nearby jeep.

Naylor climbed up onto the running board and looked inside. It had been picked clean. By who or what, he had no idea. He worked his way to the front in the hope of discovering where the truck was from, or to whom it had belonged.

The glass of the gauges was spiderwebbed with cracks, the interior of the cab rusting away. There wasn't enough sunlight to make out any specific detail.

Naylor unslung his pack so he could grab a flashlight and pull out his camera.

He looked up to check on the old man, who had already moved on from the jeep and toward something else.

Ryan removed his flashlight and put it in his mouth as he searched for his camera. There was thunder in the distance. As he heard the rumble, he glanced at his watch. Every day in the jungle the rain came at almost the same time. He looked back up for the old man but didn't see him. *He couldn't have gone far.*

Finding his camera, Ryan zipped his backpack. He positioned himself where he could get the best shot and powered up the camera.

He took his first picture and the automatic flash kicked in, brilliantly illuminating the interior of the cab. Moving a bit to his left, he had readied his next shot when there was a flash of lightning. It was followed by a scream.

Ryan ran toward the sound of the old man. His screams were like nothing he had ever heard. They weren't screams of pain. They were screams of abject terror.

He tore through the jungle with his pistol in his hand and his lungs burning. As he ran, the screams intensified. When Naylor found him, he couldn't figure out what had so frightened him until he followed the old man's eyes off and to the right. The minute he saw them, he understood why the man was so terrified.

Then Ryan saw something else entirely, and that was when his own blood ran cold.

CHAPTER 2

VENICE, ITALY
Friday, Two Days Later

Megan Rhodes studied the Palazzo Bianchi through the scope mounted on her LaRue sniper rifle. "You've still got two at the front door and two on the roof," she said via the wireless bone microphone/earpiece in her left ear. "Plus three dock boys helping guests on and off their boats as they arrive out front."

"Roger that," came the voice of Gretchen Casey over the radio. "Jules, are you all set?"

"I'm in position," said Julie Ericsson, "but I still want to know why every time we do an op involving a social function, I'm responsible for transport."

"Because you can't tell a shrimp fork from a salad fork," replied Alex Cooper, who was closing in on the palazzo from beneath the water next to Casey.

"That's cute," replied Ericsson. "You know what, Coop? Fork you."

"Easy, everybody," Casey cautioned her team.

"Let's make sure we're focused and that we keep everything simple, just like we rehearsed."

"How close are you to the entry point?" asked Rhodes.

"Thirty meters," said Casey. Like the other two women, she and Cooper had been trained at the U.S. Army's Special Forces Combat Diver Qualification Course in Key West Florida.

They were wearing dry suits and using closed-circuit Draegar Lar V "rebreathing" devices, which recycled their spent CO_2 and prevented any bubbles from rising to the surface and giving them away.

Their DSI M48 Supermasks had integrated Aquacom communications that allowed them to talk with their other team members. Underwater propulsion devices developed for the U.S. military, called Seabob US7s, pulled them silently toward their objective with zero emissions. The high-tech water scooters, built near the Mercedes and Porsche factories in Stuttgart, Germany, came complete with sonar location technology, onboard navigation, speeds in excess of thirty miles an hour, and four hours of run time. They were among the hottest, and most expensive pieces of military equipment the United States had recently fielded. Nothing was being spared for this operation.

Fifty-two-year-old Nino Bianchi was a black-market arms merchant. No matter what the conflict or the customer's ideology, he could procure almost any weapons system and have it delivered anywhere in the world. When he provided the plastic explosives used in a bus bombing in Rome that killed more than twenty Americans, the United

States decided to do something about him. And they had just the right group to do it.

America's primary counterterrorism unit, the First Special Forces Operational Detachment-Delta, also known as Delta Force, Combat Applications Group (CAG), or simply "The Unit" to its members, was created in 1977 by Army colonel Charles Beckwith. It was based on the British Special Air Service model and was designed to serve as a highly specialized force capable of carrying out direct-action and counterterrorism assignments anywhere in the world.

Divided into three operating squadrons (A, B, and C), the squadrons were then subdivided into troops and could be broken down into progressively smaller teams as their missions required. The smallest team normally consisted of four operators and was referred to as a patrol, or a "brick."

The Unit's operators excelled in a wide array of clandestine operations, including hostage rescue, counterterrorism, and counterinsurgency, as well as strikes inside hostile, off-limits, or politically sensitive areas.

Delta was headquartered in a remote section of North Carolina's Fort Bragg. There, "behind the fence" as it was called, no expense was spared in training the world's most elite warriors. The facility housed massive climbing walls, extensive shoot houses for close-quarters battle, sniper ranges, an Olympic-sized swimming pool, a dive tank, and multiple other training ranges and facilities that strove to anticipate the kinds of environments where operators could be called upon to deploy at a moment's notice.

Besides the three operational squadrons, there

were an additional nine detachments charged with providing operators with every form of imaginable support—from intelligence, training, aviation, and medical care to the most sophisticated weaponry and technology in the U.S. military's arsenal.

Never content to rest on its laurels, Delta was always exploring new ways to make itself better, deadlier, and more efficient. Taking a cue from the success of its Operational Support Detachment, which often used women to gather intelligence in advance of Delta missions, it asked one of its most aggressive and forward-thinking questions. *Why not train and field female operators?*

It was an exceedingly good idea. In fact, it was such a good idea that many within Delta's ranks were surprised that it hadn't been pursued earlier.

Women normally attracted less attention in the field than men, and when they did, it was often of a completely different kind. Give a woman a dog's leash, one person said, and she could wander around anywhere. Put a woman in a car with a baby seat and she could sit all day surveilling a target without attracting much notice. Women were welcomed in places men were not and could get away with things men could never dream of. A female operative capable of kicking in your door, shooting you in the head, or cuffing you and stuffing you in a trunk was the last thing most of the bad guys would ever expect.

With the approval of the Army's Special Operations Command under which Delta was chartered, a group of operatives agreed to become recruiters. At first they looked within the armed forces for highly skilled, highly motivated women. There were some, but not nearly enough to fully meet the objectives that had been set for the all-female squadron they were creating, codenamed the Athena Project. Thus, the recruiters were forced to look outside the military.

They were searching for intelligent, self-confident, polished women who could blend in and disappear into foreign cultures. They needed to be athletic and highly competitive. They needed to hate to lose, because Delta Operators never lost; they won at all costs. The women needed to be driven in such a way that success had become part of their DNA. They also needed to be attractive.

It was a fact of life that people reacted differently to others based upon how they looked. If the female operatives were attractive, their beauty disqualified them as a threat and there was no end to what they could achieve. Men would do things they shouldn't just to be near an attractive woman, extending opportunities and even information that would never be offered to their male counterparts. Men would try to impress them by bragging and inviting them to see things normally off-limits. In essence, men could often be counted on to act stupidly around an attractive woman. And those who didn't could very likely be counted on to underestimate a woman, especially an attractive one.

As the Delta recruiters cast their nets outside the military, they began haunting high-end female athletic events. They trolled for potential candidates at triathlons, winter and summer X Games, universities, and U.S. Olympic training facilities. The sport didn't matter as much as whether a candidate possessed the essential characteristics.

The selection and assessment process was extremely difficult. Many women didn't make the cut. Standards, though, were never dropped just to fill out the ranks.

The women who did pass the selection and assessment phases were exceptional, none more so than the brick of four women about to snatch Nino Bianchi from his extremely fortified home. They were all fiercely determined, fiercely loyal, and fiercely competitive, but other than that, they couldn't have been more different.

Alex Cooper was the twenty-eight-year-old, biracial daughter of an Ethiopian mother and an American father who owned a small restaurant in Atlanta. After high school, she went on to attend the University of Arizona as a communications major. There she became attracted to ultramarathon running—a sport that saw competitors in events racing over twenty-four hours, several days, or even thousand-mile distances. The sport suited her unwavering, granitelike determination.

She was a quiet person by nature, and her boisterous teammates were always trying to get her to come "out of her shell." They needled her constantly about being too reserved, too serious. She could be too hard on herself, and they saw it as their job to keep things in perspective for her. And as much as they teased her, they all knew how deep her still waters ran. Cooper was an outstanding operator.

So was thirty-year-old Julie Ericsson, a triathlete who had grown up on the big island of Hawaii and had studied multiple subjects at the University of Hawaii. Her father ran fishing charters, while her mother was a schoolteacher. Julie, like Alex, was about five-foot-nine. Though she was of Spanish and Welsh descent, her parents' genetics combined in such a way that she had an exotic, Brazilian look about her.

She was the epitome of grace under fire and was easily the most organized member of the team. She had a real eye for detail, with equipment and logistics being her specialty. If the team needed anything done, Julie was the person they always turned to.

Megan Rhodes was the quintessential "American" girl; blond-haired and blue-eyed. The thirty-one-year-old grew up in the Chicago suburbs. Her father was a cop and her mother passed away when she was very young. Rhodes attended college at the University of Illinois, where she continued a successful high-school athletic career as a competitive swimmer. Back in her teenage years, her five-foot-eleven height, as well as her striking Nordic features, had earned her the nickname "Viking Princess," which had stuck with her all the way to Delta. It made those who knew her laugh. Megan was every bit the Viking, but there wasn't an ounce of princess in her. She endured the worst situations any assignment could throw at them without ever complaining. A stone-cold killer when she had to be, Megan Rhodes's glass was always half full. She was always the first one to volunteer to go into a dangerous situation and was also an extremely talented interrogator.

The final woman on the team was Gretchen Casey. "Gretch," as she was known by her teammates, was Texas tough. She had grown up in East Texas and had attended Texas A&M, where she was a prelaw student. Her dad was a former Army Ranger who owned a gunsmithing business and her mother was a semisuccessful artist. Gretchen's father had her shooting from the day she could first hold a rifle. Her love of cross-country and shooting had led her to become a world-class summer biathlete who had been picked up by the U.S. Olympic Team. She competed for a while, but gave it up when she fell in love with a hedge fund manager in New York.

The relationship was good, for a while. Gretchen secured her law degree at NYU, but when she discovered that the hedge fund manager was running around on her, the Texas girl lost her taste not only for him, but for the Big Apple and the law as well.

Not really knowing what she wanted to do, she began training again and picked up her career as a summer biathlete. She was eight months into it when a Delta Force recruiter spotted her and made her an offer that sounded like it might be fun.

At five-foot-six, she was the smallest of the bunch, but height had nothing to do with her leadership abilities, which were exceptional and which had seen her put in charge of the group.

As Casey and Cooper anchored their scooters on the canal bottom, Casey said over the radio, "We're at the entry point."

Ericsson, who was cradling a small device in her lap that looked like an iPad or eReader of some sort, pressed a button and said, "Grafting a clean loop to the cameras in the boat garage now."

"Let us know when we're good to go."

"Ten seconds."

When the live security footage had been replaced by the team's repeating loop, Ericsson said, "It's all yours."

CHAPTER 3

The entry point was Nino Bianchi's boat garage. But getting in wouldn't simply be a matter of swimming under the doors and popping up on the other side. Bianchi took his security much too seriously to allow that sort of thing to happen.

The brightly painted wooden doors, which looked like any others along the Grand Canal, hid two sheets of titanium, three inches thick, descending several feet below the water level. The titanium doors came to rest upon a wall of metal bars that went all the way down and were bolted to the bedrock beneath the canal bottom.

Under the murky water, Cooper and Casey unloaded their gear. When they were ready, Casey said over the radio, "I'm going to wrap the bars."

"Roger that," replied Rhodes, who was concealed in the window of an apartment across the canal. She adjusted her face against the cheek pad of her rifle and prepared to take Bianchi's guards if they noticed what was going on below them.

Gripping the bars, Casey inched herself up as close to the surface as she dared. Though it was evening and the water cloudy, there was still a lot of ambient light spilling onto the surface. If she was seen, that would be the end of the entire operation.

Identifying the bars that they'd be working on, she wrapped them as tightly as she could with Ti wire to keep them from spreading.

Using the bars to guide herself back to the bottom, she wrapped the two bars again with wire halfway down.

Rejoining Cooper, she said, "Bars are wrapped. Let's spread 'em."

Cooper positioned a small, submersible hydraulic jack with titanium tubular extension poles between the two bars and went to work, silently creating an opening big enough for them to swim through.

They checked in repeatedly with Rhodes to make sure no one up on the dock had any idea what was going on. Each time, Rhodes replied, "You're still good to go."

After the bars had been spread far enough apart, Casey rose halfway to the surface to make sure that there was no sign of the breach. So far, so good. The wire had held.

As Cooper packed the jack back into her scooter, Casey unloaded two waterproof dry bags from hers. When they were ready, they swam through the opening, with Casey in the lead.

They quietly broke the surface of the water inside the boat garage, they came up only to eye level and took a long scan of the dimly lit room to make sure no one else was there. From what they could tell, they were alone and unnoticed.

Suspended above them, in order to keep its hull clean, was Bianchi's twenty-nine-foot 1965 Riva Super Aquarama runabout.

Casey flashed Cooper the thumbs-up and they swam to a corroded ladder at the front of the slip.

Cooper climbed out first. After removing her mask and peeling back her hood, she took off her rebreather, reached down, and accepted the two dry bags from Casey. Quickly, the two women undressed.

They wore next to nothing beneath their dry suits. Unzipping the larger of the two bags, Casey pulled out Cooper's cocktail dress and handed it to her, along with a pair of heels, jewelry, and makeup. They were followed by an inside-the-thigh garter holster, and a 9 mm Taurus "Slim" pistol.

Casey fished out her dress, heels, makeup, weapon, and holster and starting getting dressed as well.

"I hope you're right about this guy wanting to show off his boat," said Cooper.

Casey stepped into her dress. "You know what they say. The only difference between men and boys . . ."

"I know. The size of their toys."

"Don't worry. He'll want to show us his toy."

Cooper smiled. "But what if he doesn't?"

Casey turned her back so her teammate could zip her up. "Then we'll improvise. We'll tell him we want to go skinny dipping."

"In Venetian canal water?"

"Lex, you worry too much. Trust me, if we do this right, he'll follow us anywhere."

"And if we don't, this guy is going to do everything he can to make sure we don't leave this building alive."

Casey shook her head. "Won't happen."

Cooper was easily the most serious member of the team. She was a planner and didn't care much for improvisation. "Have you always been this sure of yourself?" she asked.

Handing her one of the miniature earpieces, Casey replied, "No, but I am this sure about men. Are you ready to go?"

"I'm guessing you don't have a hair dryer in that bag, do you?"

"No hair dryer," said Casey as she filled the larger bag with their dive equipment, weighted it down with a couple of items from the garage, dropped it into the water, and watched it sink out of view. "Dry suits may keep you bone dry, but the hoods are hell on your hair. Just run your fingers through it. You'll be fine."

"Easy for you to say," responded Cooper as Casey searched for a place to hide the smaller dry bag. "You always look great." In addition to being the most serious member of the team, Alex Cooper seemed to be the most critical of her own good looks.

The tarp for the Riva had been set in the corner of the garage, and Casey decided to hide the bag underneath. It contained everything the two women would need for their exfiltration: two masks, two waterproof, red-lens flashlights, and small "spare air" supplemental oxygen bottles with built-in mouthpieces for each of them. There were also restraints and a "spare air" bottle for Bianchi.

The plan was to get him back to this point, get him restrained, and get him into the water as quickly as possible. Once they had him below the surface, they would retrieve the rest of their gear, fire up their scooters, and get out of there as quickly as possible.

Casey pushed her tiny earpiece transmitter into her ear. It was about the size of a pencil eraser, and once it was in place it was virtually impossible to detect.

They tested the signal strength between them, and then outside to Rhodes and Ericsson. Satisfied that everything was ready, Casey smoothed over her rather revealing cocktail dress and said, "Okay ladies, it's showtime."

CHAPTER 4

S miling, their arms interlinked, Gretchen and Alex walked into Nino Bianchi's extravagant party.

The only thing that outshone the richly decorated palazzo was the richly decorated guests. Fit and tanned, they wore bespoke tuxedos, designer dresses, and tens of millions of dollars' worth of jewelry. Neither Casey nor Cooper had ever seen this many good-looking people in one room before. It looked like a casting call for some high-end European soap opera.

"Let's get something to drink," said Casey as she steered her teammate toward a white-jacketed server carrying a silver tray with long-stemmed champagne flutes.

Drinks in hand, they wandered the ground-floor reception area, admiring Bianchi's collection of Renaissance art. He had a lot of obvious security at the party.

"Where do you think he is?" asked Cooper.

Casey continued to admire the art. "Don't worry. He'll find us."

"And if he doesn't?"

Casey smiled. "You worry too much, Lex."

"I'm a pragmatist."

Casey laughed and took a sip of her champagne. "I've got another word for it, but as long as you keep smiling and pretend you're having a good time, I don't care what you call it."

"So I'm a planner," replied Cooper, making sure she kept smiling. "I like when things go according to plan."

"And how's that been working out for you?"

"Are you making this personal?"

Casey winked at her. "Don't you go losing that smile on me."

"I'm not like Jules and Megan. I don't just walk into a bar and five minutes later walk out with some guy."

"We can hear you, you know," said Ericsson over their earpieces.

"Yeah," added Rhodes. "And what do you mean by walk out with *some guy*?"

"Let's keep the net clear," ordered Casey, before turning her attention back to Cooper. "All I can say, Alex, is that life is what happens when you're busy making other plans."

"That's pithy. Did you come up with that one yourself?"

"It doesn't matter. I just think that if you loosened up a bit, smiled a bit more, you'd find more men being drawn to you."

"There are plenty of men drawn to me," Cooper responded.

"What is it now? Six months since you were last on a date?"

"We've been downrange for a lot of that time."

Pointing at a statue and broadening her smile, Casey said, "Not for all of it."

"You'll forgive me if I don't exactly want to swap dating advice with you, chief."

Casey rolled her eyes. "You, too? Why does everyone think I'm sleeping with him?"

It was Cooper's turn to laugh, and this time it was genuine. "You can't hide what's going on between you two."

"There's nothing to hide, because there's nothing going on," Casey insisted.

Cooper held up her hand. "Hey, I didn't ask, so don't feel like you've gotta tell. Okay?"

"Rob Hutton is our superior officer. I am not sleeping with him. Besides, the man's married. What kind of woman do you think I am?"

"Whatever you say."

Casey shook her head. "You're amazing. All of you. A man and a woman can't be friends?"

"Nope."

Casey rolled her eyes again. "There's nothing going on between us."

Cooper stared at her for several moments. Finally, she stated, "You're such a liar."

Casey's cheeks flushed.

"See. You're turning red," Cooper said with a smile. "There *is* something going on between you two."

"I'm turning red out of frustration. How's a girl supposed to defend herself against an accusation like that?"

"Just tell me it's not true."

"I *did*," insisted Casey.

"Tell me again."

"Fine. It's not true."

"I don't believe you."

Casey shook her head but never lost her smile.

"My face is starting to hurt," said Cooper. "Can we drop the fake smiles for a few minutes?"

"Nope. You catch more flies with honey."

"You really believe men care either way?"

"They care," said Casey. "Believe me. It's like turning on a magnet. If you're smiling and having a good time, men find you much more approachable. But if you stand around looking like a you-know-what, all you're going to attract are jerks."

Cooper was silent for a moment.

Casey looked at her. "Don't tell me that's some serious revelation for you?"

Cooper brushed it off. "I knew that."

It was once again Casey's turn to laugh. "Now who's lying?"

Before Cooper could respond, she caught a glimpse of someone off to her right. "Contact. Three o'clock."

Casey stole a casual glance in Bianchi's direction. He was working the room, meeting and greeting his guests. At the moment he was talking to an aristocratic-looking older couple.

"What should we do?" asked Cooper.

"Nothing," replied Casey. "Just stand here, look pretty, and smile. And it wouldn't hurt if you turned a little bit more to the side so he can see your tits."

Cooper's eyes widened in surprise.

Casey put on her biggest, brightest smile and said, "I had no idea what a basket case you were until now. Can you at least pretend you know how to be sexy?"

"I don't need to pretend. I'm just not as overt."

"Which is why you haven't been on a date in six months," chimed in Ericsson.

"And can't get a guy out of a bar in five hours, much less five minutes," added Rhodes.

"Quiet," ordered Casey. "He's spotted us."

CHAPTER 5

Is this your first time in the tank?" asked Jack Walsh as they approached the outer door of the Pentagon's ultrasecure conference room.

Leslie Paxton straightened her jacket and took a deep breath. "Yup. My first time in front of the Joint Chiefs as well."

"If it helps put you at ease, you'll only be meeting with the chairman and his assistant, the director of the Joint Staff."

"For my first national security emergency, I was expecting a larger audience."

"Don't worry about the size of the audience," said Walsh. "Just answer their questions as best you can. I'll handle everything else."

Leslie was the director of the Defense Advanced Research Projects Agency, better known by its acronym, DARPA, a research agency under the Department of Defense. She had worked as a senior scientist at NASA and as vice president for technology and advanced development at the Loral Corporation before being tapped for her current position. She was a tall, thin woman with long blond hair and a genius intellect.

Her agency's focus was on generating revolutionary capabilities in order to surprise America's enemies and to prevent them from surprising the United States. Whether it was artificial intelligence or space-based predator-style drones, DARPA was referred to at DoD as the "technological engine" that drove its radical innovation.

It was a small organization that eschewed hierarchy and government bureaucracy and prided itself on flexibility. Its eclectic staff was made up of the best researchers, thinkers, and scientists from government, universities, private industry, and even the public at large. Disciplines were just as wide-ranging, focusing on both theoretical and experimental strength.

Very little of DARPA's research was ever performed in government labs—that was for only the most sensitive and promising activities. Most researchers worked in private or in university laboratories, which was why DARPA liked to characterize itself as "one hundred geniuses connected by a travel agent."

The driving concept at DARPA was to harness the best talent, but not to isolate it. Ideas needed to flow quickly and unimpeded to allow for rapid decision making and to spur innovation.

While a key group of scientists were permanent employees meant to ensure continuity, the majority of DARPA staff was hired for four- to six-year rotations and told to be bold and not fear failure. DARPA didn't just want outside-the-box thinking, it wanted thinking where you couldn't even see the

box. That could happen only by constantly bringing in fresh ideas and perspectives, a core strength
that allowed DARPA to build incredible teams of
researchers.

DARPA was about anticipating a scientific advancement and reverse-engineering it, even if such
advancement hadn't been fully realized yet. They
also took older experimentation or scientific con-
cepts that had never come to fruition and went at
them from completely new angles.

While some projects lasted only the length of a
four- to six-year team rotation, more time-inten-
sive projects saw their teams allowed to continue
beyond that time frame so as to ensure successful
collaboration.

In order to keep itself lean and mean, DARPA
often outsourced things it required to different
branches of the Department of Defense and the
military. Regardless of where DARPA got its personnel, the number-one job of the agency's director was to hire the brightest minds with the biggest
ideas and give them everything they needed to be
successful. Leslie Paxton, like her predecessors, understood that radical innovation could come about
only from radical, high-risk investments in her
people.

Jack Walsh was the Joint Chiefs' director for
intelligence. It was he who had summoned Paxton to the Pentagon from DARPA headquarters
this afternoon. His office had been in a flurry of
activity. In fact, as Leslie had walked in, the fifty-
two-year-old rear admiral had been in the process
of throwing a staffer his car keys, saying, "Take
mine and double-park it right on their front steps
if you have to. I want those records immediately.

If anyone gives you any problems, you call my cell phone directly."

Walsh was a charming, no-BS guy. Intelligence was a people business and he excelled at it. He disliked bureaucracy but could navigate it like no one else in the military. He was as adept at cutting through red tape as he was at circumventing it when a situation called for it. Some of the country's most innovative intelligence revolutions had sprung from the mind of Admiral Jack Walsh. He was the kind of person people went to bed at night praying was working around the clock to keep them safe. And with two grown children and a failed marriage behind him, Walsh had all the time in the world to focus on keeping America safe.

No matter how many people were in the room, Walsh always made Leslie feel that she was the most important. For a man possessed of such people skills, Paxton found it hard to understand why he had never remarried. In the old-boy network of the Pentagon, he'd always treated her as an equal. He even made it a point to reach out to her and solicit her feedback on different things he was working on, something others in the DoD weren't as apt to do. He was just an incredibly good guy. And while Paxton respected the professional boundaries of their relationship, if he had ever asked her to dinner, or even to lunch, for that matter, she would have said yes in a heartbeat.

But he hadn't asked her to come to the Pentagon for a social call. He had asked her to come to assist him in making a presentation to the chairman of the Joint Chiefs of Staff in response to a developing national security emergency.

They'd spent the better part of the morning and

into the afternoon working on what they would do and what they would say. When the time neared for their meeting, she still didn't feel fully prepared.

"You're going to do great," said Jack. "Don't worry. The chairman is a nice guy; very affable. His assistant can be a real pain in the ass, but he's also a good guy. He's pretty direct, so don't let that intimidate you. It's just his style. Answer his questions as succinctly as you can and you'll be fine. Are you ready? Do you need a minute to collect your thoughts?"

Leslie straightened to her full height and shook her head. "The longer we wait the worse this is going to get."

"I agree," said Walsh as he reached down and opened the door. "Here we go."

CHAPTER 6

The chairman of the Joint Chiefs, General Red Cooney, as well as his assistant, Lieutenant General Jim Slazas, stood when Jack Walsh and Leslie Paxton entered the secure conference room. After shaking hands, Cooney invited everyone to take their seats.

"So, Jack," the chairman said, "I assume we're not here because I've been ignoring your Facebook updates."

"No, sir," Walsh replied with a smile. He had been pushing a classified DoD-wide Facebook/Wikipedia hybrid as a means of better sharing, disseminating, and understanding everything from insurgent tactics to terror cell hierarchies. Cooney had been slow to buy in and often made the project the butt of jokes in meetings. Walsh had been hearing from everyone else, though, how valuable they had found it and knew it was only a matter of time before Cooney finally came around. "If you'll permit me, I'd like Director Paxton to begin the presentation."

Paxton had been busy setting up her laptop, and once the spinning DARPA logo could be seen on the screen at the front of the room, she said, "Admiral Walsh has asked me to brief you on some rather unusual science."

"Isn't that redundant coming from DARPA?" asked Slazas.

Leslie had been determined that she was going to kill Slazas with kindness and flashed him her brightest smile. "Very true, we're in the unusual science business. But I think you'll find this case particularly interesting. Are you familiar with something called Operation Paperclip?"

"That was our effort at the end of World War II to gather up as many German scientists as we could. The goal was to deny the Soviets, as well as the UK, access to their knowledge and expertise."

"Correct," said Leslie as she advanced to her first slide. It was a black-and-white photo of 104 rocket scientists at the White Sands Proving Grounds in New Mexico. "Paperclip was created by the CIA's precursor, the OSS, and overseen by the Joint Intelligence Objectives Agency under the Joint Chiefs.

"President Truman at the time had been adamant that any active Nazis or any active supporters of Nazism be rejected from the program. He didn't care if other nations scooped them up; they were not welcome in America.

"Needless to say, both the OSS and the Joint Chiefs disagreed with the president."

Paxton advanced to her next slide. It was a picture of Churchill, Roosevelt, and Stalin. "To circumvent President Truman, as well as the Potsdam and Yalta agreements, the JIOA created false histories for the scientists. Any Nazi affiliations were either minimized or scrubbed altogether. They also scoured German political and employment records and scrubbed those as well.

"The new sanitized bios were then paperclipped, hence the code name, to the scientists' U.S. government personnel files, and they were granted their security clearance to work in the United States."

"Imagine what we could get done if the OSS was still around," mused Cooney.

Slazas nodded in agreement and said to the DARPA director, "What does this have to do with why we're sitting here?"

Paxton advanced to her next slide, a group of German scientists in a lab somewhere, surrounded by beakers and Bunsen burners. Taking a sip of water from the glass on the table in front of her, she replied, "Operation Paperclip had originally begun as part of Operation Overcast, but was eventually spun off as its own op. While Paperclip was focused on scientists, Overcast was all about locating and securing actual Nazi scientific and military technologies, of which there were a tremendous number.

"Toward the end of the war, when Hitler had been handed multiple defeats by the Soviets, he charged Werner Osenberg, the scientist in charge of the Nazis' Military Research Association, the *Wehrforschungsgemeinschaft*, with identifying and recalling from combat Germany's brightest scientists, engineers, and technicians.

"The names were compiled into what was known as the *Osenberg List*. It was a veritable who's who of the greatest scientific minds the Nazis had, and it formed the basis for Operation Paperclip. From it, we were able to recruit top scientists for our space program, such as Wernher Von Braun, as well as scientists who secretly worked on the Manhattan Project."

"Director Paxton," said Slazas, "can we fast-forward through the history lesson?"

Walsh held up his hand. "We're almost there, Jim. Trust me. This is important."

Slazas backed down and Leslie continued. "What many people don't know is that Hitler had another list compiled at about the same time. It was based on the top-secret work of a Nazi SS Obergruppen-führer who some say was the Third Reich's most brilliant scientist, General Hans Kammler. This list ranked the Nazis' most promising scientific and military projects, many of which were decades ahead of their time. With detailed overviews, status, and ratings, it was known as the *Kammler Dossiers*.

"JIOA bifurcated their operations so that the Paperclip team could focus on the scientists and the Overcast operatives could focus on the actual projects. Of particular interest to the Joint Chiefs at that time was the Nazi *Wunderwaffe* program."

"Wonder weapons," said Cooney.

"Exactly," replied Paxton as she advanced to her next slide, a Nazi flying-wing aircraft that looked exactly like the stealth fighter. "While the Nazi propaganda ministry blew a lot of smoke about the revolutionary superweapons Hitler was bringing online, there was more than a little fire there.

"Megabattleships, ballistic missile submarines, air-independent propulsion U-boats, an electric U-boat—the first ever designed to operate submerged for an entire voyage—a submarine aircraft carrier, self-propelled antiaircraft guns, supertanks, long-range bombers capable of reaching the United States, rocket-powered vertical takeoff aircraft, high-altitude reconnaissance aircraft, rocket-powered fighters, experimental helicopters, advanced artillery and missiles, an orbital parabolic mirror capable of focusing the sun's rays in a devastating beam anywhere on earth, night vision devices, a nuclear program, an antigravity program, and a host of other exotic projects we have yet to categorize."

"And that's what Operation Overcast was charged with running down?"

Leslie Paxton nodded and clicked to her next slide of three plainclothes men armed with M3 submachine "grease guns" riding in an old U.S. Army jeep somewhere in Europe. It looked to the men around the table as if it might have been taken in Paris.

"About the time Nazi-controlled Europe began to fall, the JIOA managed to steal a copy of the Kammler Dossiers. A female operative working for the OSS parachuted out of a Nazi aircraft with two bullet wounds, an SS officer strapped to her as her prisoner, and the documents chained to his wrist in a briefcase.

"Based on the information contained in the dossiers, Operation Overcast began inserting secret teams, similar to the three-man Jedburgh teams used in France, throughout Nazi-controlled Europe.

"Their assignment was to secure as much high-value Nazi scientific and military technology as possible. Raw data, blueprints, hardware; whatever they could find. Whatever they couldn't take away with them, they were to document as thoroughly as possible and then destroy, in order to prevent it from falling into the hands of the Soviets, or even the Brits. Either we got it, or no one did."

The chairman nodded and Paxton continued. "With the Soviets advancing from the east, much of Overcast's attention was focused there. As the Nazis fled the advancing Red Army, they often flooded and boobytrapped their research facilities, many of which were contained in mountain cave systems or underground bunkers. They fully believed they would eventually return and pick up on their experiments right where they had left off."

She could see Slazas getting antsy and, sensing he was ready to interrupt her again, said, "I'm getting there, I promise."

The lieutenant general leaned back in his chair and waited. When the DARPA director advanced to her next slide, his chair came forward with a thud. "Jesus Christ," he said.

"This picture was taken by one of the Overcast teams at a Nazi research facility in Czechoslovakia in 1944."

Surrounding a twenty-foot-high, fifteen-foot-wide metal structure that looked like the Greek symbol for Omega, Ω, there were countless human skeletons protruding from solid rock. They were twisted in agonizing poses and their jaws appeared locked open, as if frozen in midscream.

"This was one of Kammler's most promising pieces of technology," she continued. "It was called the *Engeltor*, or Angel's Gate. It had been based largely on the work of German physicist Max Planck, the founder of quantum theory. In essence, the Engeltor, which the Americans simply referred to as the Kammler Device, was designed to be a giant fax machine that could fax people and objects."

"Right into solid rock?" asked Cooney.

Paxton created a split screen and put up another, similar photograph. "The technology is extremely temperamental. Based on the scientists and data that American operatives were able to recover from the Third Reich, the United States built its own Engeltor. The photograph I just put up was taken in 1945, at Camp Hero on Montauk Point, Long Island."

Slazas stared in disbelief.

"As you can see," offered Paxton, "we were able to re-create similar results."

The lieutenant general shook his head. "You call those *results*? That's horrific."

The head of DARPA shrugged. "It's science. We were trying to reproduce the Kammler experiments, but without having all the pieces to the puzzle."

"The bodies in the second photo; were those American soldiers?"

"Yes. They volunteered for the assignment and knew the risks they were taking."

"But look what happened to them. They knew *that* was a possibility?"

"Yes, they did, and they also knew that it was one of the most promising pieces of technology the United States had ever worked on."

"Pioneered by the Nazis," said Slazas, shaking his head.

"As were cruise missiles, stealth aircraft, and rocket science. I would suggest our military has benefited tremendously from all of those."

Slazas knew that data collected from Nazi experiments had helped advance science, particularly medicine, but that didn't mean he had to like it.

Cooney studied Paxton. "You used the present

tense when you spoke about the technology. You said it *is* temperamental. Are we to assume that the United States is still experimenting with it?"

"Yes," replied Paxton. "We are, but with limited success."

"How limited?" asked the chairman.

"Occasionally, we're able to move very small, inanimate objects. We've also been able to move very basic living organisms, such as bacteria. Most of the advancements we have been able to make have come because of breakthroughs in the field of quantum teleportation."

"Like what the Chinese just pulled off?"

Paxton knew what the man was talking about. In the open scientific community, the record for quantum teleportation had been held by a joint U.S.-European research team that had beamed particles from one side of the Danube to the other, a distance of six hundred meters. That feat had recently been shattered by the Chinese, who had beamed particles sixteen kilometers; twenty-five times the distance achieved by the U.S.-European team.

"Exactly," said Leslie. "The potential military applications of this technology are limitless."

"Which is why we requested this meeting," said Walsh as he signaled Paxton to advance to her next slide. As she did, he said, "This picture was taken by one of our intelligence operatives in Paraguay two days ago."

Cooney and Slazas stared at the screen.

"My God," said the chairman. "Are you telling me that we've begun using human subjects again?"

Leslie shook her head. "No, sir. We don't use

human subjects. We haven't since the forties. This wasn't us."

"Then who was it?"

"We believe someone has gotten access to the technology," said Walsh.

"How? Has the program been compromised?"

"Anything is possible, but I doubt it," said Paxton, who paused before adding, "The research is part of Stardust."

The code name was immediately familiar to both Cooney and Slazas. Having realized by the 1990s that most of the United States' top-secret research programs and facilities had been penetrated by foreign spies, the U.S. government embarked on one of its most ambitious, most highly classified projects ever. Codenamed Stardust, it was the Supermax of research facilities. The idea had been to put its best scientific eggs in one basket and then build a henhouse that none of the foxes would ever be able to get into.

Chairman Cooney stared at the screen. Without turning to look at Leslie or Jack he asked, "Let's assume for a moment that the Stardust program hasn't been penetrated. Where would someone have gotten this technology?"

"I would start at the beginning," said Walsh. "At the Kammler facility in the Czech Republic."

"Why?"

"Because we could only get a three-man team in there at the end of the war. It had been flooded by the Nazis and they had a very limited oxygen supply to explore with. With the Soviets advancing on their position, they had to move fast. They removed what documents they could and then used their explosives to try to destroy the Engeltor

Kammler had built. Exiting the the complex, they called in an airstrike to seal the facility permanently.

"I think we should send a team in to make sure it has remained sealed."

"Why not use satellite imagery?"

"We tried that. The tree cover is too dense. Even if it weren't, it's an underground facility. Satellites wouldn't be able to help us see through all that rock. That's why I want to send a team in. Once they're there, they can—"

"Hold on," interrupted Slazas. "You're serious. You want to send U.S. *military* personnel. Why don't we ask the CIA to do this?"

Walsh looked to the chairman, "That's not my call to make."

Cooney knew his intelligence director well enough to ask, "I'm going to assume you have an opinion on it, right?"

"I do," said Walsh, "and while we all agree that there are some very good people at the Agency, they're not the organization they used to be. If they could do what we needed done, we wouldn't be hiring so many private intel groups."

Cooney nodded. "True."

"The CIA also has no idea of the extent of our operations down in South America, particularly around the triborder region. If we bring them in on this, they're going to end up learning a lot more about our intelligence-gathering than we want them to know."

Again, the chairman said, "I agree."

"What about informing the president?" asked Slazas.

Walsh shook his head. "I'm against it."

"Why?"

"The director of Central Intelligence is an appointee. He's an old friend and a political ally of the president's. I think if we want this done right, we have to do it ourselves and keep it as quiet as possible."

"We have a good relationship with the Czechs. Why don't we bring them in to help on this?"

Walsh shook his head again. "There's a lot we kept hidden from them at the end of the war. It'd be a big can of worms to open this late in the game. Besides, we're only talking about a reconnaissance operation."

Slazas's feelings about the subject were clear from the look on his face.

Walsh understood that they had strayed into dangerous territory, especially with a civilian in the room. Smiling, he looked at Leslie and said, "Director Paxton, could you give us the room for a moment, please?"

"Of course," replied Paxton as she unplugged her laptop and stepped outside.

When the soundproof door clicked shut behind her, Slazas looked at Cooney and said, "For the record, I want you to know I think this is a bad idea."

"I have to tell you, I'm on the fence here," added Cooney.

Walsh had expected this reaction. He pulled up a picture on his iPhone and slid it across the table. "I think this might change your mind."

Cooney looked at the photo and then zoomed in on it. "Am I looking at what I think I'm looking at?"

"Yes, sir," said Walsh. "We believe it's a bomb of some sort."

There was silence in the room. Cooney looked at Slazas, who reluctantly nodded.

Finally, General Cooney said, "If we do this, it will need to be done quietly and done *completely* under the radar. Do you understand?"

"Yes, sir."

"Whoever you send," continued Cooney, "they've got to be smart and they've got to move fast. And if things go wrong, I don't want any of it tracing back to us. That means no knuckle draggers. This cannot look military or have any U.S. military fingerprints on it at all."

"Yes, sir," Walsh stated. "You don't need to worry. I already have the perfect team in mind."

CHAPTER 7

Nino Bianchi spread out his hands as he took in the two gorgeous women standing in front of him. "Now this is why people love coming to my parties," he stated. "I always have the most beautiful guests."

"You also have a beautiful home," offered Cooper.

"Don't change the subject," said Casey. "Let him keep telling us how beautiful we are."

Bianchi laughed. "You have a lovely accent. Virginia?"

Casey laughed politely and replied, "Lower."

"The Carolinas?"

She smiled and rolled her eyes at him. "We're going to be here all night at this rate. Texas."

"Of course," said Bianchi. "Texas. And yours?" he asked, turning to Cooper.

"Atlanta."

"Two southern belles. How fortunate am I?"

"You speak English very well, Signore Bianchi," said Casey, trying to keep her mind on her assignment. Looking at him, all she could think about was the busload of Americans he had helped to blow up. If the choice had been hers to make, she would have pulled out her pistol and shot him right there in the middle of the party. "How did you become so fluent?"

The man gave a dismissive wave of his hand. "Unlike you Americans, we Europeans speak many languages. Which reminds me. What do you call someone who speaks three languages?"

Casey looked at Cooper and then back to Bianchi. "Trilingual?"

"Exactly," he replied. "How about two languages?"

"Bilingual?"

"Yes, yes. That's correct. How about one language?"

"I don't know," said Casey.

"American," whispered Bianchi with a conspiratorial wink as he began laughing.

If this guy only knew what was in store for him, thought Casey as she and Cooper laughed goodnaturedly at his joke.

"I'm sorry," said Bianchi. "That's very rude of me. But it is true. America thinks it's the center of the world and that everything revolves around it."

"Politics are so boring," said Cooper, holding up her nearly empty glass. "But champagne; that's something I can get excited about."

Casey nodded and held up her glass as well. "Can we tempt you into having a drink with us, Signore Bianchi?"

"Absolutely not," he said, his face suddenly stern. Casey and Cooper looked at him.

Then he smiled and added, "Not at least until you tell me your names."

Casey smiled back and held out her hand. "Jennifer."

"And I'm Elena," said Cooper, offering her hand to Bianchi once he released Casey's.

"Beautiful names for the two most beautiful women at my party. I want you both to call me Nino," he said, waving a waiter over. He took a glass of champagne off the tray.

Holding it up, he proposed a toast. "To beauty, to love, and to their child, ecstasy."

They all clinked glasses and took a sip.

"*Death Takes a Holiday*?" asked Casey.

Bianchi was impressed. "Very good," he said, tipping his glass in her direction. "How did you know that?"

"It was one of my grandmother's favorite films. She called it the most romantic toast she had ever heard. It made my grandfather very upset. He thought the toast he gave at their wedding was the most romantic."

Bianchi smiled. "So, what about you, Jennifer? Are you a romantic?"

He was flirting with her.

Casey replied coyly. "Romance is fine, but I think there are other things in life that are more exciting."

He liked that answer. "And you, Elena? What do you think?"

Cooper leaned against Casey and ran her fingers slowly down her teammate's arm. "I think Jennifer and I have a very similar definition of excitement."

That put the ball over the goal line. Both women

could tell by looking at him that Bianchi was hooked. Two attractive women apparently interested in each other as well as him was all it took. Men were too easy.

"Would you ladies like to see the rest of the house?"

All of the blood had been drained from his brain and rushed to the part of his anatomy now doing the thinking. This operation was going to be over in record time. All they had to do now was get him down to the boat.

"We'd love to," said Casey.

Bianchi insinuated himself between them. "Why don't we start upstairs then?"

Upstairs? That wasn't going to work. They needed to get him downstairs. Once he got upstairs, he wasn't going to want to leave; at least not until what he thought was going to happen, had happened.

Casey knocked back her champagne in a long swallow and then handed her empty glass to Bianchi. "Hold this," she said as she began to walk away.

"Where are you going?" he asked.

"To get us a little more. I'll be right back."

Before Bianchi could reply, Casey was already walking toward a bar that had been set up on the other side of the room. He watched her walk away and how the close-fitting dress she wore accented her beautiful body.

Cooper gave Bianchi's arm a squeeze. "That'll be our third glass of champagne."

"Is that a bad thing?" he asked.

Cooper smiled seductively. "Not for you, it's not. Not as long as you can keep up."

Bianchi reached down and rearranged the front of his suddenly tight-fitting trousers.

After fetching three glasses of champagne from the bar, Casey stopped halfway back and set them on a table. She pretended to adjust her dress and plucked off what appeared to be one of its decorative beads. In actuality, it was a water-soluble capsule filled with an amnesic substance called Flunitrazepam, or Rohypnol, the date rape drug.

She dropped it in Bianchi's glass and allowed it to dissolve as she walked back over to him and Cooper.

When she reached them, she took their half-empty glasses, handed them fresh ones, and then offered a toast of her own. "May we kiss whom we please and please whom we kiss."

"I like that one," said Bianchi, beaming, as they all clinked glasses and he took a nice long sip of his champagne.

As his glass came down, he then added, "Why don't I show you ladies the upstairs portion of the house."

Casey moved in closer to him and put her hand on his chest. "Do you know what I like? What I *really* like?"

"Tell me," said Bianchi, narrowing his eyes, trying to appear seductive.

"I like boats. I've always found them very sexy. I'll bet you've got a nice boat."

"I do," he replied. "But I have an even nicer library upstairs, with a beautiful view overlooking the canal."

Cooper knew she might be pushing their luck. She didn't want to make the man suspicious, but said, "I bet we can't swim naked up there."

"I actually have a tub big enough for all three of us," he stated as he linked both of the women's arms through his and led them toward the stairs. "If you're both very, very good, maybe we'll take the boat out later."

There was nothing they could do except go along with him until the drug kicked in and he became malleable enough to steer back down to the boat garage. The challenge, though, would be keeping him at bay. As they began their ascent of the staircase, he reached down and grabbed both their asses.

CHAPTER 8

The library was on the palazzo's third floor. The marble floors were covered with expensive Persian carpets. The walls were lined with ornately carved mahogany bookcases. A gilded chandelier hung in the center of the room and the ceiling boasted a bright blue fresco with rosy-cheeked cherubs peeking out from behind puffy white clouds. For a man as gauche as Bianchi, the room was incredibly elegant.

"So," he said, draining the last few drops from his champagne glass. "Who would like some more?"

Chewing pensively on her bottom lip as if she was thinking better of it, Casey finally raised her glass and said, "I'll have some."

"Excellent," he replied. He had no idea that both women had been covertly dumping out here and there as much of their champagne as they could.

Casey walked around the room admiring the books as she scanned for the security cameras she knew he had. "You have quite a beautiful collection," she said, running her fingers over the leather-bound volumes.

"I like beautiful things," said Bianchi as he produced a bottle of champagne from a minibar hidden behind a row of faux book spines.

"Is that Dom Perignon?" Casey asked, placing her hand on her hip and cocking her head sideways.

Bianchi smiled. "Indeed it is. It's a very special bottle that I've been saving for a very special occasion."

"I've never seen one that color before," said Casey.

"Or that size," added Cooper, who came over to get a better look.

"It's very rare," said Bianchi. "It is called Dom Perignon White Gold. The bottle, known as a Jeroboam, contains three liters and is—"

"Completely made out of white gold?" interrupted Casey.

The man nodded. "Like I said, I like beautiful things. I also like celebrating special occasions."

With that, the arms dealer popped off the cork and the women squealed with feigned delight as Bianchi raced to capture the overflowing champagne in their glasses. The drug was already making him a bit sloppy, and he spilled some over the top of the bar and onto the carpet.

Passing out the glasses, he said, "Here's to beautiful things."

Casey caught Cooper's eye and knew what she was thinking. The guy was a pig. But they were professionals and they weren't going to screw this up.

Setting his glass down, Bianchi reached for a remote, punched a button, and music began to pour from hidden speakers somewhere in the walls. He grabbed Cooper and pulled her into the center of the room to dance.

Pressing himself against her, he ran his hands up and down her dress and over the contours of her body.

"What about your other guests?" Cooper asked, trying to create a little daylight between them.

Bianchi scoffed. "Boring. All of them. They only come to eat my food and drink my wine. This is where the real party is."

"You can say that again," said Casey as she dropped another capsule she had plucked from her dress into the man's glass.

"Come dance with us," he said, looking up and waving Casey over. "We don't want to leave anyone out." He was beginning to slur his words.

Casey smiled and brought him his glass of champagne. He took another long drink, set the glass down, and then pulled Casey toward him so he could run his hands up and down her body as well.

She was about to reach for his glass and encourage him to have a bit more when the door of the library was thrown open and three of Bianchi's security detail rushed in. They were more thorough and more protective than had been expected. In Italian, they told their boss that they had backed up the security tapes to see when the women he was now alone with in his library had arrived, and with whom. There was just one problem. They couldn't find them. The women hadn't come through the front door like everyone else. The first time the cameras had any record of them was when they appeared in a hallway near the stairs down to the boat garage.

Uh, oh, thought Casey.

Bianchi was so out of it, he stepped forward and shoved the two women behind him to protect them from his own security people. He definitely wasn't thinking very clearly. He was furious that he'd managed to get two gorgeous ladies upstairs, had opened a forty-thousand-dollar bottle of champagne, and now his security team was destroying the mood.

For their part, Casey and Cooper didn't waste any time. Staying behind Bianchi so they could use him for cover, they moved in perfect unison as they drew their weapons from their garter holsters at exactly the same moment.

The standoff lasted for less than a second. When one of Bianchi's men reached for his gun, Cooper fired and put two rounds into where his throat met the top of his chest.

One of the other men went for his weapon and Casey took him out with two shots to the head. The third security man bolted from the room.

"We're blown," said Casey over her earpiece.

"What happened?" asked Ericsson.

"No time to explain. We need to get out of here now," replied Casey as she kicked Bianchi in the back of the knee, buckled his legs, and sent him down to the carpet.

Cooper rushed to the door of the library, counted to three, and then peeked out. The manuever was met with a hail of automatic-weapons fire from the hallway.

She pulled her head back inside just as the rounds tore up the doorframe above her.

"How many?" asked Casey as she made Bianchi lie down, face-first on the floor.

"At least one with more coming up the stairs."

"Lock the door!"

Cooper pulled one of the dead security men out of the way so she could close the library door. After locking it, she slid one of the room's heavy leather couches in front of it and jammed the two security officers between its legs to make it harder to open.

Once again, Casey scanned the walls and ceilings. "I think we're being watched."

"I figured as much," replied Cooper. "There's no way we're getting down to the boat garage. What's Plan B?"

"I'm working on it."

Hearing shouts from the hallway, Cooper said, "You'd better work fast."

Casey had Cooper watch Bianchi as she walked over and opened a pair of French doors overlooking the canal. There was a wrought-iron railing with a polished brass cap that came up about waist high.

Megan Rhodes's voice came over their earpieces. "We've got trouble at the front door. The security team has weapons drawn and they're trying to get an angle on the window you just opened."

Casey stepped back and cursed.

"What do you want me to do, boss?"

Just then Cooper said, "It just got very quiet in the hallway. I think they're getting ready to hit the room."

"They won't risk killing Bianchi," answered Casey.

Cooper drew her teammate's attention to the fact that Bianchi was lying prone on the floor and that the two of them were standing up. "If he's got cameras in here, then they know exactly where we're standing and where to shoot."

She was right. "Drag him over here," said Casey,

who then turned her attention back to her other two teammates outside. "We're going to need a hot extraction in thirty seconds."

"Roger that," said Ericsson.

Casey added, "Long-distance assistance is authorized."

"Roger that," replied Rhodes as she adjusted her rifle and placed the crosshairs over the head of her first target.

Cooper looked at Casey. "And how are we getting downstairs in thirty seconds?"

Casey looked past her and out toward the canal. "When life shuts a door, it often opens a window."

"Gretch, we're three stories up. It's going to be like hitting concrete for him."

"Then we'd better make sure he's got the wind knocked out of him so he doesn't aspirate any canal water," replied Casey as she backed Bianchi up and propped him against the railing.

Fearing for their boss's life, the security operatives in the hallway decided to move. As Casey stepped away from Bianchi, the library door was splintered with bullets.

"Extraction in ten seconds," Ericsson said over the radio.

"Tango one is down," said Rhodes, followed by, "Tango two is down."

It took Cooper only a fraction of a second to realize what Casey had planned as she leaned back and kicked Bianchi in the solar plexus, knocking the wind out of him and toppling him over the railing.

Before the arms dealer had even hit the water, both Casey and Cooper had jumped out the window after him.

CHAPTER 9

Casey and Cooper slammed into the water feetfirst. When they broke the surface, they could see Megan keeping the security men in the palazzo pinned down with a steady stream of suppressed fire from her LaRue OBR. Chunks of stone from the library window casing were raining down into the canal.

No sooner had Casey and Cooper reached Bianchi than Julie Ericsson roared down the canal and brought her Zodiac with its enormous engine to a stop between the palazzo and her teammates.

"Move! Move! Move!" she yelled as she raised a suppressed H&K MP7 to help take out any hostiles Rhodes might not be able to see.

Cooper climbed over the side and into the boat. Righting herself, she reached down to help Casey, who was holding Bianchi, and pull him out of the water. The man had landed badly and had been knocked unconscious.

Neither of the women bothered to look up to see what was going on with the arms dealer's security men. That was what Ericsson and Rhodes were supposed to do, and Casey and Cooper trusted them implicitly. All of their actions were synchronized. Even in the heat of battle, they never second-guessed their teammates.

Rhodes kept pounding away at the library window and Ericsson engaged two additional targets who had popped out of the front door with shotguns. She managed to nail them both before they could pull their triggers.

Cooper planted her feet and gave Bianchi once last tug, which pulled him the rest of the way into the boat. This coincided with Rhodes's running out of ammo and needing to do a magazine change, which meant the men in the library window were free to engage.

"Go! Now!" yelled Casey from the water as she grabbed the rope that was threaded along the exterior of the Zodiac.

Ericsson tossed Cooper the MP7 and slammed the throttle all the way to the stop.

The powerful black Zodiac reared up and raced forward as Alex Cooper drilled all of the third-story windows with rapid three-round bursts.

As they sped down the canal, Casey used her exceptionally strong arms to pull herself up and into the boat.

"We're clear," said Ericsson over the radio to Rhodes. "At the bridge in ninety seconds."

"Roger that," said Megan, who had already zipped up her red-hot rifle and was exiting the apartment across the canal from Bianchi's palazzo.

Casey reached over and checked Bianchi's pulse.

"Is he alive?" Cooper screamed above the roar of the engine.

Casey flashed a thumbs-up and was about to say something when she noticed a boat speeding down the canal in their direction. "Contact!" she yelled.

Ericsson turned and looked over her shoulder. Closing in on them was a black Donzi speedboat. "Everybody hold on," she said.

Casey used one hand to hold on to the boat and the other to hold on to Bianchi. As she did, two shooters on the Donzi let loose with a loud barrage of fire.

"So much for them not wanting to injure their boss!" shouted Cooper as she returned fire. She had only gotten off two bursts when her MP7 ran dry.

"Magazine!" she called out.

Julie Ericsson pulled two from the bag next to her and handed them to Cooper. "I'm going to try to lose them!"

Cooper nodded as she grabbed the mags and reloaded.

Ericsson sped even faster, dodging gondolas and other Venetian water traffic. Terrified onlookers screamed as they watched an almost fatal collision between the Zodiac and a smaller utility boat that had pulled out of a side canal, not expecting such a rapidly moving craft.

While Ericsson had managed not to hit the small boat, the Donzi slammed right into it and kept going.

"I'm in place," said Rhodes over the radio from her position at the Rialto Bridge.

"Sit tight!" Ericsson ordered. "We've got company."

Cooper let loose with another round of fire from her MP7. None of the rounds seemed to be able to penetrate the Donzi's windshield. "I can't drill through their glass," she shouted.

"Keep trying," ordered Casey, who had her free arm wrapped around Bianchi's torso to make sure he didn't get pitched out of the boat with all the high-speed maneuvering they were doing.

Cooper ducked as another volley of bullets let loose from the men in the boat chasing them. Preparing to return fire, she was almost tossed from the Zodiac when Ericsson spun it hard to the left to avoid hitting yet another watercraft on the crowded canal.

Ericsson spun hard left again and sent their boat flying down a different, narrower canal. The powerful Donzi followed right behind, gaining on them.

"You really need to do something about these guys, Coop," yelled Ericsson.

"I'm trying! The bullets are just bouncing off them."

"Well, find a spot the bullets don't bounce off."

"Thanks, Jules. Great idea," said Cooper as she raised her weapon and fired again.

Casey shook her head and called out to Ericsson, "We need to go back to the palazzo!"

Ericsson spun their boat to the side in order to miss hitting a trio of gondolas. "Are you crazy?"

"It's the only way we can get rid of that boat behind us. We'll blow the scooters."

Blasting down another canal, the women had to duck as they went under an extremely low bridge. Ericsson thought for sure the Donzi wouldn't even attempt it, but she watched in amazement as sparks literally flew as the boat scraped its way underneath.

"That might have weakened their windshield," Ericsson called out to Cooper.

"I'm on it," she replied, lifting her weapon and

squeezing the trigger. Immediately, the men in the Donzi fired back, and Ericsson jerked the boat hard to the left and then back right just in time to keep their boat from being torn to shreds.

She removed a small black transmitter and handed it over to Casey. "Palazzo Bianchi, coming up!"

Casey wrapped her legs around Bianchi so she could have at least one hand free. Putting the tip of the antenna between her teeth, she extended it to its full length and then flipped the power button. "Whatever you do," she ordered, "don't slow down!"

"Roger that," replied Ericsson.

"Okay, everybody hold on."

Cooper lowered her weapon and grabbed hold of one of the Zodiac's grips. Their boat skidded out into Bianchi's canal and raced toward his palazzo. They didn't need to look behind to know that Bianchi's men were still on their tail.

"We've got men on the dock! Men on the dock!" Ericsson suddenly shouted as she saw that some of Bianchi's security team had commandeered a boat that must have just arrived at the party.

Cooper leaned over the edge of the Zodiac and strafed the security team with a burst of full auto from her weapon. She succeeded in nailing two and sending the others leaping into the canal in a desperate attempt to evade harm. Little did they know that the water was now the most dangerous place of all.

Casey tightened her grip on the transmitter and made ready. The timing of what she was about to do had to be absolutely perfect. The Donzi was right behind them now; practically on top of them. As they drew even with the dock, she depressed the transmit switch and prayed to God she'd properly judged the distance. "Everyone down!"

As they passed the pier and drew even with the doors of Bianchi's boat garage, Casey felt a sudden surge of panic that she had pressed the button too soon. She braced for the inevitable, but it didn't come—at least not until they had sped past the palazzo entirely.

She turned her eyes from the houses alongside the canal to the Donzi barreling down on them from behind. It passed above the submerged scooters at exactly the right moment. Attached to the bow of each propulsion device was a classified, British-made BAE Systems "stonefish" mine meant to destroy any evidence that could point back to the team if the scooters had to be abandoned.

When the explosives detonated, the Donzi was right above them, and was tossed by the concussive pressure wave. They watched as the speedboat lost control and slammed bow-first into the next pier.

Cooper let out a cheer and flashed Casey a thumbs-up as Ericsson pointed the Zodiac toward the Rialto. Hailing Rhodes over the radio, she said, "Sixty seconds."

"Roger that," replied Megan.

Fifty-eight seconds later, they were at Venice's historic Rialto Bridge. Ericsson slowed just enough for Rhodes to jump in. Already they could see blue flashing lights in both directions and hear the sirens of Venice police boats. They had Nino Bianchi, but their job was only half done. They still had to get him to the rendezvous point and hand him off. And to do that, they were going to have to completely expose themselves.

CHAPTER 10

As they sped out into the open water, Gretchen Casey powered up the special encrypted radio she'd been issued for this part of their assignment.

Once it had reached full strength, she depressed the talk button and said, "Norseman, this is Hollow Point. Do you copy?"

She released the transmit button and waited for a response.

"Hollow Point, this is Norseman," said a man's voice. "You're coming in loud and clear. Do you have the package?"

"Roger that. Hollow Point has the package."

"What's your status?" the man asked.

"Hollow Point is fifteen minutes out, but we'll be coming in fast. Lots of local interest," said Casey, referring to all the police activity they were seeing and hearing.

"Understood. Norseman will leave the back door open for you."

"Roger that. Hollow Point out."

Turning off the radio, Casey tapped Ericsson on the shoulder to get her attention and then motioned for her to open the Zodiac's engine all the way up again. The sooner they delivered Bianchi, the better.

Ericsson expertly piloted the Zodiac through the waves. Despite several hard slams, Bianchi remained unconscious.

At fifteen minutes on the dot, Ericsson pointed to a sleek three-deck, forty-four-meter metallic luxury motor yacht that looked as if it were straight out of a Batman movie. Her name was the *Isabella*.

As the Athena Team came around from behind they found the *Isabella*'s transom garage had been left open, just as promised. Ericsson headed straight for it.

"Everyone hold on!" she shouted as they got closer.

Lining up the bow, Ericsson drove the Zodiac up and into the space that contained the yacht's tender and various other pieces of water-related equipment. The minute they were inside, the transom door began to close and Casey hopped out of the boat.

"Stay here and keep an eye on Bianchi," she said. "I don't want to move him until we know where he's supposed to go."

The other women nodded as Casey opened the door out to the deck. Coming down from the upper level was the man with the call sign "Norseman." He was several inches taller than Casey, with sandy brown hair and penetrating blue eyes. A former Navy SEAL who now worked for a private intelligence agency funded by the Defense Department, his real name was Scot Harvath.

Gretchen and her team had worked with him

recently, taking down a terrorist network involved with attacks in Europe and the United States.

"Where is he?" asked Harvath.

"We haven't seen each other in months and that's your first question? No, 'Hi, Gretch. How's it been?' "

"I'm sorry. Hi, Gretch. How's it been?"

"Not too bad. You know the way—"

"Is he still in the boat?" interrupted Harvath.

"Yes, he's still in the boat, but—"

Harvath didn't bother to wait around for her to finish her sentence. Opening the door, he stepped into the transom garage. As he did, someone else came down from the upper deck—Riley Turner. She was in her early thirties, tall and fit, with reddish-brown hair, blue eyes, and a wide mouth with full lips.

A doctor and semicompetitive winter X-Games athlete, she had been one of the earliest recruits to the Athena Project. Casey had been looking forward to seeing Harvath again, but she hadn't expected to see Riley. Though it was unprofessional, she felt jealous seeing them together. She gave Riley a hug anyway. "It's good to see you," she lied.

"You, too," replied Turner.

"You're going to want to take a look at Bianchi."

"Why? What's wrong with him?"

"We chucked him out a third-story window into the canal."

Riley didn't like the sound of that. "You what?"

"We had no choice. He's been unconscious since he hit the water. And by the way, he's under the influence of Flunitrazepam."

Turner pushed past Casey into the transom garage to examine Bianchi.

Gretchen shrugged and headed upstairs. She wanted to get out of her wet cocktail dress and into some dry clothes.

She checked all of the staterooms until she found the one Riley had taken. After satisfying herself that she and Harvath weren't sharing it, Gretchen helped herself to some of Riley's clothes and got dressed.

Grabbing some clothes for Cooper to wear, she stepped back into the passageway. When she did, she nearly ran into Megan and Jules, who were helping Scot and Riley carry Bianchi on a backboard. She stood back as they took him into a room at the end of the passageway.

Cooper came walking up behind them. "Here you go," said Casey as she tossed her the clothes she had picked out.

"Where'd you get these?"

Casey jerked her thumb over her shoulder and then asked, "What's wrong with Bianchi?"

"We don't know. Riley's just being careful."

"If he's paralyzed, I'm not going to lose any sleep over it. It'll serve him right. Do you have any idea how many people that animal has helped kill?"

Cooper nodded in agreement as Harvath came back down the passageway.

"Nice outfit," he said to Casey.

"What? This old thing?"

Harvath smiled and stepped past her. "I'm going to get us underway. There's food in the galley if you want it. When you're ready, you can come up to the bridge. I know Hutton's going to want to debrief you."

"I'm sure the feeling's mutual," interjected Cooper.

Harvath looked at her questioningly.

"*De-brief*. Get it?" she said as she pantomimed pulling someone's pants down.

"No," Harvath replied, deadpan. "And I don't think I want to."

Casey shot her teammate a withering look, and Cooper refrained from any further remarks. Instead, she said, "I think I'll change and get something to eat."

"Delta," said Harvath, shaking his head with a wry smile as he turned to go up to the bridge.

"What's that supposed to mean?" asked Casey.

He waited till he was on the stairs before replying. "It means all you think about, whether male or female, is sex."

Casey's jaw dropped, but she couldn't fight her smile. "I can't believe I just heard that. I dare you to come back here and say that to my face," she challenged, but Harvath had already walked upstairs.

Stepping into the doorway of the stateroom where Cooper was, Casey said, "Did you hear what he said? Unbelievable. And coming from a SEAL, of all people. Do those guys do anything but drink and chase women?"

Cooper was standing in front of an open closet that had been stocked with clothing. "I wouldn't mind him chasing me."

"You know what? That's a good idea. It'd be good practice for you."

"Don't worry," Cooper said with a grin. "I'm not going to cut your grass."

"My grass?"

Cooper shook her head. "I've seen the way you look at him."

"You think I'm after every guy I look at."

Holding up the outfit Casey had given her, Cooper changed the subject, "I don't know where you found this, but they already put clothes for us in the closet."

Casey was about to tell her not to worry about it when Riley came down the passageway and stopped at their stateroom. "Where's Scot?"

"I think he's upstairs," replied Casey. "What's wrong?"

"Tell him Bianchi is starting to wake up."

CHAPTER 11

As far as geeks went, Vicki Suffolk could have done worse; much worse. At least Ben Matthews was a halfway decent-looking geek. One of those Colorado guys into road biking, mountain biking, and backcountry skiing, he had a killer body, and that helped boost him from a seven to a solid eight in her eyes. Not that his rating on a one-to-ten scale mattered. Matthews was simply a means to an end.

"So?" Suffolk asked as he poured her a glass of wine. She was sitting on a stool at the kitchen counter of his loft wearing jeans and an almost see-through peasant blouse. "What are we celebrating?"

At twenty-five, Vicki was about four years younger than he. They had met in a café not far from her apartment. It was one of the free wi-fi places she used so that her internet traffic couldn't be reliably traced. She had noticed him a few times before, but she noticed everyone when she walked into a room, just like she noticed where all the exits were. It was simply how she had been trained. But it was the book he was reading on one particular visit to the café that had caught her attention. The title was very interesting, *American Conspiracies: Lies, Lies, and More Dirty Lies That the Government Tells Us* by Jesse Ventura. She filed it away in her mind and did nothing about it, until the next time she saw him. By then, she had read the same book, as well as four more listed in the bibliography, from cover to cover.

He appeared to be a creature of habit, always sitting at the same table in the corner, away from the windows and most of the bustle of the café. He struck her as a bit of a loner, which made him an even more perfect mark.

On the day she had set to make her move, Suffolk arrived at the café earlier than usual. When she got there, she took a table in the same corner and discreetly baited her trap.

Twenty minutes later, Ben Matthews walked in, ordered his usual large coffee, and sat down at his usual table.

Vicki had dressed down for the occasion; a lot more geek than chic. Her long, black hair was pulled back in a ponytail and she was wearing glasses. She had on a tight black sweater and jeans.

She didn't need to look up to know he was looking at her. She had noticed him checking her out before. He might have been a loner, but he was still a man and he definitely found her attractive.

Looking over at him, she asked, "Can I help you with something?"

Matthews immediately dropped his eyes. "No."

"There must be something you want, because you haven't stopped looking at me since you sat down."

"Actually," he said, "I was looking at one of your books."

Suffolk had a couple of conspiracy theory books, a notepad, and her open laptop on the table in front of her. "What about my books?" she asked.

Ben pointed to one of them, *The Mammoth Book of Cover-Ups.* "I read that one about a year ago. It absolutely opened my eyes to what's going on in the government."

She reached over and picked up the book he was referring to. It was one of the titles listed in the bibliography of the book she had seen him reading. "This one?"

He nodded.

"It's not bad," she replied. "I think Jesse Ventura's book was better, though."

"You've read Ventura's book?" he exclaimed. "I'm reading him right now."

Suffolk smiled and, thawing the frostiness in her voice, said, "Now *that* was an eye-opener."

Pointing to the chair across from her, Ben replied, "Do you mind?"

Suffolk invited him to sit and with that, she had him hooked. Matthews fell for her instantly.

From just that one book she had seen him reading, she had learned everything she needed to know about him. He was perfect for her plan.

Now, sitting at his kitchen counter with a glass of wine, Vicki hoped he had good news for her.

"Ben," she said. "You're killing me. *What* are we celebrating?"

Matthews smiled.

Vicki looked at him, her eyes widening. "You got it?"

Nodding, he reached into his back pocket and

pulled out his new Transportation Security Administration credentials.

"You got it!" she squealed, throwing her arms around his neck. "You got the promotion!"

Ben laughed. "Can you believe it?"

"Of course I can. They should have promoted you a while ago."

"I don't know about *that*," he said. "I haven't been there that long. But pretty cool, considering it all started over a random box of pizza."

Suffolk smiled to herself. There was nothing random about it. The TSA was so hard up for employees that they had actually started advertising on pizza boxes. She had picked the pizza delivery place on purpose. Everything she did she did for a reason.

The TSA ad was the perfect segue for suggesting that Ben take a job at Denver International Airport. If he could get wide enough security clearance, Vicki Suffolk would be only steps away from the most innovative attack the United States had ever seen.

"You know what this means, don't you?" she said.

Ben nodded, and an even bigger smile spread across his face. "Lots more airport access."

Vicki stole a glance at her watch. This was a huge development, and she needed to let her handler know. None of them had expected Ben to get promoted this quickly. But now that he had, they needed to decide what their next move was going to be. They were finally going to have someone who could get all the way inside the airport.

"Earth to Vicki," Ben said, waving his wineglass in front of her. "Are we going to toast or what?"

"Absolutely," she said, getting control of her thoughts. "Here's to your promotion."

"Here's to our exposé on what the government is really doing beneath Denver International."

They clinked glasses and as she drank, all she could think about was getting out of there and reporting in. She hadn't seen her handler in weeks. They'd communicated, but he hadn't wanted to meet in person. He'd said it was too dangerous. But with this development, he'd have to meet with her. At least that's what she hoped.

"So, I think we should go out and celebrate tonight. That is, unless you'd rather stay in," Ben said, raising his eyebrows suggestively.

There were multiple motivations that could be played upon when recruiting someone to spy— money, sex, ideology, excitement, and coercion were the primaries. If you could hit on one of those when recruiting someone, you were good, but if you could hit on more than one, you were golden, and the subject would do anything you wanted. Vicki Suffolk had recruited Ben Matthews based upon his distrust of his own government and had cemented his loyalty to her through sex.

She hadn't been able to figure him out at first. Any other man would have jumped at the chance to sleep with her. Secretly, she had suspected he might be gay. But then she started to worry that perhaps he was playing *her*. The night the thought had popped into her mind, though, Ben had taken her to bed and he had been eating out of the palm of her hand ever since.

Vicki set her wineglass on the counter. "Actually, tonight wouldn't be the best of nights to celebrate, if you know what I mean."

"Why? Are you going out with somebody else?"

Vicki slapped Ben playfully across the shoulder. *"Honestly."*

Ben was not an expert on female anatomy, but Vicki Suffolk had the most erratic menstrual cycle of any woman he'd ever met. "I understand," he said. "We don't have to have sex. We can just go out and have a good time. Or we can order in and watch a movie."

"One of my professors has evening office hours tonight. I told you about it a couple of days ago. Remember my dissertation?"

Posing as a grad student at the University of Denver was part of her cover, and the dissertation had been her go-to excuse for everything.

"Maybe you can come by after?" he said. He sure hoped so. Vicki Suffolk was one of the most sexually adventurous women he had ever been with. Until her, he had considered himself pretty straitlaced, but she had unlocked something wild in him and he couldn't get enough of her.

Vicki laughed and kissed him as she stood up. "We'll see what happens. I'll text you later."

"That's it?" he complained. "You're going? You haven't even finished your wine."

Vicki kissed him again.

"Okay, okay," said Ben, kissing her back. "I don't have any plans to go out, so you can text me as late as you want."

Vicki was halfway to the door already when she said, "We'll see, okay?"

"Right," he said, a bit dejectedly. "Drive safely."

"I will," she told him as she reached the door.

"Love you," Ben said as the door closed. He had no idea whether she had heard him.

Crossing the living room, he looked out the peephole to make sure the hallway was clear. Stepping away from the door, he pulled out his cell phone and dialed the number of someone he had very purposefully not told Vicki about.

"She's gone," he said as a voice answered on the other end. "When can we meet?"

CHAPTER 12

Where are you going to interrogate Bianchi?" asked Julie Ericsson after they had gathered back up on the bridge.

Riley had remained below to keep an eye on and assess the prisoner. He was strapped to a backboard and had regained consciousness. He had suffered several broken ribs and probably a concussion from being tossed out his third-floor window into the canal. He was in pain, but he'd live.

"All I know is that I'm supposed to sail to a town on the other side of the Adriatic called Neum and I'll get further instructions there," replied Harvath as he set the yacht on a course of south-southeast.

Megan Rhodes, Gretchen Casey, and Alex Cooper were sitting there with bottles of water and plates of food. "What do you think is going to happen to him?" asked Cooper.

"I've got no idea," he responded. "But I can guarantee you our little Q&A isn't going to be pleasant."

"Do we know who else was involved in the Rome attack?" asked Rhodes.

Harvath shook his head. "Bianchi may have provided the C4 for the bombing, but he didn't order the attack. Somebody else did. That's why I want to interrogate him myself. I think whatever those terrorist attacks were, they were only the beginning. That's what we've been trying to figure out."

"You and Riley?" asked Casey. "Together?"

"Yeah. The powers that be thought I'd draw less attention if we traveled as a couple."

"Where were you before Venice?"

"Sorrento and Sicily."

"Sounds romantic," said Casey.

"Not really," he said, changing the subject. "How's Nikki?"

Nikki Rodriguez was an Athena Team member whose life Harvath had saved on a recent assignment.

"She's doing much better," Casey replied. "The doctors say she'll be back at work sooner than they originally expected."

Harvath smiled. Nikki was a remarkable operative. "Tell her I said hello," he started to say, but he was interrupted by the ringing of his encrypted satellite phone. "That's going to be Hutton," he remarked as he tossed the phone to Casey.

Knowing that sat transmissions worked best via line of sight, she stepped from the bridge and outside onto the deck.

The night air was warm and humid, the seas calm. What little chop there was, the powerful yacht cut right through.

Lieutenant Colonel Rob Hutton's voice was so clear, it sounded as if he were standing right next to her, rather than thousands of miles away back at Fort Bragg. "How'd it go?" he asked.

"We had to improvise a little bit," replied Casey, "but it was a success. We got him."

"We're already hearing that there was a lot of shooting."

"Not our fault."

"How's the team?" asked Hutton. "Everyone okay?"

"Everyone's fine."

There was a pause. "How about you?" he asked.

Casey looked up into the sky and wondered if one of the stars she saw was the satellite beaming Rob Hutton's voice into her ear. "I'm fine, Rob."

"You're sure?"

There was no way he was in the Joint Special Operations Command center talking to her like that. He had to be standing outside somewhere, alone.

She closed her eyes and allowed herself to pretend for a moment that he was right there. She pictured his blond hair and blue eyes. His shoulders. His smile. Then she pictured his wedding ring and the moment was gone.

If Hutton couldn't be strong enough for himself and his wife, she'd have to be strong enough for all of them.

It was over a year ago that it had happened, but it still felt so fresh, so recent. It had been only a kiss, but it was the most dangerous kiss of her career. They had allowed their attraction to each other to override everything else, and they had stepped over the line.

No sooner had the kiss begun than Gretchen had broken it off. She sensed afterward that, if she hadn't, he would have. Hutton loved his wife and Casey knew that. She also knew that he loved her, too. Regardless of what her feelings for him might have been, though, she swore she'd never let it happen again. It was one of the hardest resolutions she'd ever made.

"I'm fine," she replied. "Bianchi's a bit beat up, though."

"Who did it? Rhodes? Cooper? I'll bet it was Ericsson again, wasn't it? Damn it, Gretchen. You need to keep your operatives on a much tighter—"

"Rob," Casey interrupted, "relax. Nobody physically beat him up."

There was silence for a minute before Hutton said, "Oh. I'm sorry. It's just that I thought—"

"I kicked him in the chest and knocked him out a third-story window."

"You what?" he shouted. "Damn it, Gretchen. You could have killed him."

"He'll be fine."

Hutton and Casey had been down this road before. "So once again the ends justify the means?" he asked rhetorically.

"Defenestration was the safest and most expedient option at the time. I exercised what I believed to be sound operational judgment."

"Save it," said Hutton. "You're not on the record."

Casey shook her head. She knew why he was upset. They weren't fighting about who left the cap off the toothpaste. She colored outside the lines a lot. That's what made her and the team successful. No, this wasn't because of what she'd done to Bianchi or any of her unorthodox behavior on countless other operations. It was because as much as she wanted to, she refused to let Hutton get that close to her again.

"I haven't looked in the bags below deck, but I assume everything we need to get home is in there," she said, changing the subject. "Clothes, money, passports, the usual?"

Hutton wasn't in the mood to fight her. It wouldn't get him anywhere. "It's all in there," he said, his tone softening. "But we're going to arrange to get more."

Casey didn't like the sound of that. "More for what?"

"I just heard from the Pentagon. There's something they need you to do before you fly back."

CHAPTER 13

With a top speed of over forty knots, they traversed the Gulf of Venice in under two hours. Harvath and Riley dropped the team in the Slovenian coastal town of Koper. The idea had been to get them out of Italy as quickly as possible.

It was dark when they arrived and found the car with German plates that had been left for them. After throwing their bags in the trunk and climbing in, Ericsson slid behind the wheel and drove them inland toward the A1. Rhodes acted as copilot as Casey and Cooper slept in back.

It was a boring, pitch-black, nine-hour drive that cut across Austria to Salzburg, skirted Munich, and went up through Germany before crossing into the Czech Republic.

Despite the coffee and energy drinks they'd purchased while gassing up the car and stretching their legs, everyone was exhausted. Even if they hadn't had to drive nine hours, they still would have been wiped out. The Bianchi assignment had required absolute, laserlike focus from all of them. Each had performed at her physical and mental peak. What the women needed now were hot showers, a week of doing nothing, and probably more than a couple glasses of wine. What they had been given, though, was another assignment.

They had stopped in Munich for breakfast, and by the time they pulled into the Czech town of Zbiroh, it was late morning.

Sixty kilometers from Prague, Zbiroh was in the southeast of the country and the landscape looked very much the same as it had in Germany before they crossed the border; rolling green foothills, forests, and farmland. After they left the somewhat industrial city of Pilsen, there was nothing but small villages, cows, and Eastern Orthodox–inspired churches.

"Okay, who's up for shopping?" joked Rhodes as they took a drive through the rather austere couple of blocks that passed for Zbiroh's center.

"First guy we see with a full set of teeth is all mine," said Ericsson.

"*If* you can pry him off his sister," added Cooper.

Casey shook her head. "What a bunch of big-city snobs."

"Wait a second," countered Rhodes. "I grew up in the Chicago *suburbs*."

"Same thing."

"No it isn't."

"Don't bother arguing with her," said Ericsson. "As far as Gretch is concerned, she's got all of us beat in the small-town-girl thing."

Casey laughed. "If the Choo fits."

"You're unbelievable," replied Rhodes, unwilling to let it go. "My dad was a cop. Julie's dad was a fisherman, and her mom taught school. Alex's mom was an immigrant and her parents saved all they had to open a restaurant. You can't get any more red, white, and blue than that."

Ericsson threw up her hands. "You've done it now, sweetheart."

"What? Why do you guys just roll over for her?"

"Because they know," said Casey.

Rhodes let her mouth hang open as if she was heavily medicated and slurred, "That East Texas is the best place in the whole world."

Casey ticked the points off on her fingers as she spoke, "One gas station and *only* one gas station. It's where you get your gas, get your car repaired, and fill up the air in your bicycle tires or the inner tube you're taking swimming.

"There's only one store for groceries and if they don't have it, you don't need it. If you don't dress and prepare your own game, the store's butcher will do it for you. He'll meet you in back, unload whatever you've got in your truck, and call you when he's got your steaks, burgers, sausages, and jerky ready to be picked up.

"The town has one doctor. He delivered my mother *and* he delivered me. He's eighty-eight years old and he *still* makes house calls.

"When our sheriff sees a ten-year-old boy walking down the road with a rifle he doesn't call a SWAT team, he asks the boy how the hunting is.

"We have one church and that church still puts on socials year round and picnics in the summertime.

"We have front-porch swings because we like to see our neighbors pass by and we like to ask them how they're doing. We know everyone's names and they know ours. And yes, just about every single house flies the American flag.

"So with all due respect to Honolulu, Atlanta, and Chicago, I think I've got all of you beat."

"We had a Williams-Sonoma," snarked Rhodes.

Casey smiled. "You didn't have Mayberry. *I* had Mayberry."

"But if you wanted your ears or anything else pierced in Mayberry, you had to see the vet, right?"

Casey shook her head. "Someday, when you finally come down to visit, you'll see for yourself."

"Let me know when the Victoria's Secret opens," said Rhodes, "and I'll be on the first covered wagon down there."

"I hate to interrupt," said Cooper, who was now taking her turn driving, "but do we all have a feel for the layout of this place?"

"I haven't seen the public pillory yet," offered Ericsson.

"Or where they burn the witches," chimed in Rhodes.

Casey ignored them. "I think we're good, Alex. Let's head for the hotel."

Cooper nodded and made a left turn. She followed a narrow, winding road up to the top of the forested hill overlooking the town. There they were greeted by the statues of two enormous lions flanking the entrance of the majestic Zbiroh castle.

"Wow," said Ericsson. "I'm not surprised the Nazis commandeered this place during the war."

"As monstrous as they were, the SS seemed to appreciate the finer things in life, but that's not why they picked this castle," said Casey, who had been filled in, to a certain degree, by Hutton. "It is sitting on top of one of the largest quartz deposits in Europe. This hill functioned as a huge radio wave amplifier, and the SS used it as an electronic listening post."

"But what's that got to do with the abandoned bunker we're supposed to check out?" asked Cooper as she steered the car toward the south wing of the castle where the Château Hotel Zbiroh was housed.

"Apparently, radio wave intercepts weren't the only things the quartz helped amplify."

When Casey didn't elaborate, Rhodes asked, "So are we supposed to guess what else the Nazis were working on here, Gretch?"

In the parking area, several fit, serious-looking men with short, military-style haircuts, wearing plain clothes with tan tactical boots, had just taken up positions around a black Range Rover and distracted her. "I'm sorry," said Casey. "A Czech-speaking SS Obergruppenführer named Hans Kammler had been sent into Czechoslovakia after the Nazis invaded to take over one of its largest industrial-engineering companies, called Škoda.

"Kammler wasn't a soldier, he was an engineer and a scientist. Some say he was Hitler's most brilliant. He set up his offices in the city of Pilsen, which we passed about twenty miles back, but he lived here at the castle.

"He was in charge of the Third Reich's most avant-garde, cutting-edge scientific programs. He claimed that in addition to the quartz found throughout this region, he had discovered other 'miraculous minerals,' as he put it, that unlocked doors to things never before seen in science.

"With the assistance of the Škoda staff, he began

building bunkers and cave complexes throughout the region where he could protect his research, not only from aerial bombardment by the Allies, but also from the prying eyes of Allied spies, who very much wanted to get their hands on anything and everything that Kammler was working on.

"One of the bunkers he had created was on the grounds here at the castle."

"But what specifically was he working on?" asked Cooper.

"Hutton said that information was on a need-to-know basis."

"And we don't need to know."

"Exactly," replied Casey. "What I did manage to get out of him was that it had something to do with bending or absorbing radar waves. That was it."

Rhodes looked at Casey. "The Soviets took Czechoslovakia from the Nazis over sixty years ago. Why is there this sudden interest in Kammler and Zbiroh now?"

"The castle has the deepest well in Europe; over 550 feet. The well has all sorts of tunnels and passages splitting off from it. Most were sealed with concrete and steel by the Nazis before they fled. Almost all of them were boobytrapped. Whatever the Nazis were doing here, they believed they would eventually return to pick up where they left off.

"According to Hutton, the United States slipped a team in here just as the Nazis were leaving. Based on documents captured from one of Kammler's lieutenants, we uncovered the location of one of the Nazis' most secret research complexes.

"With the Soviet Red Army advancing, Kammler's team abandoned the facility and blew up the entrance. There was a much smaller, very well-hidden secondary entrance, which took the team two days to find.

"When they got inside, they discovered that the complex had been flooded. Scuba equipment was air-dropped to the team, and they salvaged the documents they could and then photographed as much as possible. Because of sheer size, they were not able to extricate any of the equipment.

"They'd only brought a certain amount of explosives with them, so they had to choose between trying to blow the submerged equipment and collapsing the hidden entrance to the complex.

"They decided to destroy the equipment, but were only partly successful. The Red Army was almost on top of their position. After they had called in two airstrikes, the third finally hit the target dead center and completely sealed off the secret secondary entrance."

"So we're here to make sure the doors are still closed? Why?" asked Cooper. "It doesn't make sense. Like Megs said, this research facility is more than sixty years old."

Casey shrugged. "Ours is not to reason why. We've been tasked with reconning the complex and reporting back. That's what we're going to do."

"And after that," said Ericsson as the women watched a handsome man exit the hotel and climb into the black Range Rover idling in front with his bodyguard detail, "I think I may have found my full set of teeth."

As Casey watched the Range Rover roll away from the front of the hotel, a bad feeling started to well up from deep within the pit of her stomach.

CHAPTER 14

There was no need to draw straws. Jean "John" Vlcek was Julie Ericsson's contact, so she needed to be the one to go meet him. And as usual, wherever Julie went, so did Megan Rhodes.

Vlcek had pitched a fit about having to leave his zip code. It wasn't until Julie played the age card and asked him if he was worried that he couldn't find decent senior discounts outside Prague that he agreed to meet the women halfway, in a town called Beroun.

Vlcek was a former Delta operative who had served in the Bosnian invasion, taken a liking to that part of the world, and decided to retire there. He was a part-time consultant to the Czech firearms manufacturer CZ and held a minority interest in a tequila bar and music venue in Prague. He had also been one of Julie's first instructors when she had joined Delta. It was precisely how she knew he was so sensitive about his age.

A gentleman and a professional, Vlcek had ar-

rived at the bar well in advance of Ericsson and
Rhodes. It would have been impolite to make the
ladies wait for him to get there, and old habits
died hard, so he arrived early enough to recon-
noiter the bar, get a feel for the clientele, and
make sure it wasn't under any sort of surveillance.
When Julie and Megan walked in, Vlcek stood to
greet them.

He was in his fifties, with long gray hair that he
kept tucked behind his ears. He sported a gray Van
Dyke and had piercing blue eyes beneath thick gray
eyebrows. His nose was long, but not unattractively
so. He was good-looking, in a rugged sort of way.
"Hello, Ms. Ericsson," he said, putting his arms out
for a hug.

Julie walked right up and embraced her former
instructor. "It's really good to see you."

"How's the leg?"

Ericsson had been shot a couple of months back
when the team had been taking out a terror cell in
Chicago. She stepped back from him, tapped her
leg, and replied, "Good as new."

"Ah, to be young again," said Vlcek.

He was staring at her teammate when he said
that, and she couldn't tell if he was referring to the
ability to heal quickly or his interest in Megan. She
decided to give him the benefit of the doubt. "John,
this is Megan," she said. "Megan, John."

"Damn, you're tall," said Vlcek.

"It's a pleasure to meet you, too," replied Rhodes.

"And good-looking, too."

So much for the benefit of the doubt. "Easy, big
fellah," said Julie.

"How do the boys at the Unit get any work done
with you ladies around?"

Megan didn't miss a beat. "All their trousers have bull's-eyes painted on the flies," she replied. "And we've got Tasers."

"Ouch," said Vlcek as he placed his hand over his crotch, and Megan winked at him.

A waitress came over as they took their seats, and the trio ordered coffee. They made small talk and caught up until she came back, and then they got down to business.

"Were you able to get everything on the list?" asked Ericsson.

"All business, this one," said Vlcek to Megan. "I bet she does all the heavy lifting for your team."

"We all do the heavy lifting. That's why it's called a *team*."

Vlcek dismissed the remark with a wave. "What I mean is that she's happy doing what needs to be done, even if it's not the most glamorous stuff. I'll bet she does most of the team's driving, right?"

Megan's eyes widened. He had her nailed. "Totally."

Vlcek smiled. "Driving is often one of the team's most important jobs. She never screws it up and she's always where she's supposed to be when she's supposed to be there. Am I right?"

Ericsson tried to interrupt, "John—"

Vlcek kept going. "She may pretend not to like some of the work, but if you're smart, you've made her the rock of your team. She's someone you'll always be able to count on. It came through on her pysch profile and I saw it for myself firsthand. Julie was consistently the most dependable person I ever trained—male *or* female.

"The shrinks said it had to do with being the oldest and helping her mother raise four brothers and sisters. That's BS. Julie is a thinker; a detail person. She sweats the small stuff, but it doesn't paralyze her. She may go out drinking with you all and get crazy, but don't let that fool you. She's going to know how many drinks you've had, who owes what, and who's walked in and sat where since you've been there. She's also going to make sure all of you get out of there and get home safely. That goes double when you're under fire. I would have put her on one of my teams in a heartbeat."

Rhodes was stunned. Finally, she said, "Wow. That's one hell of an endorsement. If I wasn't so good at reading people, I'd say you were just desperate to get her into the sack."

"Megan!" chastised Ericsson, her cheeks flushing. "John was my instructor. Our relationship has always been 100 percent professional."

Vlcek looked at Rhodes and it turned into a leer. "You, on the other hand, I didn't train, so anything that happens between us I'm happy to make one hundred percent personal."

Megan, the consummate tease, leered right back at him. "You promise?"

"You've got big stones, don't you?" he asked. "Not afraid of anything or anyone. No problem pulling the trigger and always the first one through the door. Am I right?"

Megan shrugged. "I'm really the shy, retiring type."

"I am right. Stone cold killer, it's written all over you. I'll bet your dad was an accountant, or a lawyer, or something like that."

"Nope."

"He wasn't a priest, was he?"

Rhodes laughed. "He was a cop."

Vlcek hadn't been ready for that response. "Seriously?"

"Seriously."

"Did you have any brothers?"

"Only child. And he raised me by himself."

Vlcek raised his hand like an imaginary pistol and pulled the trigger. "That explains everything." Leaning forward, he added, "I'll also bet you've got a thing for older male authority figures."

Megan winked at him again. "A girl's gotta have some secrets."

Ericsson rolled her eyes. "Can we get back to the list, please?" she interjected.

Vlcek, whose eyes were still locked on Megan, said, "Sure."

Julie waved a hand in front of his face to break his stare and get his full attention. When he finally broke off looking at Rhodes and turned to face her, Ericsson repeated her question. "Were you able to get everything on the list?"

Vlcek nodded. "Yup. No problem."

"Good. What can you tell us about Zbiroh? We've been given very little background."

"The man who owns the castle is supposedly a Czech organized crime figure."

"Supposedly?"

"I don't know the guy. All I know is that in the Czech Republic, if you're successful, everybody thinks you must be corrupt. It's a mind-set held over from the communist days. The only thing people seem to be able to agree on is that he's a pretty unsavory character. His name is Radek Heger," said Vlcek as he punched up a picture on his phone and showed it to them.

Rhodes recognized him right away. "We saw him when we were pulling up to the hotel," she said. "He got into a black Range Rover with his security detail."

"All ex–Czech Special Forces," stated Vlcek. "They not only do his security work, they also are in charge of excavations at the castle."

"What kind of excavations?" asked Ericsson.

"The whisper is that Heger didn't buy that dilapidated castle to turn it into a hotel or to help preserve a piece of Czech history. He bought it so that he could exploit any of the treasure the Nazis might have left behind."

Rhodes took a sip of her coffee and said, "Why hire ex-SF personnel for that?"

"Because the crazy Nazis boobytrapped everything. The men Heger hired have EOD experience. They know how to dispose of all the hand grenades and other explosive devices the Germans rigged their tunnels and vaults with."

"If there's anything of value at the castle, why didn't the Czech government go after it themselves?" asked Ericsson.

"Easy. They didn't have the money or desire. Nobody knows if there's anything there at all. The place was crumbling, and when Heger offered to buy it, the government said yes, provided Heger completely restored it and opened at least part of it to the public. They also strong-armed him into the hotel that now takes up the south wing."

"But obviously he believes there's something there, or he wouldn't have gone to all the trouble and expense."

Vlcek nodded. "There's lots of stories about gold and priceless pieces of art being hidden there. In the waning days of the war, villagers saw tons of things being transported up to the castle, but when the Nazis fled, they did so empty-handed. So whatever was up there must still be up there."

"Anything else you can tell us?"

"Besides the fact that the castle survived a couple of near misses from bombing runs at the end of the war, that's about it."

They drifted back into small talk as they finished their coffees. By the time they walked outside, they didn't know much more about what they were looking for, or what had gone on at Zbiroh Castle, than when they had arrived.

In a secluded area ten minutes outside of town, they transferred the gear Vlcek had procured for them into the trunk of their car.

Giving him one last hug, Julie Ericsson said, "It was good seeing you again, John. Thanks for your help."

"It was good seeing you, too," he said. "Be careful. And tell the rest of your team to be careful, too. If even half of what they say about Heger is true, you're better off staying as far away from him as possible."

Vlcek then gave Rhodes one last, long look from head to toe and said, "See ya, Stretch," before getting into his beat-up car and pulling back out onto the road.

Megan pretended to hold a phone to her ear and teasingly whispered, "Call me."

As Vlcek disappeared from sight, Rhodes looked at her teammate. "God, that guy has you pegged."

Ericsson didn't respond.

Megan was about to say something else until

she caught the look on Julie's face. Reality was already settling back in. The visit with John Vlcek was over. It was time to face what they had all been quietly trying to ignore. There was something about this operation that they weren't being told.

CHAPTER 15

S he's not going to screw up," said Ben Matthews, as he and his partner, Dean Pence,
sat in a dark blue Mazda in a parking garage
downtown. "She's a professional."

Pence was fifteen years Ben's senior, with black
hair graying at the temples. They were discussing
Victoria Suffolk.

"Really?" replied Pence. "Supposedly, so were
those Russian spies the Bureau caught in New
York."

Matthews nodded. Pence had been at the FBI
a lot longer than he had. If anyone knew how the
espionage game was played, it was Pence. In fact,
this entire operation had been his idea.

Neither of them really knew what the government had built beneath Denver's sprawling international airport. All they were certain of was that it
had attracted a lot of attention from foreign intelligence agencies.

Matthews figured that it probably served as

some sort of continuity-of-government facility, a place the United States could evacuate members of Congress and other key political figures to if there was ever a major threat to the nation. Of course, they'd have to have enough advance knowledge to get them from D.C. to Denver, but that didn't seem impossible.

Pence, though, disagreed with him. He figured it was some sort of modernized command-and-control structure meant to replace North American Aerospace Defense Command's operations in the aging Cheyenne Mountain Complex. *What better place to coordinate the nation's air defense from, than an airport?* he had asked.

Whatever the U.S. government *or* the U.S. military was doing beneath Denver International, they certainly had gone to interesting lengths to camouflage it.

Matthews could remember visiting the once top-secret congressional fallout shelter beneath the Greenbrier Hotel in West Virginia. In the late 1950s, at the behest of the U.S. government, the Greenbrier had built an entirely new wing to disguise the massive excavations needed to construct the bunker. The public had absolutely no knowledge of its existence until an investigative reporter, acting on an alleged tip, blew the lid off of the program in the mid-1990s.

But for some reason, the powers-that-be behind Denver International had taken a completely different approach.

In February 1995, despite massive protests, the city of Denver closed its previous airport, Stapleton International, and opened the brand-new Denver International, or DIA, as it was commonly called. It was the largest international airport in the United States and was allegedly built to allow Denver to step into the future, yet with fewer gates and fewer runways, the new airport actually had reduced capacity.

It was built in a severe high-wind area that often forced the delay and cancellation of flights. Originally budgeted at $1.5 billion, by the time it was completed, the price tag had risen to $5.3 billion. Some said that was due to incompetence. Others said it was by design.

Despite the fact that the fifty-three-square-mile site was perfectly flat, great effort was made to raise some areas and lower others. When all was said and done, over 110 million cubic yards of earth had been moved, the equivalent of one-third of the earth moved for the Panama Canal.

The construction had begun with five unusual buildings built below grade. As soon as they were completed, they were deemed to have been built incorrectly. But instead of being demolished or retrofitted, the buildings were simply buried.

There were up to eight levels of sub-basements beneath the airport itself and almost ninety miles of tunnels, many large enough to drive semi trucks through. Air vents and exchangers could be seen popping up from the ground at even the most remote, barren corners of the enormous property.

Surrounding the entire fifty-three square miles was a continuous barbwire fence. But the barbed wire was not angled out, as it was at other airports. It was angled in. And things only get odder from there.

Satellite imagery showed that the runways had been laid out in a rough swastika pattern.

Inside the airport were two enormous, highly

disturbing murals, which many claimed to be a manifesto hidden in plain sight.

In the first mural was a Nazi soldier wearing a gas mask with dead women and children scattered around him. In the second, a city burned in the background as Third World populations died and a handful of the elite, in specially sealed containers, were saved from the raging apocalypse. Had Ben not seen these murals for himself, he never would have believed they existed. They were right there, out in the open for anyone traveling through the airport to see.

Embedded in the floor near the murals were the letters Au Ag, which was the abbreviation for the deadly toxin Australian Antigen. In other places bizarre acronyms like DZIT, DIT, and GAII appeared.

Then there was the granite cornerstone in the main terminal, supposedly laid by the Freemasons and packed with Masonic symbolism. Engraved upon it were the words "New World Airport Commission," despite the fact that there was no record of any such commission ever having existed. Ben had researched for himself.

Mysterious electromagnetic pulse phenomena supposedly had cracked airplane windshields and caused people to fall ill. Fifteen acres of Teflon-coated radar and infrared-signature-resistant woven fiberglass covered the roof. The queen of England and other elites were rumored to be snapping up real estate around DIA, while contractors and construction workers had been allowed to work only for short periods on the project before being replaced, allegedly so that they didn't grasp the scope of what they were working on.

Throw in what appeared to be open-air elevator shafts big enough to swallow 747s, along with a terrifying thirty-two-foot-high statue of a rearing blue horse with glowing red eyes that airport officials claimed was necessary to ward off evil spirits, and you had a conspiracy theorist's wet dream.

It was almost too much in Matthews's eyes, which was exactly what made him suspect that was the government's intent. So many crackpot theories had exploded around DIA that every single one of them was laughed off by anyone with half a brain. Little green men could walk out of baggage claim and hail a cab, and the whole thing could be reported on the front page of the *Denver Post*, complete with photos, and not a single sane person would believe it.

It reminded him of Edgar Allan Poe's "The Purloined Letter" in which a stolen letter, packed with sensitive information, is hidden right in plain sight. In Ben's estimation, whoever was responsible for what was happening beneath Denver International was either absolutely nuts, or incredibly brilliant. Though he was unaccustomed to attributing brilliance to the government, he had a feeling in this case that it might be merited.

Which brought Ben back to what he and his partner were doing right now. When Vicki Suffolk had become known to the Denver FBI field office, courtesy of one of Pence's local informants, the elder FBI man had suggested they try to flip her, to double her back against the Russians. The SAC, or special agent in charge, a woman by the name of Carole Mumford, hadn't been so keen. She didn't want her career tarnished by greenlighting some elaborate op against nothing more than another Facebook-obsessed, low-level Russian Mata Hari. The spy ring the Bureau had recently rolled up in New York was an embarrassment, both for Russia and America. Permission for Pence's op was denied. Permission to surveil the subject, though, was authorized, and Pence and Matthews had been given the job.

Over the course of their surveillance, they had learned very little about Victoria Suffolk. All they knew was that she was interested in Denver International Airport.

That was enough for Pence. His gut told him that there was something special about this case; something big. He felt certain it was going to make both of their careers. Mumford, though, didn't see it that way. She remained unwilling to allocate further resources to Victoria Suffolk unless Pence and Matthews could bring her something substantive. This left the two FBI agents in a difficult position.

They had been approved only to surveil Suffolk, nothing else, but the surveillance wasn't producing. After three weeks, Pence sold Matthews on expanding their efforts by putting some teeth into what they were doing. That's when they began pushing the envelope. And as many people who fall from lofty heights eventually realize, the sins begin small, but from little sins, bigger sins soon grow.

Pence was the one who had bugged her apartment and her car without a warrant and without the FBI's approval. But from that, they learned that Suffolk was looking to place someone in DIA. That was why Matthews had studied up on all the conspiracy theories surrounding it. Pence had a pretty good feeling that if they dangled Ben in front of her, she'd take the bait, which was exactly what she had done.

Warrantless eavesdropping was the first of Dean Pence's sins. Ben Matthews's sins began when he first took Suffolk to bed. She had made so many advances, he was worried she was getting suspicious. He told himself that if he didn't sleep with her, it might blow the entire operation. It was a lie and he knew it, but he couldn't help himself.

Not only did he know it was wrong, he also knew what Pence would do to him if he confessed, so he lied to his partner as well. This entire operation felt cursed, and part of him wished that he had never met Victoria Suffolk.

Dean Pence looked at his watch. "If she can lead us to her handler, there could be a whole network of Russian spies we could take down."

Once again, Ben shook his head and repeated. "I'm telling you, she's good. I don't think she's going to make that kind of mistake."

Their meeting was pretty much over. If Matthews was going to get out to DIA in time for his shift, he had to get going.

After an uncomfortable pause, Pence said, "Ben, I need to ask you something."

Ben was now looking at his own watch. "What is it?"

"Are you having sex with her?"

"Who?" replied Matthews. "Suffolk?"

"Who else?"

Ben looked his partner right in the eyes. "I am not having sex with Victoria Suffolk."

"Not that anyone would blame you," said Pence. "She's extremely good-looking."

"Dean," Ben insisted. "I'm not having sex with her. Okay?"

"You'd tell me if you were, right?"

"Of course I would."

Pence shook his head. "I don't know. Maybe this is a bad idea. You're still raw from your divorce. Dropping you into a situation like this isn't fair."

The elder FBI agent was right. It wasn't fair. Ben's divorce had been beyond messy. His ex had kicked him in the teeth so hard and so many times it was a wonder he didn't need to eat all of his meals through a straw.

His wife had been the one who cheated, but throughout the bitter, scorched-earth proceedings, she had blamed all the problems in the marriage on Ben.

All things considered, was he vulnerable? Absolutely, but divorce or no divorce, there weren't many men who could say no to a woman like Victoria Suffolk. The fact that Ben Matthews hadn't even caught as much as a second look from a halfway attractive woman in the eight months since his divorce had begun to nudge him dangerously close to the desperate column.

Women like Suffolk didn't happen to men like Ben Matthews, at least that was what he believed. Sleeping with her was wrong on multiple levels and he knew it. It was something that had been bothering him more and more. Nevertheless, he had yet to find the strength to bring it to a halt.

Determined to shield himself and the relationship from criticism by Pence, Ben lied a final time. "I'm *not* having sex with that woman."

His partner studied him. "That's almost believable," he joked. "Wag your finger and say it like Bill Clinton this time."

"I'm going to be late for work," replied Matthews as he opened the door and stepped out of the car.

Pence put the Mazda in reverse and followed him. Rolling down the passenger window, he said, "Ben, for what it's worth, I do believe you."

"You don't sound like it," replied Matthews as he pulled his keys from his pocket and unlocked his truck.

"You're a big boy, Ben. You can make your own decisions. Just be careful, okay?" cautioned the elder FBI agent. "I've got a bad feeling that Victoria Suffolk is going to turn out to be a very dangerous woman."

CHAPTER 16

Jogging in the Arapaho National Forest was one of Vicki Suffolk's favorite things to do. Today, though, she wondered if maybe it hadn't been such a good idea. She had a very bad feeling that someone or *something* was following her.

It was the same trail she always took and one she had never seen anyone else on. The feeling coming over her was not one of regret that her private corner of the world had suddenly been discovered. This was a visceral feeling of being stalked.

She had already doubled back twice, trying to flush out whoever was behind her, but that hadn't worked. Part of her mind wondered if maybe her imagination was in overdrive, but her instincts quickly shut down that dissenting opinion.

The one thing she had been taught was to always remain calm. The moment she let fear take over would be the moment she lost. That was easier said than done. Her heart was pounding and the adrenaline was coursing through her bloodstream. She could almost sense the thoughts of the thing pursuing her. It was powerful, hungry, and extremely cunning. *It had to be a bear.*

Unlike her beta-male, conspiracy-obsessed "boyfriend," Ben, Vicki Suffolk didn't have a problem with guns. While she kept hers a secret from him, she never went jogging, especially in a national forest, without it.

Unzipping her runner's pack, she withdrew her Glock Slimline 36. It held six rounds of .45 caliber ammunition in a single-stack magazine. *Would six rounds plus one in the chamber be enough?*

She drew the pistol and turned to face whatever was pursuing her. The forest grew quiet, all of its creatures seemingly holding their breath in unison. It was as if someone had just hit the Mute button.

Was that really it? Or was her mind playing tricks on her? She waited, straining her ears for any sound of approaching danger. She peered into the forest around her, hoping to catch a glimpse of what was following her. She heard nothing and she saw nothing, so she did nothing.

She stood frozen for what felt like an eternity. Whatever was out there was patient, very patient.

A wind blew down along the path and teased the hairs on the back of her neck. Her skin, which had been covered with a thin film of sweat from jogging, was now cold and clammy to the touch. She could feel a chill spreading throughout her body.

The anxiety she was experiencing seemed to be playing itself out in the clouds above the tops of the trees. They were gray and telegraphed a rapidly approaching storm. A storm meant rain and rain meant acoustic cover for whatever was following her.

Taking her eyes off the path for a moment, Vicki

glanced uphill. There was an abandoned miner's cabin only a few hundred yards away. She couldn't see it from where she now stood, but she knew it was there. It would keep her dry. It would also give her a tactical advantage over whatever was out there stalking her. Cautiously, Vicki made her way toward the cabin.

Fifty feet from the door, she heard a branch snap somewhere behind her. The rational part of her brain told her that if there was a bear back there, she'd never outrun it. All she could hope was that her shots would all find their marks and that seven rounds of .45 would be enough. She gripped her pistol tighter than she ever had in her life and picked up her pace. She needed to get to safety.

The trail gave onto a clearing beneath the trees. It was covered in pine needles and fallen branches. Up ahead was the abandoned cabin, its windows broken and its roof falling apart. Vicki didn't want to look over her shoulder, but she knew she had to. If a bear was indeed after her, she'd need to turn and shoot.

Vicki risked a glance back. There was nothing there. No bear, no nothing. Part of her said she was overreacting. Another part, her primal instinct, screamed at her to run. *Run!*

Vicki listened to that primal voice and ran like never before. She barreled into the front door of the cabin and sent it exploding inward, almost knocking it off its rusted hinges.

As soon as she was inside, she slammed the door and flattened her back against it. Her eyes scanned the room for something to place against it. *Something. Anything.* There was nothing. The cabin had been stripped bare.

She knew she'd be no match for any bear that wanted to come through the door. She wouldn't be able to hold it shut. She simply wasn't strong enough.

Bolting to the other side of the tiny cabin, she slid to the floor and placed her back against the wall. If it came through the front door, she'd have a clean shot. It could come through one of the broken windows as well, though it would have a much harder time of it.

Sitting there on the floor, her heart thumping and the sound of blood rushing in and out of her ears like the ocean, she knew she had to calm down. She had to get control of herself. *Deep breath,* she thought. *Start with one deep breath.*

She took in a long, deep breath and held it for a count of three and then slowly, silently let it out. She counted to five and then repeated the process. From above the dilapidated roof, there was an ear-splitting crack of thunder. The cabin grew dark.

Outside, the wind moved the branches of the heavy trees. It also moved the cabin door. As the door creaked in on its hinges, Vicki Suffolk caught a glimpse of something on the threshold and her heart caught in her throat.

CHAPTER 17

Lying just beyond the open cabin door was a bouquet of Rocky Mountain Irises. Gathering them up, Suffolk stepped outside, her heart beating even faster than before. *Where is he?* she thought to herself.

With her gun an afterthought as it dangled in her hand, she stepped outside. The trunks of the trees near the cabin were too narrow to hide behind. She tried to lick her lips, but her mouth was dry.

She spun quickly around, but there was no one behind her. Walking to the corner of the cabin, she peeked around it, but there was no one there either. Her legs were weak and her stomach was churning, but she pressed on. She walked behind the cabin, but saw nothing. Finally, she came the rest of the way around to the front door. As she did, the rain came down in a torrent.

Her heart was pounding against her chest. "Hello?" she called out into the storm. "Hello?"

There was flash of lightning as the bolt struck somewhere close by. Barely a second had passed before thunder rocked the ground. That was the moment she felt the hand on the back of her neck. He had come from behind, from inside the cabin. He must have slipped in while she was walking around the outside.

As his grip tightened on her, his other hand reached down and took away her gun. She didn't struggle. Slowly, he drew her back inside.

She knew what would happen next and she resigned herself to it. She had no idea if the man was wearing a mask or not. Just in case, she knew it was better to keep her eyes shut tight; to not look at his face.

His backpack lay cast aside. On the floor he had hastily unrolled his sleeping bag. He laid her down and once she was lying flat on her back he raised her arms above her head. He grabbed both her wrists with his powerful left hand as if he knew that she was going to fight him when he began to undress her. And fight she did.

When his right hand slid underneath her jog bra, she brought her left knee up hard into his side. He muttered some sort of curse and threw himself on top of her, straddling her legs. She fought hard and snapped her teeth wildly, hoping to get a piece of him.

When she heard the click of his knife locking into place, she froze. He kept her arms pinned above her head and he waited. Outside the lightning flashed, the thunder roared, and the rain poured down.

He drew the flat of the blade along her lithe, tight stomach and then slowly moved it upward. She didn't fight. She lay still. The entire time she kept her eyes tightly shut, not wanting to risk seeing his face.

He cut the jog bra from her body and cast it to the side, exposing her breasts. He did the same to her running shorts.

She felt him slide out of his trousers and then and only then did she open one of her eyes, but only part way. He was wearing a ski mask. *He had remembered.*

CHAPTER 18

They lay on the floor of the cabin panting, working to catch their breath as their heart rates came back to normal.

"You can take the mask off now if you want," said Vicki.

Peter Marcus pulled the mask from his head and tossed it toward his backpack. His hair was drenched with sweat.

"I could have shot you," she said as she drew herself closer to him.

Marcus smiled. "But you didn't."

"But I could have."

"And that's what made it exciting," he said, and then added, "for both of us."

"Do you remember the first time you gave me Mountain Irises?"

"I do," he replied. "I also remember showing you how their roasted seeds could be used as a coffee substitute."

"Ummmm," she said, closing her eyes.

They lay in silence next to each other, listening

to the storm rage outside. The gusts of wind were so strong they shook the little cabin.

Vicki ran her fingers across his chest. "I don't suppose you've got any Power Bars in your pack, do you? I'm starving."

"Why don't you go check?"

She gave him a long kiss on the mouth and then pushed herself to standing. Even in the almost pitch-dark he could see how beautiful she was.

She picked up the pack and looked inside. "Oh, my God," she said. "Are you kidding me?"

"Did I do well?" he asked.

"I love it!" she cooed as she pulled a bottle of wine and a small cooler bag from his backpack. "It's a little early in the day, but who cares, right?"

"Bring the whole pack over," he told her. "There's silverware and dishes and a picnic cloth in there."

"Picnic blanket," Vicki corrected.

"Picnic blanket," Peter repeated dutifully.

Suffolk handed him the bottle of wine along with the corkscrew she had found at the bottom of the pack with a few other items. He laid out some candles and lit them.

"Can you find my cigarettes, please?" he asked.

"You're smoking again?"

"Victoria, you're not my mother."

"Of course not. I'm way too young to be your mother," she responded. "Seriously, Peter, I thought you had quit."

"Please, Victoria. May I just have my cigarettes?" he asked.

Suffolk rummaged around in the backpack.

"They're in the outside pocket," he said.

When she found the pocket in question, she unzipped it and pulled them out. "I really thought you had quit. You said you were going to do it for me."

Marcus shrugged.

"You know what? You're going cold turkey. Right now."

"What if I get a craving?" he said with a smile.

Vicki smiled back at him and said, "You let me worry about your cravings." With that, she crushed the cigarettes and pitched them over her shoulder.

"I wouldn't do that if I were you," he said.

"Peter, please. How stupid do you think I am? You trained me, after all. Do you really think I would leave something like that behind? We'll take it all with us when we leave. Speaking of which," she said as she gestured to her naked body, "you better have brought an extra set of clothes for me."

Marcus began working on the wine bottle. "We're in the middle of a forest. There's bound to be a few fig leaves around."

Vicki laughed and kept digging. She found a shirt and pair of women's running pants, brand-new, with the tags still on them. Thanking her paramour, she set them off to the side.

As Peter poured them each a glass of wine, he said, "Bring the cigarettes over to me, would you please?"

"No," replied Vicki.

"Trust me," he said as he handed her a glass.

Vicki gave in and reached over to pick up the crumpled package. "I don't even like touching these things," she said as she offered it to him.

"Open it up."

She started to ask why, but the look in his eyes stopped her. Gently, she lifted the lid. The inside was stuffed with cotton, like you would find in an aspirin bottle. "Peter, what is this?" she asked.

"You'll see."

Pulling out the lumps of cotton, Vicki quickly realized that the package hadn't contained cigarettes at all. "It's gorgeous!" she said as she removed the necklace. "Where did you find it?"

"Do you remember that jewelry store you liked?"

"The one in Naples?"

He nodded. "The woman remembered you. In fact, when I walked in, the first thing she asked me was where you were."

Suffolk smiled as she held up the necklace and put it on. "You're a liar, but I still love it. When were you in Naples?"

"About a month ago," he replied. After a beat, he added, "Alone."

"I'm not naïve, Peter."

"It's true."

Vicki allowed herself to believe it and she pressed the necklace to her bare chest.

"How about you?" he asked. "Your reports have been very professional, very clinical. Are you sleeping with him?"

Suffolk took a sip of her wine as she decided how to respond. "That's what you wanted, isn't it?"

Peter Marcus smiled. "You're a very attractive woman, Victoria."

"You didn't answer my question."

Marcus took a sip of his wine. It was important that she felt the decision pained him and that he had trouble talking about it. "We don't make the rules of the game. We are just forced to play by them."

"Oh, puh-lease!"

He loved how direct she could be. "Okay, yes. I

did say that you were authorized to sleep with him. Secretly I hoped it wouldn't be necessary, but perhaps it was. At least you appear to have been successful. I will comfort myself with that."

Suffolk moved back over and rubbed her body against his. "You can also comfort yourself with the fact that when I was in bed with him, the only way I could do it was if I pretended I was with you."

She leaned over, her breasts brushing against his chest, and kissed his lips. As the tiny tea candles burned, they ignored the food and made love once more.

An hour later, the wine almost gone, Marcus stared at the ceiling and said, "We need to have a talk."

Suffolk propped herself up on an elbow. "About what?"

He took his eyes from the ceiling and looked at her. "What you're going to do with Ben Matthews's body."

CHAPTER 19

Gretchen Casey phoned down to the hotel's concierge and asked him to prepare a list of restaurant and nightclub suggestions in Prague. When the women stepped out of the elevator and crossed the lobby forty-five minutes later, heads turned so fast you could hear necks snapping.

Considering what these women did for a living, they certainly wouldn't have described themselves as being dressed to kill, but everyone else would have. High heels, perfect hair and makeup, and dresses that left very little to the imagination screamed: big night on the town.

Everything came to a stop as the four gorgeous women walked across the marble floor to the concierge desk. They made small talk with the staff as the concierge handed Casey the list he had prepared and then handed them a map and highlighted the route to Prague.

Outside, the valets had the ladies' car ready and

waiting. They wished the women a pleasant evening and seemed to take an unusual amount of care
in seeing that their legs were fully tucked into the
vehicle before closing the doors.

Once they had driven about a hundred yards,
the women all burst out laughing. "They're going
to be mopping up the drool out of that lobby for
a month," joked Rhodes from the front passenger
seat.

Cooper looked over her shoulder and out the
rear window. "The valet who opened my door was
kind of cute."

"Now that we know you like them that young,"
said Ericsson as she turned out onto the road, "we'll
stop hitting bars and start taking you to high school
football games."

After the laughter in the car subsided, Cooper
said, "Okay, maybe not *that* young."

"Stick with the young ones," said Casey, looking
out her window. "The older they get, the more of a
pain in the ass they become."

"Ain't that the truth," replied Rhodes.

"Whatever happened to if he's older, he'll hold
her?" asked Ericsson, trying to catch Casey's eyes in
the rearview mirror.

Rhodes didn't give her a chance to answer. "If
he's younger, he's *probably got the hunger,* if you
know what I mean," she proclaimed.

That got a laugh from everyone but Casey, who
was still staring out the window, preoccupied with
her own thoughts.

The wooded hotel grounds were quite extensive,
and after about two kilometers, Ericsson pulled the
car off onto a barely visible dirt road. She drove
slowly, the headlights bouncing with each rut and

pothole they hit. Above them, the thick canopy of trees blocked out the night sky.

As a clearing approached, Ericsson slowed down and pulled in. She drove over uneven ground for about fifty yards until the car was completely hidden from the road and then shut off the ignition. "We go the rest of the way on foot."

"Not in these shoes we don't," said Cooper.

Julie hit the trunk release button. "Boots and clothes are in back," she replied. "Megan and I cached the rest of the gear up ahead."

The women stepped out of the car and grabbed their backpacks from the trunk. As the car had been under the hotel's control, nothing out of the ordinary had been left inside. If anyone had searched their vehicle, all they would have found was hiking gear.

Once they had changed, Megan Rhodes clicked on her flashlight and used its filtered beam to guide them deeper into the woods.

The equipment John Vlcek had provided had been organized in several black duffel bags, which were hidden well out of sight. Even in broad daylight, they would have been difficult to find unless you knew exactly where to look. Rhodes and Ericsson quickly divided up the gear.

In addition to night vision goggles, or NVGs as they were known, Vlcek had provided them with .40 caliber CZ Rami pistols and extra magazines, as well as encrypted radios and a few other items Hutton had asked for. After checking their weapons and loading the gear in their packs, they recached the duffel bags and Megan Rhodes once again took the lead, using a pre-programmed GPS to guide their way.

Hans Kammler had done an excellent job of hiding his research facility in the 1940s. Even modern satellite technology was unable to pick it up.

The warm day had turned into a rather cool night. The women were glad to have brought several layers. As they followed Megan, keeping about five yards between team members as their training had taught them, they maintained complete silence. Their senses were acutely aware of every sound and every movement in the forest around them. Casey had been very clear; they were operating blind and had to remain prepared for anything. The lack of information still weighed heavily on each of them, though no one said anything. No one needed to. They'd worked together long enough that they could almost read each other's minds.

After fifteen minutes of walking, Megan signaled the team to stop. As they did, she waved for Gretchen to come forward. Casey did as Megan asked, but it wasn't until she was standing right next to her that she saw what her point woman was looking at—a high chain-link fence topped with razor wire. And it was relatively new. Whoever had placed it there, it certainly wasn't the Nazis. Someone was trying to keep people from going any farther.

Rhodes motioned for the team to stay put while she investigated. Ericsson and Cooper turned to guard against possible ambush, while Casey scanned what part of the forest she could see beyond the fence.

Megan returned a few moments later. "I don't see any cameras, and the fence doesn't appear to be electrified," she said. "But that doesn't mean they don't have buried seismic sensors, or something else I'm not picking up. I did, though, notice several large signs warning people not to trespass."

"Well, that does it for me then," joked Ericsson. "I'm going back. I'm tired anyway."

"It is getting pretty late," said Cooper, adding to the humor.

Casey ignored her teammates. "Do we have any wire cutters?"

Rhodes nodded and swung off her pack. Lifting the top, she sifted around until she found a pair of C7 Swiss wire cutters, about the size of a large set of pliers, which could cut through wire up to three-eighths of an inch thick, and pulled them out.

Gretchen walked the fence until she found a support pole and began clipping there. A few minutes later, she had made an opening large enough for them to squeeze through one at a time if they took their packs off.

Once they had all gathered on the other side of the fence, Casey gave the signal for Rhodes to lead them forward.

They walked for less than five minutes and came to another fence. No one needed to say anything; they were all thinking the same thing. Whoever had built these fences was serious about keeping people out.

As before, Megan checked the fence and once she deemed it was okay, Gretchen went to work cutting just enough to get them through one at a time without their packs.

If someone was serious enough to have erected two fences, there was no telling what other measures they had taken. The women's already heightened senses were even more keenly alert.

As they walked, they came upon a large stone

with an odd symbol carved upon it. "Runic letters," said Rhodes. "Nazi occult stuff."

Casey had a real thing about the occult. She didn't like it at all. She felt a chill race down her spine and tried to shake it off. Getting Megan's attention, she signaled for her to move out.

They passed several large piles of oddly shaped rocks. The rocks were jagged and misshapen as if they had been chiseled, or more than likely blasted out of the earth. They were getting closer. They all could feel it.

It didn't just come from the piles of rocks or the runic symbols. There was an aura to this place, an aura of pure evil. The deeper they pushed into the woods, the colder the air became and the more unsettled they all felt. Death seemed to hang in the very air itself.

The path suddenly sloped downward and curved to the right, and that's when they saw it.

CHAPTER 20

The opening to the tunnel was big enough to drive a truck through. Above it, carved in relief, was a Nazi eagle emblazoned with the immediately identifiable letters SS.

They were standing on the remnants of what once must have been a paved road of some sort. Rocks were scattered everywhere and several trees had been sheared in half. *Had someone used explosives to blow the rocks away from the bunker entrance?* Unless someone had come spinning through the forest with a buzz saw set at random heights, it was the only thing that made sense. As the rocks had been blasted away from the entrance, they had exploded outward, snapping the enormous trees like matchsticks.

"Looks like we found it," said Ericsson.

Cascy and the others nodded.

While they had no idea what kind of research had gone on inside the underground complex, they knew they were staring at a piece of history; a piece of history few even knew existed.

"Are we going to stand here all night?" asked Rhodes. "Or are we going to go inside and look around?"

"We're going to have to leave one person outside to stand guard," said Gretchen.

Reflexively, she began to look in Ericsson's direction until Cooper said, "I'll do it. I'll stay outside."

"Okay then," replied Casey. "Megan and Jules, you're with me."

As Alex took up her position at the entrance, the three other women struck off down into the tunnel.

"Remember, the Nazis boobytrapped everything. So be careful."

"Roger that," said Rhodes and Ericsson in unison.

Their night vision goggles cast an infrared beam that helped illuminate the tunnel. Alex Cooper watched from her position until her teammates disappeared from view, swallowed by the darkness.

As the three women walked, they noticed the composition of the tunnel walls changing. The solid stone was soon studded with minerals as they went deeper.

"Quartz?" asked Rhodes as she reached out to touch some of the crystalline formations they were passing.

"Either that," replied Casey, "or Kammler's *miraculous minerals*."

"This place has got a very bad vibe to it," said Ericsson.

Vibe was the right word, thought Casey, and it was definitely bad. The tunnel seemed to pulse with an ominous force all its own.

"Hey, Jules," said Rhodes. "If we find anything in here with a full set of teeth, it's all yours, okay?"

"And I'll make sure to send anything that's younger or has a hunger right your way," Ericsson replied.

Something along the ceiling caught her eye and Casey looked up. They appeared to be murals.

The other two women followed her gaze.

"Man, the Nazis were sick," said Megan as she stared at a rearing horse with glowing eyes leading a dancing column of skeletons. "I thought this was supposed to be some sort of scientific facility."

"It was," answered Gretchen.

"So what's with the paintings?"

"I've got no idea. Let's keep moving."

"Shouldn't we be getting video of this?" asked Ericsson.

"Probably," agreed Casey, who stopped to remove the digital night-vision camera from her pack.

Turning it on, she pointed it toward the ceiling and then pressed the record button. "Okay, let's move," she said.

Every thirty feet was another set of blast doors that had been propped open. A string of lightbulbs ran down the tunnel's left side. Up ahead, they could see what looked like a guard station of some sort carved out of the solid rock.

"Would it surprise anyone if suddenly three SS officers just stepped right out in front of us?" asked Rhodes.

Casey instinctively reached for her pistol just to make sure it was still there.

"How deep into this place do you want to go?" Julie asked.

"As far as we can," replied Casey.

The answer was good enough for Ericsson, who kept checking behind them, to make sure they weren't being followed.

They stepped into the old stone guardhouse. There was a desk with a field telephone that was vintage World War II. There was also a cot, a table with two chairs, and a bookcase lined with moldy, German-language books. On one of the walls was a small control panel with a series of buttons and dials that looked as if it might have been responsible for the opening and closing of the heavy blast doors they had been passing through.

"Check this out," said Rhodes as she dusted off the desk. "More runes."

Casey looked down and saw the strange string of symbols that had been carved with the point of a knife. "More Nazi occultism. Terrific. Let's keep going."

They exited the guardhouse and continued walking deeper into the tunnel.

"When do you think somebody opened this place back up?" asked Ericsson.

Casey shook her head. "I don't know. It's hard to tell."

"Weeks? Months? Years?"

"Jules, I don't know."

"Sorry, I didn't mean to—"

"I'm not angry," replied Casey. "I'm just trying to process what I'm seeing too, okay?"

"Okay."

"I've got about as much of this figured out at this point as you do."

"I got it," said Ericsson. "Enough said."

Casey chastised herself for not being more professional, but Ericsson had a bad habit of asking dumb questions when she was on edge. Gretchen didn't need that now.

The trio moved on in silence. Above them, the Nazi murals grew more macabre. Casey continued filming, just as she had in the guardhouse. She had no idea if any of this would be of value back home, but she had her orders.

Up ahead, they came to their first obstacle—a set of blast doors that were closed. Rhodes tried to push them open, but they wouldn't budge.

"Maybe they left the key under the mat," said Ericsson.

"What mat?"

"Found it," said Casey, as she ran her fingers down along the outline of a smaller entrance that had been cut into one of the blast doors.

Ericsson came over, flipped up her NVGs, and lit up the lock with her filtered flashlight.

"What do you think?" Casey asked after a couple of moments.

Ericsson studied the rest of the door for any sign that it was wired, either with boobytraps or with alarm sensors, and then finally said, "I can do it."

Taking off her backpack, she removed a small zippered case. Holding the flashlight in her mouth, she unzipped the case and pulled out a small steel lockpick gun.

Kneeling, she adjusted the flashlight and then slid the tension wrench into the lock and applied a slight amount of downward pressure. Next came the pick gun. Once it was inserted, she began pulling the trigger. The noise it made resembled a stapler being depressed over and over.

She adjusted the tension wrench a couple times and then felt the lock give way.

Removing the equipment from the lock, she said, "We're in."

Casey and Rhodes drew their weapons and pointed them at the door as Ericsson stowed her gear and then slung her pack over her shoulders.

Flipping her NVGs back down, she reached for the door handle and waited. All three took a deep breath and then Casey whispered, *"Go."*

CHAPTER 21

Ericsson pulled on the handle and the door swept back soundlessly on perfectly greased hinges.

Rhodes stepped through the doorway, followed by Casey and Ericsson, who closed the door behind them. They then moved forward slowly, purposefully.

"Wasn't this place supposed to have been flooded?" asked Rhodes.

Casey nodded. "Part of it," she said as she looked around at the large room they were now in. It appeared to be an airlock of some sort. There was a large freight elevator at one end and across from it an oval, pressure-style door with a wheel that acted as a handle. Casey walked over to it and cranked the wheel until the lock released. When it did, she pulled the door open and a blast of damp, moldy air rushed out.

Inside was a concrete landing and a flight of stairs going down. Casey motioned for the team to follow her.

As they descended, the smell of mold grew stronger. At the bottom of the stairs they found another door like the one above. Rhodes and Ericsson made ready while Casey turned the handle. When the lock *clanked* into place, she nodded to her teammates, opened the door, and they swept into the hallway on the other side.

With its tiled floor, concrete walls, and bulkhead light fixtures, it looked as if they could have been in some European hospital's basement. As Casey turned off her night vision goggles and flipped them up, Rhodes and Ericsson followed suit. They removed the filters from their flashlights and let the powerful beams illuminate the hall.

It had been underwater for a long time and most everything was discolored. Heavy metal doors lined both sides. One by one, the women searched the rooms.

They were in offices of some sort. There were desks, lamps, filing cabinets, and typewriters. There were also microscopes, calipers, and surgical instruments. From the rusted wastepaper cans to stacks of German newspapers molded together by water, it all formed a bizarre sort of time capsule. There was no doubt that they were indeed inside Kammler's secret research facility.

The women checked the drawers of the desks and file cabinets, but they were all empty. Someone had cleaned the entire place out.

At the end of the corridor were two more hallways, one to the right and one to the left. They stayed together and explored the one on the left first. There was a cafeteria, a more formal private dining area, and a kitchen in between that served both. There had been a hierarchy here, and it was obvious in the tin lunch trays in the cafeteria and the neatly stacked, SS monogrammed china in the private dining room.

There was a library and a communal gathering area. After that came the bedrooms. There were some that had only one bed, but the majority had two to four. There were communal bathrooms with sinks, toilets, and showers. At the very end of the hall were what appeared to be a barracks with row upon row of bunk beds.

As they explored, Casey made sure she kept capturing everything on video. The bunker felt like some sort of strange museum, as if someone had raised a Nazi version of the *Titanic* and had drained all the water.

The other hallway was considerably longer and was lined with all sorts of laboratories. Each seemed to be dedicated to a different field: chemistry, physics, biology, electronics, medicine, and more. There were rooms with stainless-steel autopsy tables and rows of freezers. The women could only imagine what kind of horrors had taken place there.

The few scattered pieces of equipment that had been left behind, while no doubt quite advanced at the time, appeared quite primitive more than sixty years later.

At the very end of the hallway was a set of heavy double doors. Rhodes pulled them open and the trio walked into what looked like some sort of early 1900s zoo. They passed cage after cage made of thick iron bars. Casey badly wanted them to have been for monkeys, or apes, or any sort of wild animal Kammler's people might have been experimenting on, but she knew they weren't. These were for holding human beings.

On many of the floors were words in a language she couldn't understand. There were hash marks in one of the cages as well. What had someone been counting? The number of days in captivity? Maybe the number of days since a loved one had been taken away?

Two cages later lay a little girl's doll. *There had been animals here all right,* she thought, *but the animals had been the ones outside the cages.* She could think of nothing worse than torturing a child. The anguish people had been forced to suffer at the hands of the Nazis was beyond imagination.

At the end of the rows of cages, they passed through an open doorway and into a communal shower. As they looked up at the large shower heads protruding from the ceiling, they all were thinking the same thing. Had this shower been used to gas prisoners? There was no telling. All Gretchen Casey knew was that the more she saw, the sicker to her stomach she was becoming.

To their left was a large, metal door. It was hung on a track with pulleys and a cable that ran into a conduit and disappeared into the wall at the far end of the room. Rhodes tried to slide the door open, but it wouldn't budge. Unlike the other doors they had encountered, this one seemed to have rusted to such a degree that it couldn't be moved, not even with all three women working on it at once.

They gave up and walked to the end of the shower room. A small flight of tiled steps led up to a door, which they were able to open.

On the other side, they found themselves in a wide, semicircular room reminiscent of an airport control tower. Desks, which appeared to have held all sorts of equipment at one point, were pressed up against large glass windows. It seemed to have been designed as an observation station. *But designed to observe what?*

Casey walked over to one of the windows and tried to use her flashlight to illuminate what was on the other side. It was no good. The thick glass acted like a mirror and bounced most of the light right back in her eyes.

Using her flashlight to guide her, she walked over to the door at the far end. She had no idea what kind of experiments the Nazis had been working on, but there was something about the scope and layout of this observation station that told her whatever they were observing from here was very important.

Opening the door, she felt a cold rush of air from the other side. She raised her flashlight and cast its beam into the darkness. What she saw was amazing.

The observation station was built overlooking a giant cavern. Looking up, she saw that the ceiling was almost entirely covered with some sort of crystal formations. As she played her flashlight across it, the light was refracted into a prism of colors. The ceiling was like a giant disco ball.

"You girls should see this," Casey said over her shoulder.

There was a viewing platform underneath the observation room's window and she stepped out onto it. She was joined by Rhodes and Ericsson, who also cast their flashlight beams upward.

"What is this place?" asked Julie.

"I don't know."

They swept their flashlights in a wide arc and the walls of the cavern, just like the ceiling, burst to life, refracting the light in all directions.

"What's down there?" Ericsson asked, shining her light down below.

It was hard to see, but about thirty feet down was a large platform or stage of some sort.

Rhodes had already walked to the other end of the viewing platform. "I've found some stairs over here," she called out.

When Gretchen and Julie joined her, they saw that the rusted door they couldn't budge from the inside fed to a ramp of some sort that led down in the same direction as the stairs. It must have been used for moving equipment.

Megan, who always preferred to be on point, stepped onto the stairs and began to lead the way down.

The stairs had been carved out of the sheer rock wall. There was a railing, but as it had been submerged for God only knew how long, she didn't put too much faith in it. Instead, she chose her steps carefully, as did Ericsson and Casey. They were less concerned with where they were than where they were going.

With their flashlights lighting up the stone steps, they took them one at a time. It wasn't until they reached the very bottom that they paused to look around.

Casey was the first to see them. Rhodes was the first to choke back a scream.

CHAPTER 22

Despite all the mayhem they had seen as operators, nothing could have prepared them for what they found. It was beyond horrific; beyond grotesque.

Human skeletons protruded from the rock walls surrounding the platform. It was as if they had been fused with the cavern itself. The mouths were wide open in silent screams.

"What did those bastards do?" asked Rhodes.

Casey was having trouble speaking. Her heart rate had spiked and it was all she could do to keep things under control. She was plenty tough, but this went beyond rational explanation. Her mind was screaming for her to get out of there. She was scared, but she was also in charge. She had to control her fear and not let it control her.

"Jules, are you okay?" she asked, reaching out and putting her hand reassuringly on Ericsson's arm.

Julie nodded, slowly.

"What the hell did those bastards do?" Rhodes repeated.

"I have no idea," replied Casey.

"People just don't grow out of walls."

"I know."

"So what happened? What the hell happened?"

"Megan, you've got to calm down," said Casey.

"What do you mean, *calm down*? Look at these skeletons. Look at their mouths all open. It's like they were alive when this happened. This is beyond horrifying."

She was right. The word *shocking* didn't even come close to describing what they were looking at. There were skeletons of adults as well as children. *What the hell had Hutton sent them into?*

"I'm going to video all of this and then we're going to get the hell out of here," said Casey, asserting her command. "You two can go back upstairs if you want. You don't have to stay down here."

"No," replied Ericsson, pulling herself together. "We don't split up."

"She's right," said Rhodes. "We stay together."

"Good," answered Casey.

After filming all of the bones protruding from the walls, she focused on the platform itself. There were two discolored patterns in the cement where some large object or objects had once sat. Looking more closely, she could see that those objects had been bolted down.

Casey shot several close-ups of the marks and then said, "Okay, that's it. We're getting out of here."

They were pretty far below ground, but she tried to raise Alex Cooper over the radio anyway. As the quartz was so well known for amplifying radio signals, she thought it was worth a try. Cooper didn't answer. Casey decided to leave it until they got back up into the tunnel and beyond the airlock.

Everyone was shaken by what they had seen. It was a shock to all of them. Despite Rhodes's love of being on point, Gretchen ordered her to fall back. Casey would lead her team out.

They were cautious, but they mounted the steps a lot faster than they had coming down. Though they had witnessed something beyond their worst collective nightmare, all of them had a very bad feeling that the true evil of the facility had not entirely been revealed to them.

"By the way," said Rhodes as they got to the observation platform, "there's no way in hell I'm sleeping in that hotel tonight."

"I agree," added Ericsson. "I say we get in the car, drive, and don't stop driving until the sun comes up."

Casey was with them. "I'm all for that," she said, as she pressed on.

They moved through the observation station, out the door, and down the short flight of stairs into the shower room. From the shower room, they moved past the cages, and though Casey didn't want to, she allowed her eyes to be drawn to the little girl's doll again.

They left the cages behind and stepped through the double doors into the long research corridor. As they passed the various labs, Casey forced herself to slow down. *Was there anything she was missing? Were there any clues to who had been here? Any clues to who had opened this place up and cleaned it out?* That was their job. That was why they had been sent here.

She shone her flashlight into each of the rooms they passed. She didn't expect to suddenly spot something they hadn't seen the first time around, but she felt that she should at least try to bring back something useful regardless of how disturbing the scene in the cavern had been.

They kept moving, and with each room they passed, Casey allowed herself to become more convinced that there wasn't anything of value left here.

Soon, they arrived at the office corridor. At the end of it was the hatch, and on the other side of that were the stairs up to the airlock. Then it was the tunnel and finally they'd be away from this place.

They stepped through the hatch and climbed the stairs up toward the airlock. When they reached the landing, all of them were breathing more heavily than normal. They were all in incredible shape, but considering the stress they were under, the distance, and the number of stairs they had climbed, as well as the speed they had been moving, it wasn't surprising that they were all a little short of breath.

The women moved through the doorway and into the airlock. After passing through the blast door, they quickened their pace up the tunnel. None of them looked up at the ghastly murals. They had seen enough to last them a lifetime.

Passing the guardhouse, Casey said, "Everybody okay? We're almost out."

"Ask me how I'm feeling once we get out of here," said Rhodes.

Gretchen looked back at Ericsson, "You all right?"

Julie nodded. "I'm okay,"

"Good," replied Casey as she reached for her radio and hailed Cooper. The reception was terrible. There was a lot of static and she couldn't understand what Alex was saying. *So much for the quartz improving radio reception,* she thought.

Soon enough, they began to smell the forest and

knew that they were almost out. Had it been daytime, they would have been able to use the sunlight spilling in to gauge how much farther they had to go.

As it was, all they had to go on was their memory of how long the tunnel was and the radio signal, which was starting to become clearer.

They knew they were just about there when they picked up an audible snippet of Cooper's voice.

"Say again," replied Casey over her radio.

When no response came, Gretchen said, "We're going to be on top of you any second now. Be ready to move."

There were a couple of radio clicks, but that was it.

"On our way out," said Casey. "Do you copy? Over."

They were twenty yards from the tunnel entrance when they heard Cooper's voice again, but this time it didn't come over the radio. This time it came in the form of a scream.

"Run!"

CHAPTER 23

Armen Abressian blinked his eyes and looked at his watch. It was late. *Business never sleeps*, he thought to himself as the phone on the nightstand kept vibrating.

He picked it up and placed his feet over the side of the bed. He was a handsome, powerfully built man in his early sixties with gray hair, a thick beard, and deeply tanned skin. When he spoke, he did so with a soothing, basso profundo voice coupled with a slight accent that was difficult to place.

Looking out over the twinkling lights of the Bosporus, he activated the call and said, "I'm here, Thomas."

"I'm sorry to bother you, Armen. I assume you have a guest," said Thomas Sanders, Abressian's second in command.

Abressian looked over at the gorgeous creature in his bed. She was less than half his age and worth every penny. He'd have to see if he could hire her for another night. Things were not moving as quickly as he had planned.

"What is it I can do for you, Thomas?"

"We have a problem."

Another one? It had been just over twenty-four hours since Nino Bianchi had been abducted from his home in Venice. While no one knew for sure who had done it, it smacked of the Israelis, especially as they had used women to pull off the job. That would be just like them. And the timing couldn't have been worse. Abressian still had one more shipment he was expecting from Bianchi.

Turning his attention back to Sanders, he replied, "What is the problem?"

"It's Professor Cahill."

Of course it was. "What has happened now?" Abressian asked calmly.

"The Bratva want him."

Bratva was slang for the Russian mafia who ran the town of Premantura at the southern end of Croatia's Istrian peninsula. There wasn't a single official or law enforcement officer in the area who wasn't on the Bratva's payroll. It was a place where people learned to keep quiet. The locals kept to themselves, minded their own business, and didn't ask any questions. That was one of the reasons Abressian had selected it. Via his relationship with the Russians, he was able to purchase a significant amount of goodwill. Professor Cahill, though, had been burning through it very quickly.

When it came to quantum physics, George Cahill was a genius. When it came to everything else, he was an idiot.

Abressian had discovered him toiling away in a physics lab at the Australian National University.

Technically, he was on unpaid administrative leave. Cahill had been reprimanded twice for his substance abuse, but when it came to light that he had been involved in several inappropriate relationships with students, he was removed from his duties until he could complete a rehabilitation program with a full review of the charges against him. But Cahill's situation had rapidly deteriorated.

It seemed that the harder his demons rode him, the faster he descended into a hell of his own making. Incredible brilliance often dwells on the razor's edge of madness, and this was certainly the case with George Cahill.

When Armen Abressian had found the twenty-nine-year-old Cahill, he was being beaten outside a seedy bar on the outskirts of Canberra. The wheels had completely come off Cahill's axles. Abressian suspected the man might have been bipolar or sociopathic, prone to incredible mood swings and incredibly self-destructive behavior. Alcohol, drugs, prostitutes, and gambling had sucked the young genius into a suicidal black hole from which not even the faintest hope of escape appeared possible. That is, until Abressian had made Cahill the offer of a lifetime.

Cahill had a bad habit of blaming his problems on others. He claimed that because the university didn't give him enough support and leeway to pursue his research, he hadn't been able to make greater headway. He saw other, far less intelligent professors soaring to academic heights and pawned it off on their ability to play "the game." Everyone knew that university life was all about publish or perish, but until you could *prove* your hypothesis, there was nothing to publish. The more frustrated he became, the more depressed, and the more depressed, the more self-destructive.

What Abressian offered him was an opportunity to be his own boss, to prove to everyone that he had been right; that he was smarter than everyone else. It was a chance for redemption. Abressian had appealed to both the man's intellect and his ego, and Cahill had accepted.

Cahill tendered his resignation at the university and with Abressian's help, disappeared.

When he arrived at the facility in Croatia, Cahill had been sober for a month and a half. He was filled once again with purpose. He had been given something people rarely ever receive in life: a second chance.

The project began well, very well indeed. Cahill oversaw a team of brilliant scientists provided by the project's funders, a mysterious organization known as the Amalgam. They were a group of powerful elite who kept their membership and their agenda secret.

The only thing they demanded was results. To that end, whatever Cahill needed, Sanders and Abressian made sure he received. No matter how obscure or expensive a piece of equipment, all he had to do was ask and it would arrive within twenty-four hours. Cahill found it all so perfect that he felt it was like falling in love.

Of course, his feelings of euphoria had everything to do with the fact that he had made significant strides in the beginning. With the schematics and other information the Amalgam had been able to secure, he had rebuilt Hans Kammler's badly damaged Engeltor device. By manipulating the properties of certain "miraculous minerals" the scientists working at Zbiroh had discovered, he was able to transport small, inanimate objects to the Amalgam's receiving site on a small island in the Andaman Sea.

But then Cahill's progress began to slow. When it came to a complete halt, his feelings of euphoria soon crashed and were replaced by depression.

He began drinking again, heavily. He also began gambling. Much to his surprise, he was somewhat successful. Little did he know that Mr. Sanders had been arranging for the games to be fixed in his favor. Abressian had placed Sanders in charge of the project. It was up to him to make sure it succeeded.

Sanders had rigged the games in the hope that if Cahill hit a winning streak, his creativity would be reignited and his mood would improve. But instead of focusing on work, Cahill focused on women.

The Russians were all too happy to supply him with as many as he wanted. With Cahill getting lucky in cards and in love, Sanders encouraged him to refocus his energies on the project. The scientist, though, wasn't "in the mood," so Sanders cut him off. No more gambling and no more women.

When Cahill went on strike, Sanders had him roughed up. His pride and his body wounded, the scientist dutifully returned to work, but made no headway. The only change was in his mood, which had become increasingly more malevolent; darker. The man probably needed to be under the care of a doctor.

"Did you hear what I said, Armen?" Sanders asked, interrupting Abressian's thoughts. "Viktor wants to see you personally about it."

Viktor Mikhailov ran the Russian mafia in Croatia. He was an extremely dangerous man, but he could also be very reasonable. A former Russian intelligence operative, he understood the art of compromise.

Abressian closed his eyes and massaged the bridge of his nose. "I can't leave Turkey right now," he said as he closed the bedroom door and walked into the suite's sitting room. "We'll just have to pay off whatever debt the professor has again incurred."

"Armen, three of Viktor's girls have gone missing over the last week," said Sanders.

Abressian opened his eyes. *"Missing?"* he repeated.

"As in *gone*. Vanished."

"And he thinks Cahill had something to do with this?"

"Apparently, the professor was the last one seen with any of them."

Abressian had known a lot of psychopaths during his life. In fact, he actively employed a good number of them, but Cahill didn't fit the profile. He had problems, sure, but he wasn't a killer. It didn't add up. "Have you talked to George about this?"

"After the first time Viktor's men came around, I asked him."

"And?"

"And," replied Sanders, "he told me he had no idea what happened to them."

"Do you believe him?"

"No. And there's something else you need to know. There was a fourth girl. She went missing last night."

"Where was the professor?"

"I don't know," said Sanders. "Out."

Abressian was silent for several moments before

he exhaled and said, more to himself than to his aide-de-camp, "What has he done?"

"I think you and I both know the answer to that question."

"No," said Abressian. He refused to believe it. "Laboratory animals maybe, but not a human being. Not *four* human beings."

"Did anything come out on the other side?"

"No," replied Sanders. He didn't say anything else after that. He knew his employer was thinking exactly what he was thinking. Whether those girls had stepped through the device willingly or had been pushed, they were gone. And they'd never be seen again.

"I'm going to need time to figure this out," Abressian said.

"There's no time, Armen. Viktor wants his girls back. The only reason he hasn't snatched Cahill and started torturing him yet is out of respect for you. If he does get his hands on him, Cahill will tell him everything. And I mean *everything*," said Sanders, drawing out the last word.

Abressian didn't need to be reminded what was at stake, or the price he'd be forced to pay if they failed. "We need to make sure that doesn't happen."

"What would you like me to do?"

"For starters," said Abressian, "lie. Tell him you know for a fact that Cahill couldn't have done anything to those girls because he was with you."

Sanders laughed nervously. "I don't think Viktor would believe me."

"Make him believe you."

"I'll try. In the meantime, what should we do about Cahill?"

"I don't want him out of your sight," replied

Abressian. "If you have to handcuff him to your wrist, you do it."

"So I have your permission to restrain him?" asked Sanders.

Abressian exhaled. "You have my permission to do what's necessary," he said. "But use your brain. That's what I pay you for. Let's not let the situation get any further out of control."

"And if Viktor calls and asks for you again?"

"Tell him I am still out of town, but that I will meet with him as soon as I get back."

"I will do that," said Sanders.

"What about that other assignment we discussed?"

"The new one in Prague?"

"Yes," said Abressian. "You were planning to use that same Czech again, Heger. Correct?"

"Yes."

"And you'll run him through our man in Belgrade so it doesn't trace back?"

"That's my plan. I expect to hear something tonight."

Abressian nodded. "Good. Any further word on what happened in Venice?"

"Still nothing," said Sanders, "but I have feelers out. I'm confident we'll hear something soon."

Armen wasn't so sure. Bianchi might not ever resurface again, and that meant they wouldn't get their shipment. "Keep pressing. We need that delivery."

"I will," replied Sanders, who then changed the subject. "How's Istanbul?"

"Don't ask. Just do what I have requested. I will be back as soon as I can." And with that Abressian hung up the phone.

He thought about returning to bed and the beautiful young woman who would graciously and professionally perform any act he wished, but he wasn't feeling aroused. He was feeling overburdened and stressed.

He decided on a swim. Perhaps then he could clear his head and get answers to the problems that seemed to suddenly be mounting up against him.

CHAPTER 24

Alex Cooper had no idea Heger's men were there until their red dot lasers lit her up like a Christmas tree. Their message couldn't have been any clearer—*Make one false move and you die.*

She had been so well concealed that it took her a moment to realize how they had found her. Setting down her weapon, she stood and raised her hands above her head. That was when the men materialized.

All of them were wearing night vision goggles. But unlike Cooper, they hadn't activated their infrared illuminators. She might as well have been sitting there waving a flashlight back and forth.

She had tried to communicate with Casey, Ericsson, and Rhodes, but the radio signal was too weak to reach all the way down into the complex. She caught the tail end of Gretchen's message just as one of the Czechs, a tall man with a crew cut and pockmarked face, took her radio from her. He and his colleagues were wearing the same tactical boots she had seen on the men getting into the Range Rover with Heger outside the hotel earlier.

Casey had said they were on their way out. Using their distress code—a word meant to convey that the operation had been compromised—was impossible. So, she did the next best thing and yelled for the rest of her team to run.

The shooting started almost immediately, and Casey, Rhodes, and Ericsson dove for the ground. There was no cover to be had anywhere. They were sitting ducks, and what was worse was that tunnels had a bad habit of funneling gunfire right at you.

They had all drawn the pistols Vlcek had given them, but they knew their weapons were no match for the fully automatic weapons they could hear being fired just outside.

Casey tried once more to raise Cooper over the radio, but quickly gave up. There was no answer. If she was still alive, she'd be in the fight. The only problem was that none of the three women in the tunnel could hear Cooper's pistol being fired.

"We've got to get to Alex," said Rhodes.

Casey nodded and the trio popped up onto their feet, but stayed as low to the ground as possible. Rhodes charged right out in front.

As the gunfire continued, all three of the women picked up speed. They could now see Alex Cooper engaged in serious hand-to-hand combat with what appeared to be one of Heger's men. Another was already sprawled on the ground nearby.

She delivered a series of punches, culminating with a jab that dropped the man right where he stood. Reaching down, she seized his CZ Skorpion EVO submachine gun, took cover behind a large rock, and began firing in controlled, three-round bursts.

When Casey, Ericsson, and Rhodes ran up, they glanced at the two men. One had night vision goggles on and was bleeding profusely from his nose. There was no telling if he was alive or dead. The other man had had his head wrenched to the side and his NVGs thrown clear. He lay on the ground with his eyes wide open. He was definitely dead. Alex Cooper's bad side was a very dangerous place to be.

A fusillade of bullets erupted around them and the three women dove for cover near Cooper. Casey grabbed the pant leg of the dead man and dragged him behind the rock, stripped him of his weapon and extra magazines, and got in the fight with Alex.

Casey didn't have time to put on her NVGs, so Cooper called out where to fire. "Three o'clock! Eleven o'clock! Ten o'clock!"

Rhodes dragged the other man behind the rock with them and felt for a pulse. He was still breathing. She stripped off all of his extra magazines and handed them to Ericsson so she could feed them to Casey and Cooper as needed.

Rhodes found a bundle of plastic FlexCuffs in the man's pocket and, rolling him onto his stomach, bound his wrists behind his back. She relieved him of his sidearm, an auto knife, and another knife in his boot, then put her knee in his back and got her NVGs on.

Ericsson had hers on now, too, and took the Skorpion from Casey, who immediately pulled her NVGs from her pack. "How many are there?" yelled Ericsson as Cooper continued to fire.

"At least six, maybe more," she said.

"How did they know we were here?" she asked as she engaged two men creeping up on their position and nailed both of them in the head. The men fell to the ground dead.

Cooper swung her weapon to the right and nailed one of the Czechs in the throat. "There must have been an intrusion device we didn't see."

Rhodes leaned her body well beyond the boulder and fired four shots. It was an overly aggressive move that almost got her killed. Dust and rock chips exploded all around her. One bullet missed her head by millimeters.

"Let's switch it up," she said, tapping Ericsson on the shoulder.

Casey and Rhodes were the team's best shooters, and Cooper and Ericsson now handed the submachine guns over to them. Julie placed her knee in the unconscious man's back.

"How much ammo do we have left?" asked Casey.

"One mag apiece," answered Ericsson.

"Let's make them count," she said, as she indicated to Rhodes what she wanted to do.

Rhodes nodded and transitioned to her pistol. She counted to three and then said, "Go!"

Leaning out from behind the rock, Rhodes swept the pistol in a wide arc and laid down a wave of suppression fire as Casey ran for cover on the other side of the tunnel entrance. Once she had fired her last round, she ducked back behind the rock and transitioned to the Skorpion. Now, Heger's men were really going to get it.

Seeing that the Czechs were using night vision goggles, none of the women had activated their illuminators. While that made it more difficult for them to see, it also made it more difficult for them to be seen. Cooper, who had learned the hard way that the men were wearing NVGs, had already shut her illuminator off.

Casey and Rhodes waited for the men to show themselves. They had very little ammo left. They needed to use it sparingly.

Cooper looked at Megan and said, "I'm going to flank them." It was a good idea, especially as the men were probably planning on doing the same to them.

Rhodes got Casey's attention and signaled to her what Alex wanted to do. Casey gave them the thumbs-up. Ericsson wanted to go too, but someone needed to keep an eye on the prisoner. Rhodes couldn't focus on Heger's men and their prisoner at the same time. Besides, there was still a chance someone might come over the top of the tunnel behind them, and they needed Julie to be the eyes in the backs of their heads.

No sooner had Rhodes given her the signal to watch their six o'clock than Ericsson's pistol flew up and she pulled the trigger twice, double-tapping one of the Czechs, who had come over the hill behind them.

His lifeless body toppled over and landed on the ground in front of the tunnel.

Before the man had even made impact, Cooper took off running.

Casey saw movement down the path from them and squeezed her trigger. "Gotcha," she said as another Czech fell.

Rhodes kept her weapon up and ready. She knew they were still out there; they were just too well hidden for her to see. That gave her an idea.

"Jules," she said. "When I say go, activate the illuminator on the dead guy's NVGs and toss them off to my three o'clock."

"Roger that," said Ericsson as she kept her pistol trained on the hill behind them and reached over for the abandoned night vision goggles.

"Ready?" asked Rhodes.

Ericsson felt along the device until she found the illuminator and then replied, "Ready."

Megan tightened her grip on her weapon and said, "Okay, go!"

Ericsson tossed the NVGs as Rhodes had instructed and it had exactly the intended effect. One of Heger's men fired and gave away his position.

"Czech-out time," whispered Rhodes as she pulled her trigger and nailed him with two rounds to the chest and one to the head.

Her shots were immediately followed by multiple rounds from Cooper's .40 caliber pistol.

Minutes felt like hours as they sat with neither sight nor sound of any of Heger's men. There was no telling how close they were, or how many remained.

Suddenly, they heard Cooper's pistol fire again, but this time it came from much farther off in the woods.

Several minutes later, Cooper came back. "TNT," she said as she approached, using their code for *there's no threat* to indicate she was coming in alone.

"I took out another one, but two others got

away. I think one of them might have been Heger. I'm not sure."

With the toe of her boot, Rhodes kicked the night vision goggles off their prisoner. "We're going to clear that mystery up real fast."

"But first," clarified Casey, "we need to get out of here and get someplace safe."

CHAPTER 25

Someplace safe" was the home of John Vlcek. And while Rhodes prepared their prisoner, whom they had driven to Vlcek's bound and gagged in the trunk of their car, Gretchen Casey used Vlcek's computer to Skype with Robert Hutton back at Fort Bragg.

"You knew that stuff was there," said Casey angrily. "All of it."

They were each wearing a headset and using a secure webcam feed. The digital encryption was quite good and Vlcek had several additional features enabled that helped to make sure their communication was as watertight as possible.

"All I know is what I was told," replied Hutton.

Casey studied his face on her screen. She was looking for any indication that he wasn't telling the truth. "Who ordered this operation?"

Hutton hesitated and then, referring to the Special Operations Command, said, "SOCOM."

"Who told them to order it?"

"I don't know."

There was something in his face, just a flash of it. "You're lying to me."

"No, I'm not."

Casey leaned forward toward the camera mounted on Vlcek's computer. "Who was it, Rob?"

After a moment, Hutton relented. "It came from the Joint Chiefs."

"Who specifically?"

"Jack Walsh."

"The director for intelligence?"

Hutton nodded. "Yes."

"The same Jack Walsh who helped stand up the Athena Project?"

"Yes."

Casey leaned back in her chair and shook her head.

"What's that supposed to mean?" asked Hutton.

"It means I'm tired of being lied to. SOCOM didn't task us. Jack Walsh called you directly and *you* tasked us."

Hutton didn't respond right away. He didn't need to. She could read it on his face. "What aren't you telling us, Rob?"

Casey had already uploaded all of the video from the Kammler bunker and had briefed Hutton on both the firefight and the prisoner they had taken. All her cards were on the table.

"I told you what you needed to know to get the job done."

"Really?" asked Casey. "We walked into a firefight with .40 caliber pistols against eight heavily armed Czech Special Forces soldiers. Does that sound to you like my team had everything they needed?"

Hutton tried to reply, but Casey held her finger up to stop him. "Don't."

"Don't what?"

"Don't give me the line about following orders and compartmentalization. We were outmanned and outgunned because we were not fully briefed. This operation made no sense from the get-go and I should have pressed you for more details."

"You did," Hutton said with a laugh.

"Then I should have pressed harder," replied Casey. "That's what I get for trusting you."

The reaction in Hutton's eyes said it all. It was visible for only a moment and he masked it quickly, but the barb had found its mark.

"You're an operator. You follow orders. You don't question them," he finally said.

Technically, Hutton was correct. An operator's primary obligation was to follow orders. But the men and women of Delta were selected for their intelligence and ability to think for themselves. They were so highly prized because they didn't need their hands held. They could be dropped behind enemy lines or into some of the harshest environments in the world and be trusted to complete the mission; any mission.

In fact, most male operators had at least two disciplinary actions in their Army file before arriving at Delta. The women of the Athena Project were different. They hadn't come up through the regular Army; they'd been recruited from outside. They hadn't yet been given a chance to be insubordinate or disobey a direct order just because their instincts told them they knew better.

It was a double-edged sword for Hutton. He'd

been an operator as well. He knew what it was like being mushroomed; being kept in the dark and fed crap. But now that he was on the other side, sending teams out on assignments rather than being sent himself, he had to find the right balance.

He also knew that it was important for his operators to trust him. He'd never led women before. It was a steep learning curve. He'd made more than a few mistakes, but one thing that had become clear to him was that he couldn't lie, not if he intended to maintain both their trust and respect.

He also knew that telling Gretchen that her job was to follow orders and not question them was weak. Her response drove that home.

"Up yours, Rob," she replied.

"Damn it, Gretchen," he said. "This is how it works. I can't always give you all the information."

"Well you could have given us more."

The statement hung in the air between them for several moments.

Finally, Hutton relented, "I don't have all of the pieces, but I'll give you whatever I can. What do you want to know?"

Casey adjusted her headset and leaned back in toward the computer. "Why now? Why after sixty years did this suddenly become so important?"

Hutton looked at her and smiled. "You're a smart girl, Gretch. What do you think?"

"I think the fact that the place was empty means that someone cleaned it out."

"And?"

Gretchen couldn't believe where this was going. "*And*, something somewhere must have happened that made Walsh want us to go look to see if anyone had breached that facility."

Hutton closed his eyes and nodded.

"Something bad?" she asked.

Opening his eyes, he looked right at her and said, "You have no idea."

CHAPTER 26

Casey listened as Hutton quickly rehashed the history of Operations Overcast and Paperclip, as well as how the Kammler Dossiers had been acquired. He then explained what specifically had been discovered at the facility at Zbiroh.

"Kammler named the project Engeltor, or the Angel's Gate," he said. "It had been conceived of as a hybrid between two experiments; one dealt with antigravity and another that was looking to camouflage aircraft and ships from enemy radar by bending light around an object to make it invisible. Both involved quantum physics and unified field theory. Combing them resulted in the Angel's Gate."

"Did any of it work?"

"Apparently, some of it worked well enough to attract the attention of the U.S. government. And while an Overcast team went after any and all documents and equipment they could find, the Paperclip folks went after the scientists who had been working on the project.

"Everything was brought to the Montauk Air Force Station, or Fort Hero as it was called, at Montauk Point on the eastern tip of Long Island. Just like the Manhattan Project, security at Montauk was extraordinarily tight. And human nature being what it is, speculation ran wild among the people of Long Island about what was going on. To divert attention from the real focus of the project, the government seeded rumors and disinformation everywhere.

"There was talk about exotic psychological warfare techniques and even time travel experiments being carried out in a secret underground facility beneath the base. Real science-fiction kind of stuff. The crazier the conspiracy theory, the more the military would promote it. Anything to throw people off. Some of the theories, though, were not that far from the truth. Have you heard of the Philadelphia Experiment?"

"You mean that story from the 1940s about a ship disappearing from the naval yard in Philly, appearing in Norfolk, Virginia, and then back in . . ." her voice trailed off.

Hutton finished her sentence for her. "Back in Philadelphia again with crew members' twisted bodies fused to different parts of the ship."

"That actually happened?"

"No, but something very similar did and word unfortunately leaked out. The story of the Philadelphia Experiment, like the other conspiracy theories, was created to take attention away from what the military actually was doing at Montauk Point."

Casey tried to take it all in. "So what actually *were* they doing?"

She watched as Hutton looked over both his

shoulders before he responded. "Something called quantum teleportation."

"Teleportation?" asked Casey. "As in beam me up, Scottie? You've got to be kidding me."

"I'm not. The Germans' achievements were remarkable."

"Is that why those bodies were fused to the walls in Zbiroh?"

"Yes," he said. "As their experiments picked up speed, they ordered boxcar after boxcar of human subjects from concentration camps across the Third Reich."

Casey shuddered. "They even used children."

"I know," Hutton replied, his head bent. "It was terrible."

"And we just reproduced those horrible experiments?"

"We tried, for a while."

"That's disgusting," stated Casey.

"Our volunteers were willing. That's the difference. They knew the risks."

"But still."

Hutton nodded. "The German scientists brought to Montauk swore that the Engeltor could work; that it had worked. In fact, there was a rumor circulating near the end of the war. It claimed that three thousand Germans had disappeared right before being captured by Patton's Third Army. The group was made up of scientists, SS personnel, men, women, and children. They allegedly disappeared into an underground facility and sealed the entrance behind them with explosives."

"Mass suicide?"

"That's not the way the story was told. That facility was a gateway of some sort. No trace of those people has ever been found."

Casey said, "But the Montauk experiments sound like they were a bust."

"The researchers there believed they were somehow missing a step; that some critical piece of data had been lost and if it could be rediscovered, the device would work perfectly.

"Considering that we didn't get all of the Nazi documents and all of the scientists out of Europe, our military was willing to concede that the researchers might have been right."

If she had not seen the skeletons embedded in the walls of the facility at Zbiroh herself, she wouldn't have believed any of it was possible. "So what ultimately ended up happening?"

"The research was scaled back. At the time, it was deemed too dangerous."

"*Scaled back*, not abandoned?"

Hutton shook his head. "Are you kidding? Why abandon it? Imagine the military applications of this technology. Imagine being able to move troops and materials anywhere, instantly. Better yet, imagine being able to *fax*, for lack of a better term, a bomb or even a laser beam anywhere with absolutely no warning."

Casey had seen and deployed with multiple pieces of technology that at one point in time must have seemed like the stuff of science fiction. In fact, half the "futuristic" devices from the TV show *Star Trek* could now be seen in the real world: magnetic resonance imaging, flip cell phones, the military's laser project known as the Personnel Halting And Stimulation Response (PHASR) rifle, the military's universal translator known as the Phraselator, global positioning via satellite, ultrasound surgery, the list went on and on. Even Lieutenant Uhura's wireless earpiece wasn't much different from the Bluetooth earpiece Casey used today. Why *not* teleportation? "Yes," she agreed. "If you could pull that off, it would be incredible."

"The United States doesn't have a choice," replied Hutton. "Quantum teleportation has become the most aggressively pursued field of military research on the planet. It's like the race for the atom bomb. This technology is the ultimate game-changer. Can you envision what the world would look like today if our enemies had developed the bomb before us?"

It wasn't a pretty picture. "Is that what we're talking about? Is that why we were sent to Zbiroh?"

Hutton nodded once more. "While there have been huge leaps forward in quantum physics, especially in the last year, Kammler's research, his device, is really the platform upon which any serious program would have to be built."

"You knew the facility in Zbiroh had been breached."

"We had our suspicions. That's why we sent you. *Now* we know."

"How do you know, though, that the program back in America hasn't somehow been compromised?" asked Casey. "I mean, we spend hundreds of billions of dollars on R&D and the Russians, Chinese, and even the Israelis only spend in the millions on espionage and they have been robbing us blind."

"True, but we don't think the program has been penetrated."

Casey laughed. "Rob, our enemies have all of

our nuclear secrets, why wouldn't they be able to get this research as well?"

"Because the U.S. military took unprecedented steps to hide it," said Hutton.

"Like what?"

"Now we're drifting outside my pay grade."

"You know something, though," said Casey. "I can tell."

"I only heard RUMINT," he replied, using the acronym for rumor intelligence.

"What rumor?"

Hutton lowered his voice. "That back in the 1990s the U.S. military realized that, just like you said, we were getting robbed blind. A decision was made to identify the most promising research in the country and move it somewhere where nobody would be able to get to it."

"Sounds similar to what Kammler was charged with," said Casey.

"I hadn't thought about it that way," replied Hutton, "but I guess you're right."

"So where was all of our greatest research moved to? Area 51?"

Hutton smiled. "Good one."

"Come on," pressed Casey. "You've got no idea? You have to. You and Walsh are pretty tight."

"All I have are rumors," he said. "Some say it's hidden beneath the Greenbrier in West Virginia in the old congressional fallout shelter. Some say the Yucca Mountain nuclear waste repository is a smokescreen for it. Hell, I've even heard some joker claim that Richard Daley helped get it hidden beneath the White Sox's Comiskey Park in Chicago."

"Well, if anybody could have pulled that off,"

said Casey with a smile, "it would have been Mayor Daley."

"Whatever they're up to," Hutton continued, "you can imagine there's a ton of disinformation being put out around it."

Gretchen thought about it for a moment. "If you were going to hide something like that, where would you put it?"

He didn't need to ponder the question. He was military through and through. "Somewhere out in the middle of nowhere. A place where I could see people coming from miles off. A place where I controlled all the property and had great interlocking fields of fire." As he looked at her, he could see the wheels spinning. "You don't agree, do you?"

"No," said Casey as she shook her head. "I think it'd be better to hide it right in plain sight. I might even draw a little attention to it just to throw people off balance."

"Why?"

She shrugged. "It's probably just me. I can't think of anything more mind-numbing than to be kept on some dusty military base day in and day out the way they were with Manhattan Project. Of course, you've gotta have security, but if you can allow people to come and go, live somewhat normal lives, that has to be good for productivity, not to mention people with families."

"So you're a *yes* on the Mayor Daley and Comiskey Park theory then."

Casey ignored his joke. She knew what would happen if the conversation got too personal. To stop that from happening, she brought them back to the business at hand. "What happened that made Walsh dispatch us to the facility at Zbiroh?"

Hutton knew he couldn't keep it from her any longer. "Somebody else is pursuing the technology."

"I kind of figured that."

His face was deadly serious. "This isn't just anybody. This is someone who has gotten their hands on Kammler's technology."

"How do you know for sure?"

"Because they've started sending through human subjects. And the results have been exactly the same; disastrous. Worse still, the bodies are fresh, so we know it happened recently."

Casey was at a loss for words.

"And that's not all," added Hutton.

"There's more?"

"I saved the best for last. Whoever is doing this, they've also been trying to get a bomb through."

Casey's eyes went wide.

This time, it was Hutton who leaned in toward his camera. "We've got to find out who this is, and we need to stop them."

"Agreed," replied Casey. "One hundred percent. Where do you want us to start?"

He looked at her, but he was all business. "Have Rhodes start with the man you brought back in the trunk of your car. Find out everything he knows about who stripped that facility at Zbiroh bare."

"And then?" she asked, even though she had a good feeling she knew what the answer was going to be.

"And then we're going to make sure nobody ever gets the ability to fax a bomb or a laser to *us*."

CHAPTER 27

The swim did little to clear Armen Abressian's mind. When he climbed out of the water, there was a message waiting for him on his phone. Thomas had called again.

"I'm here, Thomas," he said, calling the younger man back.

"I thought you'd want to know that Viktor came by a half-hour ago. He was drunk and so were his men."

This wasn't good. "Tell me what happened," said Abressian.

"I did just what you told me. I told Viktor that Professor Cahill was with me and that while I was sorry to hear about his girls disappearing, Cahill couldn't have had anything to do with it."

"Did he believe you?"

Sanders laughed. "No. In fact, he told me to my face that I was a liar."

"Then what happened?"

"Then he said he wanted to talk to you. I told

him you were out of the country, but that I expected you back soon. I told him you were sorry to hear about his girls having gone missing, but that you're also certain the professor had nothing to do with it."

"And what did he say to that?" asked Abressian.

"He seemed a lot less prepared to call you a liar than he was me."

Armen smiled. Mikhailov was no fool. "Was that it?"

"No. He wanted to see Cahill. He wanted to talk to him, himself."

"You told him that wasn't possible of course."

"Of course I did. Had I produced Cahill, they would have shoved him in the trunk of Viktor's Audi and we never would have seen him again."

"Good work, Thomas. What about the extra security we discussed?"

"I've doubled the number of men."

"Then everything is okay for now," replied Abressian.

"There's one other thing," said Sanders.

"I'm listening."

"I was hoping to get confirmation on that new assignment in Prague. The artifact the Amalgam wants recovered."

"Yes," said Abressian. "We were going to use the Czech."

"Well, I heard from our man in Belgrade. Apparently, there was an incident at the hotel in Zbiroh tonight."

"What kind of *incident*?"

"There were reports of gunfire on the property. Apparently, the police are involved now, but the details are still very sketchy."

"What about our Czech?"

"Our man in Belgrade says he can't reach him. He has talked with a couple of hotel employees who said he was there shortly before the shooting, but that no one has seen him since. Our man in Belgrade says the Czech's entire network has gone dark. He can't reach any of them."

This was not good. First Nino Bianchi, now Radek Heger. It might be coincidental, but Abressian had learned not to believe in coincidences. Those who did, ended up dead.

"I think I am going to check out of my hotel," said Abressian.

"Do you need me to make other arrangements?" asked Thomas.

"No, just keep focused on what I have asked you to do."

"Okay, what about the job in Prague? Should I look for someone else to handle it?"

"Let's put Prague on hold for right now," replied Armen. "We need to finish our current job first."

"Does that mean you'll be putting Istanbul on hold then too?"

Abressian cast his eyes up toward the hotel and thought about the beautiful young woman in his bed. Finally, he replied. "Yes. I'll let our clients here know that we'll have to reschedule."

"Should I send the plane for you?"

"Please."

Armen spent the flight back to Croatia thinking about his problems. The one immediately at the forefront of his mind was Viktor Mikhailov.

Abressian's initial reaction was to find someone to take the fall for the disappearance of Mikhailov's women. He'd make it look like a murder/suicide and then burn the house down around them so that the bodies couldn't be identified. At first blush, it seemed like the most expedient path. There was no way he was going to let that Russian mobster get his hands on Professor Cahill. It made no difference what insanity Cahill had committed, he was too valuable.

He was also all too human. If Mikhailov got his hands on him, Cahill would barter with anything he had to save his own skin. That would mean spilling everything he knew about the project.

The Amalgam wouldn't like that. Abressian had been hired because of his almost supernatural ability to keep things quiet. There were no such things as leaks in his operations. He hired only the best people and he'd had a perfect record because of it. This modus operandi had begun to translate into some very good money. He had no desire to see that stop now.

What's more, he knew how angry the members of the Amalgam could get. The punishment for failure would be worse than anything some Russian like Mikhailov could ever dream of dishing out.

As he sipped his Turkish coffee and stared out the plane's window, he wondered if maybe his first impulse hadn't exactly been the soundest. Perhaps rushing to stage a murder/suicide was the wrong play. Mikhailov was many things, but he wasn't a fool. Underestimating him could be a big mistake. Abressian would have to tread carefully.

He had toyed with the idea of offering a cash settlement to compensate for the loss of the women, but that road was fraught with peril. It meant first and foremost admitting that Cahill was guilty.

If Mikhailov got the bit between his teeth, there might not be any amount of money in the world that would satisfy him. He would be out for blood and that would cause a lot of problems. Buying him off was not the way to go.

Threatening him wasn't the way to go either. Mikhailov was Russian mafia. He had been with the KGB and had risen through its ranks as it morphed into its current incarnation, the FSB. He'd been threatened countless times in his career. Inferior opponents had very likely threatened to harm, or like most bombastic Russian underworld figures, threatened to kill him repeatedly. If Mikhailov was half the man he was thought to be, he would laugh at threats of violence to his person.

Abressian reflected on what Mikhailov actually knew. Regardless of what his gut was telling him, all he knew was that his girls were missing and that Cahill was the last person to have been seen with them. He didn't have any further evidence than that. He had no bodies. And if what Abressian and Thomas suspected was true, he never would. Those bodies were gone forever; never to be found.

But the fact that his girls were gone and Cahill was the last to have been seen with them would be enough for a man like Mikhailov to convict and pass sentence. And, as Abressian already knew, Cahill would admit to all of it as he offered anything and everything to the Russian to avoid his wrath.

Armen had been at this game long enough to know how men like Viktor Mikhailov operated. Last night he had shown up drunk and had gone away peaceably and without Cahill. They probably weren't going to get off that easy again.

The only way they were going to get Mikhailov

to stop pursuing the professor was to convince him that he had nothing to do with the women's vanishing act.

As the words hung in his mind, Abressian shook his head. That was literally what they were looking at: a vanishing act. It was almost unfathomable that all of their success could be undone by the idiocy of someone as bright as George Cahill.

This was technology that was going to reshape the entire world. Governments, armies, fealty to the concept of the nation-state—all of it was about to change. Mankind was about to be reborn.

Granted, the birthing process was going to be painful. Many would die, but many more would survive. And those survivors would see a cleaner, more equitable, more peaceful world. At least that was what Abressian had been told by the members of the Amalgam. Personally, he very much doubted that.

The hegemonic, megalomaniacal aspirations of even the brightest, most well-intentioned elites had always ended the same way. Nevertheless, the Amalgam's money was as green as anyone else's. And suppose they were right?

Suppose this time history would be wrong and the members of this incredible cabal would be successful. Why not be on the winning side? After all, Armen Abressian was a free agent. The boutique organization of intelligence and special operations personnel that he had built was his business to run as he saw fit. He could make and reshape his allegiances as the times and his conscience dictated. There really was no downside for him.

That said, at present there appeared to be very little upside either. Not unless George Cahill finished his work. And Cahill couldn't finish his work if Viktor Mikhailov was gunning for him.

Picking up the plane's satellite phone, he depressed the speed-dial button assigned to Thomas. The man picked up on the second ring.

"Yes, Armen," he said.

"Thomas, I have made up my mind."

"What have you decided?"

"We need to take care of Mr. Mikhailov."

"I agree," replied Sanders. "But I don't think right now is the time for us to go to war with the Bratva."

"We're not going to go to war."

"Okay," said Sanders. "Then what do you want to do?"

Abressian took another sip of his coffee. "First, I'm going to try to reason with him."

"And if that doesn't work."

"Then we'll just have to help him see the light."

They discussed details before hanging up the phone. Nothing was to be done until Abressian was back. He would handle everything in person. It was the only way to secure Mikhailov's full cooperation.

Having decided upon a course of action, Armen was then free to focus on his next most pressing matter—Bianchi.

It was said, especially in his world, that a healthy dose of paranoia was necessary for survival. While he was always vigilant, he never allowed himself to become paranoid. Under any other circumstances, he might have been willing to pin his deepening concern to paranoia, but not now. Not when Bianchi had been in the process of delivering their final shipment of merchandise.

Abressian had to assume the worst. The shipment probably wasn't going to make it. And that
meant the other targets the Amalgam had selected
would have to wait. For now, Armen's entire focus
would be on stepping up the operation in Colorado. It was important that the first blow be the
most devastating.

CHAPTER 28

The former Czech Special Forces soldier had been kept hooded. He had no idea where he was or who had him. He had no idea whether the rest of his colleagues were alive or dead, much less where they were.

He had been doing private security for one of the Czech Republic's wealthiest men, Radek Heger, who was also one of its most dangerous.

Megan Rhodes of course had a pretty good grasp of these facts as well. While she couldn't put herself completely in the mind of the man she was going to interrogate, it was important to know as much about him as possible. In particular, she needed to know what he valued.

One look at his wallet revealed that his name was Pavel Skovajsa and that he was thirty-six years old. That was a good start. One look at his cell phone told her everything else she needed to know.

Rhodes had exceptional instincts, which she figured she probably got from her father, the cop. Not only could she tell if people were lying, she also was fairly adept at discerning when they were telling the truth. That was the fine line one had to walk in the role of interrogator.

Another excellent trait she possessed was the willingness to get physical with a subject. As the tallest member of her team, she was the most physically imposing. This was important, especially when dealing with men. If they didn't fear her, they wouldn't respect her.

Her father had taught her how to take care of herself. The Army had taken those skills to a whole other level. She wasn't particularly fond of torture. Slapping some guy around, as her father used to put it, to gain a little cooperation was one thing. Pulling out teeth and toenails was something completely different.

There was also the risk that if you applied too much force, too much pain, people would tell you anything just to get you to stop.

Rhodes had been taught a wide range of interrogation methods. She had been subjected to most of them herself, so she could better understand them and the effects they had on their subjects.

What she had learned was that even with the harshest of interrogation methods, the ideological puritans, particularly the Muslim fundamentalists, were some of the hardest to break. Every time she had been required to interrogate one of them, she could tell the moment she walked into the room what it was going to take to get him to submit. It was like a sixth sense. Even though she was always right, she didn't just go from zero to sixty; not unless there was a severe, ticking-time-bomb scenario where they needed the information the subject had immediately.

She sized up Pavel Skovajsa quite quickly. She knew that he was an idiot, or if not an actual idiot, he was quite careless.

Megan nodded and John Vlcek snatched the hood off the man's head. He was bound to a chair in Vlcek's darkened basement. Vlcek remained standing behind him while Rhodes sat on a chair several feet in front with a bright desk lamp shining in his face.

"Where am I?" Skovajsa said in Czech. "Who the hell are you?"

"Do you speak English?" asked Rhodes.

He called her a very nasty name and Vlcek slapped him in the back of the head.

"I'm going to ask you again," said Rhodes. "Do you speak English?"

Skovajsa dropped his head. "Yes," he said. "I speak English."

"Good. Now, I am going to be very clear with you. The rest of your team is dead. All of them. My people are now going after their families." She flipped open his cell phone, looked at it, and then tossed it to Vlcek.

Vlcek held it up so he could see the picture. "These are your little girls?" asked Rhodes.

Skovajsa didn't reply.

Rhodes nodded at Vlcek, who advanced to the next picture. "This is your wife, along with your two little girls. Correct?"

The man still said nothing.

Rhodes nodded again. Vlcek advance to the next picture and kept advancing. "And either these pictures are of the model in your nude portrait class, or this considerably younger woman is your girlfriend."

Once again, the man cursed her in Czech and once again Vlcek slapped him in the back of the head, this time with the cell phone in his hand.

"Mr. Skovajsa, if you tell me what I want to know, you, your children, your wife, and even your girlfriend will be allowed to live. If you do not, you will all be killed, but not before your wife and children are made aware of what kind of man you are. Do we understand each other?"

Skovajsa didn't respond.

"I'll take that as a yes," said Rhodes. "How many years have you worked for Radek Heger?"

He was reluctant to answer, but he finally replied, "Five years."

"Tell me about the bunker."

"I don't know about any bunker."

"Sure you do. That's where you tried to apprehend my friend and she head-butted you, knocked you out, and then broke your colleague's neck when he tried to shoot her. Any of this coming back to you?"

He was about to curse her again, but thought better of it when he sensed Vlcek drawing back his hand. "I know the bunker," he admitted.

"See, this isn't so hard."

There was a sneer on the man's face.

"Now," said Rhodes. "What happened to everything that was inside? Where did it go? Who took it?"

"I don't know."

"I'm not going to ask you again, Pavel. This will be your family's last chance."

"I don't know," he growled.

Rhodes nodded at Vlcek, who set the phone down and picked up a roll of duct tape. Tearing off a piece, he placed it over Skovajsa's mouth and then tossing the roll aside he picked the man's phone back up.

Activating the speaker phone feature, he dialed Skovajsa's wife and woke her out of a sound sleep. In perfect Czech, Vlcek then said everything Rhodes had told him to say.

"Yes, there's been an accident . . . Your husband was drinking. We think it is better we bring him home to you. If the police get involved it will be a lot of trouble. Yes, he is injured . . . He is bleeding . . . You can probably clean him up. I don't think a hospital will be necessary . . . The car, though, was very damaged . . . The problem is that your husband tells us he doesn't want to go home for some reason. He is worried we will wake your girls. He is telling us we should take him to some woman named Margita?"

Skovajsa was fighting against his restraints and screaming from behind the tape. Vlcek had to move away from him with the phone lest his wife hear him making such a commotion.

"I don't know if Margita is a whore, Mrs. Skovajsa," continued Vlcek. "Oh, I'm sorry, you are confirming that she is a whore . . . *His* whore . . . I see . . . Well, we'll let you settle that with him . . . Now, he seems to have left his wallet somewhere this evening and he will only give us Margita's address . . . Yes, if you will give us your address we will bring him straight to you . . . Thank you, yes. I know that area. We will come now . . . Good . . . It is up to you, but you may not want the neighbors to see any of this . . . You have a garage and will leave the door open? Excellent. You are a good wife, Mrs. Skovajsa. He doesn't deserve you. We will see you soon."

When Vlcek finished the call, he hung up the phone and tossed it back to Rhodes. She studied Skovajsa's face. She had no intention of harming his family, but he didn't know that. All he knew was that his wife had now had her worst fears about his having a mistress confirmed. She had also just given out her address and was probably at this very moment going down to open the garage door so these strangers could gain access to the house. Any illusions he may have had about his family's safety were now completely shattered.

Rhodes nodded and Vlcek snatched the tape from Skovajsa's mouth. The minute it was off, he began talking. "They took everything out of the bunker several months ago," he said.

"Who did?"

"I don't know."

Megan shook her head. "I'm very sorry for your family, Pavel."

"I don't know!" he shouted. "I'd never seen them before. They came with lots of equipment. First they cleared several tons of rock from the entrance. Mr. Heger then sent my team in with diving equipment to search for any explosives, any boobytraps. Then we figured out how to drain the water.

"Once the water was out, everything was packed into crates and loaded onto trucks. That's all I know. I swear I have told you everything. Now, you have to swear to me you will not hurt my family."

"That's a good start, Pavel," she replied. "But we're not done yet. We're not even close."

Skovajsa was beyond angry. "Damn it!" he shouted. "I did what you asked. What else do you want?"

Megan leaned forward, her head and shoulders silhouetted by the light from behind, and said, "I want your employer. I *want* Radek Heger."

CHAPTER 29

According to Skovajsa, Heger kept a safe house in a rough, industrial area outside Prague known as Kladno. After what had happened at Zbiroh, that was where he would be headed.

The safe house was where Heger and his men planned their operations and stored their weapons, vehicles, cash, and other items. Standard operating procedure was to evacuate to that location and wait twenty-four hours for the surviving team members to assemble. Anyone who did not make it would be presumed dead or in custody.

Skovajsa confirmed they would not go looking for any bodies in Zbiroh, at least not right away. It was pointless to go looking while it was dark. What's more, they had no idea who they were up against or if those same people would be waiting for them to come back and pick up their dead.

That gave the Athena Team an even greater sense of urgency. They needed to hit Heger tonight, while it was still dark and before he realized that Pavel Skovajsa had been taken prisoner.

Based on the information Skovajsa gave them, the team put together an operations plan detailing their plan of attack. To say they were going to be winging it was an understatement. The way these things normally worked was that they first gathered extensive information about the neighborhood, the building they'd be taking down, the strength of forces at the objective, and so on. It was all about compiling the most complete profile possible and then rehearsing till they could do the entire operation in their sleep. That was not going to happen tonight, though.

The plan was something Casey liked to refer to as CBS—cute but stupid. Vlcek made sure they had all the gear they needed. He even provided them with a lower-profile car with Czech plates so that they didn't have to drive the same vehicle they had been using in Zbiroh.

They changed into their evening wear once again and headed outside to the car. As much as Vlcek wanted to go with them, someone had to stay behind and keep an eye on Skovajsa. The last thing they needed was him getting loose and warning his boss that the team was coming.

Kladno was about twenty-five kilometers north-northwest of Prague and known for its drugs, its gangs, and its rave parties. When the four very attractive women rolled through in their beat-up VW Passat, anyone who saw them would figure they were on their way to a party or to score illicit substances. No one would figure they were there for a fight.

Using Google Earth, Julie Ericsson had mapped

out their entry route as well as multiple exits. Without driving by Heger's safe house, she took a quick spin of the surrounding area just to familiarize herself with it. Rhodes was sitting next to her with a fake rave flyer they had put together on Vlcek's computer. Cooper and Casey sat in the back seat.

Once she was confident she had a good enough feel for the area, Ericsson said, "Let's go find ourselves a party."

They drove two blocks and then turned onto Heger's street. His safe house was a defunct steel forge that sat among a string of decrepit factories and warehouses along both sides of the street.

The women had to give Heger credit. Most thugs would have had two slabs of beef standing around outside in leather jackets looking imposing. Not him. There was no visible security presence whatsoever. Had they not been given the address, they would have driven right by it.

Ericsson pulled over to the curb and the women all got out. This time, they really were dressed to kill. In addition to the short dresses they had been wearing when they'd left the hotel in Zbiroh, they now had their backpacks with them—a fashion staple for many female rave goers—and a perfect place to conceal their weapons. They had also ditched their high heels and were wearing the boots they'd worn while exploring the Kammler complex. As they had overdone their makeup to top things off, no one would doubt that they were on their way to an underground rave party.

Looking at Cooper, Casey said, "I want everyone to remember to smile. Okay?"

"Why do you always look at me when you say that?"

Rhodes jabbed Alex in the ribs and replied, "Because the *I'm a tough bitch don't bother me* face just isn't in this season."

"You really think that's the way I look?"

Ericsson put her arm around her. "You're just so damn serious all the time, Coop. You need to lighten up."

Alex looked around. "You realize where we are and what we're about to do, right?"

Casey wanted to get the team moving. "It's called acting. Sometimes you've got to fake it until you make it. Are we all ready?"

The women nodded, and this time it was Casey who took the lead. Navigating a narrow gangway that led to the entrance of the old forge building, she kept her eyes peeled for security cameras. The team made sure to look as if they were having a good time. They laughed and weaved a little, as if they'd been drinking.

At a heavy iron door, the women adjusted themselves and took a deep breath. The key to success in any operation of this kind was speed, surprise, and overwhelming violence of action.

When she was sure her team was ready, Casey pounded three times on the door and stepped back. Seconds later, a slot opened and a man's eyes looked out. Casey smiled and tilted her head to the side, her hair spilling over her shoulder.

The man didn't say anything, but he didn't retreat inside and close the slot either. Casey raised her eyebrows suggestively and lifted a bottle of slivovitz, a strong Czech liquor made from plums. The man behind the door said something in Czech.

"We're here for the party," said Casey.

"Fuck off," the man said in halting English, before slamming the viewport closed.

"Get a load of the mouth on that guy," said Rhodes.

Casey walked back up to the door, pounded again, and stood back. Several moments went by.

"These guys have got to be spooked," said Ericsson. "Four hot chicks and a bottle of booze, but nobody's opening the door?"

Casey took the rave flyer from Rhodes and pounded on the door again. She didn't stop pounding till the slot opened and they could see the man's eyes again. She held up the flyer. "We're here for the party," she repeated.

"No party here," the man replied before slamming the slot closed.

"Everyone get ready," Casey said quietly. She then wound up and began pounding on the door with a vengeance.

After a minute and a half of her thundering assault, locks could be heard from inside rapidly being thrown back. Cute, but stupid. It worked every time. It also helped that Heger and his men were trying to lie low and didn't need a bunch of drunk women outside their safe house making a racket.

When the door opened, the very large man on the other side was not happy.

Stepping onto the threshold he spat, "I say you to fuck off. *Now fuck off.*"

No sooner were the words out of his mouth than Casey slammed the bottle against the side of his head. The man stumbled backward as she delivered two punches, one to his windpipe and one to his solar plexus, driving him the rest of the way inside.

CHAPTER 30

Two men inside the building immediately raced for their weapons. Their sawed-off shotguns would have been devastating had Alex Cooper and Julie Ericsson not shot them both first.

The team was no longer simply carrying "company guns," as Vlcek called the CZ pistols given to them earlier. Cooper and Ericsson were carrying extremely quiet, .22 caliber suppressed SIG Mosquito pistols, while Casey and Rhodes had suppressed Uzi 9 mms.

Rhodes pulled out a roll of duct tape and bound and gagged the man who had opened the door. He had one hell of a gash across his forehead, but he was alive, which was more than could be said for his two partners. She left him hog-tied, facedown on the ground, and then got back up and joined her teammates.

According to Skovajsa, Heger would be holed up in an office converted into a makeshift apartment near the rear of the building.

The walls of the entrance area where the two thugs lay dead and the other bleeding were covered with posters depicting scantily clad women hoisting mugs of Czech beer. There was a tattered couch, a couple of crummy folding chairs, and a cheap coffee table. Directly across was a very large and no doubt very expensive flatscreen television.

Priorities, thought Casey to herself as she led her team deeper into the building.

A door at the rear of the reception room opened onto a loading bay area. There were crates and pallets stacked everywhere. Computers, stereos, televisions; Heger seemed to have a little bit of everything. In the corner, parked next to a yellow forklift, were two Kawasaki Ninja motorcycles that probably belonged to the guards. Beyond that were several pumps, hoses, and an array of marine salvage equipment, which had most likely been used to drain the water from the Kammler complex back in Zbiroh.

On the opposite wall were the building's circuit breakers. It had been decided that Cooper would stay back to shut the power down when she got the signal. Casey had not intended the assignment to be a punishment for what had happened outside the bunker. In fact, it was just the opposite. She was sending the message that what had happened at Zbiroh was water under the bridge and that she still trusted Cooper to watch their backs.

For her part, Cooper didn't know what to think of the assignment. She knew Gretchen well enough to know that she didn't do things out of spite, but she felt as if she was being left out of the actual takedown of Heger and, right or wrong, that bothered her.

Clipping their radios to the outside of their packs,

the women slid their NVGs, then their headsets on and tested their gear. When everyone was good to go, Casey gave the order to move out.

From the loading bay, Casey, Ericsson, and Rhodes slipped into the main part of the building. It was a large, wide-open space with a glass-paned skylight that ran down the center of the roof. Several of the panes were broken and there were puddles in different spots across the dirty concrete floor.

At some point, a bulldozer appeared to have been brought in to push debris into six or seven large piles. Some of the refuse, like old department store mannequins and broken carousel horses, seemed oddly out of place.

They moved through the building's cavernous interior like ghosts, remaining in the shadows and not making sound. When they neared the last pile of rubble, they could make out several parked cars, including Heger's black Range Rover.

To the right of the cars was the collection of offices Skovajsa said Heger had retrofitted. Casey powered up her NVGs and signaled for Ericsson and Rhodes to do the same.

They crept as close to the offices as they could and then Casey radioed Cooper to kill the power. Seconds later, all the lights in the entire building went out and Casey, Rhodes, and Ericsson burst through the main office door. It was then that they realized Skovajsa had lied to them.

There was a desk and a couple of file cabinets, but other than that, the room was completely empty except for a heavily fortified door at the other end. Casey didn't waste any time. She charged right at it. Ericsson and Rhodes followed.

The three operators were halfway across the room when bullets began coming through the drywall. While Rhodes and Ericsson took cover, Casey went for the door and tried to kick it in. It didn't work.

With bullets popping and snapping all around her, Casey suddenly thought of the sawed-off shotguns up front and wished they had brought one with them. The subsonic 9 mm ammunition she and Rhodes were using wasn't going to help much with the hinges on the fortified door.

They had lost the element of surprise and they were taking withering fire. Pinned down at the door, Casey waited for a lull in the shooting and then ran for one of the filing cabinets.

When she got there, she hailed Alex again over the radio.

"Where are you?"

"I'm halfway to your position," Cooper replied.

"We need you to go back and grab those shotguns from up front. Hurry!"

"Roger that," replied Alex, who turned around and ran back toward the front of the building.

"When we get back to Prague, Skovajsa is a dead man," Rhodes said.

Before Casey could respond, the shooting started up again.

"There's got to be another way in," yelled Ericsson.

Casey judged the distance to the door they had come in from and then replied, "When I say *now*, I want you two to make a break for it. I'll try to keep them pinned down."

Ericsson and Rhodes nodded.

Casey waited for another lull and when it came,

she said *"Now!"* and began shooting. She put her shots high so as not to accidentally kill Heger. They needed him alive.

As Ericsson and Rhodes tumbled out the door, they were greeted with more gunfire, this time coming from the direction of the cars. With no other choice, they scrambled back inside.

"There are two more shooters outside," said Rhodes. "By the cars."

Casey squeezed herself up against the filing cabinet as another round of gunfire tore through the room. "They're going to make a run for it!"

The bullets came in wave after wave, pinning them down. When they finally stopped, there was the sound of squealing tires outside.

"They're running," yelled Casey. "Go! Go! Go!"

Ericsson and Rhodes leaped up from behind the desk and took off with Casey right behind.

When Rhodes peeked out the door, there was a quick burst of fire and then silence as Heger's last shooter hopped into a car and sped out of a rolling garage door that had been opened.

They had taken two vehicles: Heger's black Range Rover and a yellow Porsche 911.

Rhodes fired at the vehicles even though she knew they were out of range. Casey was in the process of telling her to cease fire when the trio heard a high-pitched whine quickly approaching.

When Alex Cooper sped by them on one of the Kawasakis from the loading bay, she had to be doing at least sixty miles an hour. By the time she hit the street outside, she was up to seventy-five.

CHAPTER 31

Neither Heger's supercharged Range Rover nor the Porsche were any match for the racing-inspired motorcycle Cooper was piloting. There was no way they could outrun her, but they could run her off the road. And that's exactly what the driver in the Porsche tried to do.

Had the driver been thinking, he would have realized that he would be better off keeping his vehicle steady so his passenger could lean out the window and try to shoot her. Twice she saw the passenger begin to poke his head out, but twice he was forced back inside by the driver's overly aggressive maneuvers.

As the Porsche slowed, Cooper had no choice but to slow down as well. The streets were too narrow to try to pass. One wrong move and that would be it. And while she had slipped on a helmet sitting near the bikes, at these speeds it wouldn't make much of a difference.

They took three turns, and each time the driver of the Porsche tried to slam on his brakes to cause her to crash, but each time Cooper was ready for him. The only problem, though, was that she was losing sight of Heger and the Range Rover. She was going to have to do something about this Porsche.

At the next intersection, as the driver slowed down and she saw the passenger attempting to come out of his window yet again with his weapon, she decided to make a very bold move. Instead of slowing down, she gunned it.

With oncoming traffic there was not enough room to pass the Porsche, at least not on the street, so Cooper leaped the motorcycle up onto the sidewalk. If one person stepped out in front of her, it would be all over.

She pressed herself tighter against the bike and gave it even more gas. Out of the corner of her eye, she could see the yellow Porsche keeping right up with her on the street. It was time to lose them.

An intersection was coming up. She prayed to God that it would be clear. Flying off the curb at over eighty miles an hour, she shot right through it against the light.

There was the screech of tires and the wailing of car horns as drivers slammed on their brakes and twisted their steering wheels to avoid hitting her. But as they swerved to avoid Cooper on her Kawasaki, what they never saw was the yellow Porsche 911 that was speeding right up the street behind her.

The driver of the 911 tried to steer around the roiling mayhem of the intersection and ended up hitting a blue Smart car. Whether it was the Porsche's speed, the angle at which it hit, or most likely both, the 911 was sent airborne and slammed into two parked cars and a tree. Both the driver and the passenger were probably killed on impact.

Her head down, Alex Cooper raced after Heger's Range Rover. She picked up sight of it again, just as it was entering the highway headed west out of town.

At first she had no idea if the Range Rover knew she was back on their tail, but her question was quickly answered as the driver punched the accelerator and picked up speed.

Unlike the team in the Porsche, the men in the Range Rover had a much better plan for handling her. It began with shooting out their own back window. Sitting in the cargo area was a man with two pistols. Taking aim at Cooper, he began firing.

Bullets pinged off the road and two even struck the front fairing of her motorcycle. She swerved back and forth as best she could to avoid being shot.

When the man stopped to reload, she flipped on her high beam and aimed the motorcycle right for him.

It seemed to do the trick, as the man instantly stopped what he was doing and raised his arm to shield his eyes. She knew the ploy would work only once. Rolling the throttle down, Cooper hung on as the bike raced forward.

Nearing the Range Rover, she swung to the left, shooting the beam from the headlight into the driver's-side mirror so he would be unable see where she was and run her off the road.

With her heart pounding in her throat, Cooper pulled one of the sawed-off shotguns from her backpack, pointed it at a rear tire of the Range Rover, and fired.

The tire exploded in a maelstrom of smoke and black rubber, but it kept going.

Heger's luxury SUV had run-flat tires. But that didn't mean he could run forever, especially at these speeds. The question was, who would be forced to stop first? Cooper was determined it would be Heger. And there was only one way to make that happen. She said another prayer, this time that Heger was wearing his seatbelt.

She goosed the motorcycle forward and prepared to shoot out a front tire as well, but then noticed that because of the range, the beam from her headlight was no longer being reflected into the driver's eyes. Changing her point of aim, she shot out the man's mirror, just as he swerved the Range Rover at her.

Motivated by nothing other than self-preservation, she dropped the shotgun, which clattered down the road behind her, and applied the rear brakes. The bike fishtailed wildly underneath her and for a fraction of a second she saw her life pass before her eyes, convinced she was going down.

But as quickly as she had begun to lose control she regained it. The motorcycle straightened itself out and she was headed forward again. The only problem was that she was staring right at the man in the cargo area, who had both of his pistols pointed right at her chest. Before she could slam on the brakes once more, he began firing.

She weaved the bike from side to side at incredibly dangerous angles, almost laying it down.

Cooper felt one of the rounds slap against her helmet. It was all she could do not to lose her vision for all the stars she suddenly saw.

Two more rounds connected with the motorcycle itself and this time they did damage, *serious* damage. While she didn't know what exactly had been struck, there was a distinct change in the whine of the motorcycle's engine and she could feel it gumming up on her.

She also noticed that the Range Rover was pulling away. She was going to lose Heger. Already once tonight, when his men had gotten the jump on her at Zbiroh, she felt that she had let her team down. She wasn't going to let them down again.

Downshifting the Ninja, Cooper gave it more gas and felt it lurch forward. She began closing the distance with the SUV and as she did, she reached over her shoulder and pulled the second shotgun from her backpack.

The man in the cargo area fired two more shots from each of his weapons and then his slides locked back. *He was empty.* Cooper didn't hesitate.

Racing up behind the Range Rover, she leveled her weapon at the man's chest and pulled the trigger. It was a direct hit. Then, sweeping the bike once again to the left, she raced forward.

Taking out a front tire of the vehicle was no longer an option. Her motorcycle wasn't going to make it much farther. It was time to make the SUV stop. When she was just behind the driver, she raised the shotgun and pulled the trigger.

The Range Rover careened toward her once again, but this time she couldn't avoid making contact.

Dropping the second shotgun, Cooper latched on to the handlebars and tried to keep from losing control. But just as quickly as the black truck had come at her, it veered wildly off in the other direction.

She could see Radek Heger in the passenger seat, frantically trying to grab the wheel from his dead driver and regain control of the vehicle. He failed miserably.

Jerking it too hard, he sent the Range Rover spinning completely out of control.

Cooper watched as the vehicle flipped in the air and landed on the ground. It rolled nine times before coming to a dramatic, smoldering stop in a wide field sixty meters off the side of the road.

There was no telling if Heger was alive or dead. But one thing was for sure. If he was alive, what should have been the end of a nightmare scenario would be just the beginning for him.

Pulling her dying motorcycle off onto the shoulder, Cooper took out her cell phone and called Casey, explaining what had happened and where the team could come find her.

With that task complete, Alex removed her silenced SIG pistol from her backpack, took out a flashlight, and struck off for the wreck.

CHAPTER 32

The former monastery had also been a winery before falling on hard times and going out of business. It was composed of a cluster of buildings set atop a hill and surrounded by a high wall. From both a functional and a security standpoint it was exceptional. All of the staff had a place to sleep, there was a communal dining area, a space devoted solely to the project itself, offices, and a large central court for their vehicles and the mobile generators they had brought in. In a word, it was perfect, and that was why Armen Abressian had chosen it.

The extra cover he received from Viktor Mikhailov had proven extremely valuable as well. When Mikhailov had inquired what Abressian was doing at the old monastery, Armen had avoided answering. When the Russian pushed him, he answered in such a way as to leave the ex-KGB man relatively certain Abressian was refining heroin.

Mikhailov didn't really care what Abressian was doing—at least he hadn't until four of his girls had gone missing. Armen had paid handsomely for the Russian's "protection" and his agreement not to stick his nose into what he was doing. That arrangement had worked out quite well. In fact, it very likely would have continued working had Cahill not vanished those four women.

Abressian shook his head. They were so close to achieving success. Cahill of all people should have been much more careful. He had suddenly made things incredibly difficult for all of them. Armen didn't relish having to deal with Mikhailov. But before he did that, he needed to speak to Cahill. Sanders informed him that despite the hour, he was still working. Abressian wondered if it might be some sort of penance as he headed off to confront him.

The only indoor space large enough to house the project was the monastery's former church, also known as a katholikon. And no matter how many times Armen visited, he was still struck by what a powerful image it presented. It was as if the church itself had been built to house the magnificent device, which now fit so perfectly where one altar had once stood—science overtaking and replacing religion.

Cahill was alone. Armen found him at a work station near the enormous Kammler Device. He had on his usual "business suit" of faded blue jeans, a T-shirt and Chukka boots. Abressian could make out the Maori tribal tattoo on his upper arm. They were the only ones there.

"George," Abressian said as he approached. "You and I need to talk."

Cahill was studying some waveform pattern on one of the multiple computer screens on the desk. "Armen," he replied with his Australian twang as he turned. "It's about time you got back here."

He appeared to be in one of his moods. His hair was unkempt, his eyes wide and bloodshot. There were several crushed, empty energy drink cans on the floor that had missed landing in the trash receptacle. Abressian wondered how long he had been up this time. "Let's sit down, George," he offered.

"Whoa, whoa, whoa," stated Cahill. "You come into my lab and pretend to give me orders? Who do you think you are?"

All of the personality traits had been there from the beginning—his glib, superficial charm and grandiose sense of self, his shallow emotions and constant need for stimulation, his promiscuity and impulsiveness, his contempt for those who sought to understand him, the rapidity with which he blamed others for his own failings; the way he tried to manipulate and con those around him— too often you didn't know you had been taken for a ride until it was too late.

"George," said Abressian. "There are four women missing from the village."

"No," he replied. "There are four *whores* missing from the village. And I already talked to Sanders about this."

"Well, now you and I are talking about it."

Cahill slammed his fist on the desk. "You need to make up your damn mind, Armen! Are we talking whores, or are we talking about the greatest scientific advancement mankind has ever seen? Let's talk about that, huh? Let's talk about power. Let's talk about power like no one has seen since they split the atom!"

"Tell me what happened to the women, George."

"You mean the whores."

"I mean the women. Four human beings. What happened to them?" asked Abressian.

Cahill flipped open the minifridge next to the desk and pulled out another energy drink.

"Stop drinking those."

Cahill mocked him. "Stop drinking those," he repeated and then opened the tab and took a long swallow. Afterward he said, "You don't tell me what to do, Armen."

"Did you push those women through the device, George?"

The scientist turned and looked at the Engeltor. He threw his arms out to his sides, tilted his head back, and closed his eyes as if he were communing with something. Just as quickly as the odd behavior had started, it stopped.

Cahill snapped his head forward and said with a laugh, "Armen, my good man. I didn't push anyone. They all walked through! They completely did it on their own."

My God, thought Abressian. "You made them do it, George. Whether you threatened them or you lied; somehow you manipulated them. They didn't do it knowingly."

"Poh-tay-toe, Poh-tat-toe," he intoned. "For Christ's sake, Armen. You certainly know how to ruin a celebration, don't you?"

The older man was getting extremely angry, but he refused to allow it to show. "You have no idea the trouble you have caused."

The physicist shrugged and took another sip of

his drink. "You're the one who wanted to make an omelet. It seems a bit hypocritical to be crying over the broken eggs."

"You have endangered the welfare of the project."

"I'm a scientist. An incredibly brilliant scientist. You need to accept that," said Cahill.

Sociopath or not, Abressian couldn't believe the man's arrogance. "You still haven't gotten the machine to work, so don't tell me how brilliant you are."

The scientist threw his half-empty energy drink toward the trash can and started laughing. Bringing his hands together in an overexaggerated clap he yelled, "Boom!"

Abressian stared at him. Cahill had fallen into the abyss of madness.

"Say it again!" yelled Cahill, a smile growing on his face from ear to ear. "Say it again!"

Abressian watched as the man put his hands up in front of his chest and began a little dance in front of his computer screens.

"Tell me how I haven't gotten the machine to work," Cahill repeated. "Go ahead. Tell me."

"George?" Abressian said gently. "Do you have news for me?"

"I certainly do," said the scientist as he did a turn and then smiled at his employer. "You're an asshole."

The older man smiled back at him. "It works, doesn't it?"

"I don't want to talk about that. Let's talk about how stupid I am."

"You're not stupid, George," said Abressian.

Cahill was serious again and stopped dancing. "You're damn right I'm not," he replied.

"How? What changed?"

"I had the balls to break a couple of eggs."

"I don't understand," said Abressian.

"The Engeltor. It needed a sacrifice. A blood sacrifice," replied Cahill.

Armen stared at him.

The physicist stared right back. "You think I'm crazy, don't you? I can see it in your beautifully bearded face."

Abressian sensed Cahill was ramping back up again, his mood elevating.

"We're only missing about a hundred pages out of the damn owner's manual for this thing and that got me thinking while you were gone."

"Thinking about what?" asked Armen.

"What if there was a way," said Cahill, as he punched his fist into his palm, "to pop the clutch on this thing? I mean seriously, Armen. We're so close. I was ready to whack the thing with a hammer and give it a couple rounds of percussive maintenance. But then I thought, what's the one thing we haven't tried to send through?"

"People," replied Abressian as he felt a chill run down his spine.

The physicist nodded. "Guess what happened after that?"

Armen shook his head.

"The bombs started going through."

Abressian's mask slipped and he was suddenly visibly upset. "How many did you send?"

"All three of them."

The older man clenched his fists and fought back the urge to beat Cahill to death. "Those were the only devices we had remaining," he said. "They are now half a world away. We can't simply ask our colleagues at the Andaman site to pop them in the mail and send them back to us."

"What do they cost you?" Cahill asked nonchalantly. "A thousand bucks apiece? Buy some more from wherever you got the others."

Abressian wanted to lash out at him, but the scientist had no idea what had happened to his connection for those devices. "We don't simply run down to the store and pick those things up, George."

"Well, that's your problem, not mine. I've got your machine working again. It seems Andaman is receiving at a 66 percent success rate. That means we only lost one out of the three devices we sent through."

"I know what a 66 percent success rate means. What happened to the stray device?"

Cahill shrugged. "I have no idea."

"No hypothesis? No guesses?"

"Who cares?"

"I care, George," replied Abressian. "It's sloppy."

"You and your friends are about to begin wielding one of the most powerful weapons the world has ever seen. I wouldn't care so much about how sloppy it is. You should be quite pleased with a 66 percent success rate. Two out of three ain't bad. Consider the one you lost as the cost of doing business."

The man had made a reasonable point and Abressian nodded.

"Now," said Cahill. "All I need are a few new bombs and the address to which you want them sent. After that, history will take care of the rest."

CHAPTER 33

So how exactly do these work?" asked Ben as he examined the devices disguised as smart phones that were arranged on his kitchen counter.

"Apparently, they can triangulate to create some sort of underground geopositioning system," said Suffolk. "They pick up on atmospheric signals like lightning strikes, gravity fields, and geomagnetic noise."

He looked at her. "How's that going to tell us what's going on beneath Denver International?"

Vicki smiled. "Think of them as highly sensitive listening devices. They have the ability to pick up cellular conversations, radio transmissions, computer activity; even electromagnetic phenomena. How much they're able to pick up, though, depends on how deeply you can penetrate the facility beneath the airport."

"What if there's nothing there?" he asked. "What if it's a big hoax after all?"

"You're not having second thoughts, are you?"

"No. I'm just—"

She leaned over and took his earlobe between her teeth for a moment. After she was sure she had him hot and bothered, she let go and said, "Ben, this is the only way we'll be able to discover the truth."

Matthews smiled. "How about we continue this conversation in the bedroom?"

All this guy thought about was sex. It made Suffolk laugh to herself. *Don't they all?* Even the debonair, sophisticated Peter Marcus was an animal around her. She'd never been sure if Peter's seducing her had been part of his effort to recruit her, or if it had just happened.

The sex between them was intense, and he matched her spirit of adventure in lovemaking quite well, but more than that, he was the first man to ever appreciate her for who she truly was. And because of that, Peter Marcus had represented a turning point in her life.

He cared for her, maybe even loved her, but he didn't try to possess her. In fact, he understood that she needed to be free. He was good to her, really good. Somehow, he had been able to break her long history of abusive relationships with men.

They had met when she was doing a study abroad program in St. Petersburg, Russia. Originally, he told her that he was a banker, but when he finally admitted what he did for a living, she wasn't upset. In fact, she found it incredibly romantic, dangerous, and exciting.

Thanks to her mother, she possessed both Canadian and American citizenship. Even though she lived right across the border in Vancouver, she had never had any desire to visit the United States. With their imperialism and warmongering, not to mention how they treated their poor and downtrodden, who would want to? She was quite content to remain in Canada. But then Peter had recruited her and had changed all of that.

Being a spy was terribly exciting, and Peter had received special permission to train her himself. He came to Canada when he could, but mostly she traveled to the United States to see him. It was all so clandestine, and it made their time together even more electrifying.

And while she preferred to use her wits to get what she needed, she liked the fact that he didn't mind if she slept with other men. He understood that if she used sex to get what she needed, it was only because that's what was necessary for the assignment. She made sure, though, to stress that she took no enjoyment from it, even if it meant she was lying to him.

And with that willingness to lie to the man who had marked such a turning point in her life, she realized that she had reached another turning point and that she was slowly beginning to come more fully into her own.

Turning her mind back to Ben, she said, "I'm not going anywhere near a bedroom with you until you answer my question."

"Okay yes," he said, wrapping his arm around her waist. "I will plant them as *deep* beneath the airport as I can."

Suffolk smiled.

"Where'd you get these things anyway?" he asked, reaching over with his other hand and picking up one of the devices.

"I told you. I know a guy at the university who tinkers with all this stuff."

The woman was an incredible liar. Ben set the device back down on the counter. He didn't want to look at it. He didn't want to look at any of them. As soon as he walked those into Denver International for her, that would be it. The whole operation would be over. Pence had marked that as their endpoint, the moment at which they would present their full case to their SAC in order to arrest her.

Of course, Pence still had no idea that he was sleeping with her. That was something they were going to have to deal with. But not right now. All he wanted was to freeze this moment, so that no matter what happened, he'd never forget how she looked, how she smelled, how she felt pressed up against him.

He'd already told several lies, and there'd be many more before the case against Vicki Suffolk was closed. Instead of telling yet another one, he simply pressed his lips against hers and drew her closer.

As he did, Vicki could feel how badly he wanted her. She decided to give in. This would probably be their last time. She was almost done using him.

CHAPTER 34

John Vlcek had been rightly impressed with Megan Rhodes's interrogation skills. She hadn't even touched Pavel Skovajsa. All the intimidation, except for a couple of slaps to the back of the man's head by Vlcek himself, had been psychological. None of it had been physical and none of it had been torture.

With that said, he doubted Radek Heger would be as easy to break, and he told her so.

Rhodes smiled. "I've got more ability in my little thumb than you'll ever know."

"Honey, I don't know what the rest of them look like in that village back in the Amazon you come from, but trust me, there ain't nothing little about you or your thumb," replied Vlcek, smiling right back at her.

"Your fascination with my height aside, I'll bet you dinner that I can get what I want out of Heger."

"Without laying a hand on him?"

"And without *you* laying a hand on him either," said Rhodes.

Vlcek didn't believe she could do it. "You're on," he stated. "And I expect you to dress *very* nicely for our dinner because you're going to be taking me someplace *very* special."

"We'll see, cowboy," she said as she opened the door and headed down the stairs to the basement. "Just make sure you keep your cool no matter what happens during the interrogation, okay?"

"Anything you say, Thumbelina."

Megan shook her head and then focused on putting her game face on. Interrogation might have been something she was extraordinarily gifted at, but it required the right mind-set. It was all about power, even if it was just the perception of power. Power perceived, she had been taught, was power achieved.

Alex Cooper was standing outside the door to the room where Heger was being kept.

"Has he been prepped?" asked Rhodes.

"Just like you requested," she replied. "We moved Skovajsa into the other room."

"Hey," said Vlcek. "I don't want to end up being the creepy guy with a bunch of people tied up in his basement. Okay?"

"Too late," stated Rhodes as she reached out and laid her hand on Cooper's shoulder. "You did an awesome job tonight," she told her teammate.

Cooper was uncomfortable with compliments. "Are you going to need any help in there?" she asked.

Rhodes shook her head and jabbed her thumb over her shoulder at Vlcek. "As long as he doesn't faint on me, I think we'll be okay."

"All right then," replied Cooper. "Gretch has got first watch upstairs, so I'm going to grab something to eat and then get a little sleep. Try to keep the screaming to a minimum."

"A tall drink of water and a screamer," said Vlcek as he shot Rhodes a look. "Apparently dreams do come true."

"I wasn't talking about her," said Cooper.

"He knows that," replied Rhodes. "He can't help himself. Just ignore him."

Alex shot Vlcek a look of her own and then headed up the stairs.

"There's earplugs in the nightstand if you need them," he called after her. "But I don't mind if you want to listen. Everybody loves an audience."

Rhodes looked at him. "Are you done now?"

"What'd I do?"

Ignoring him, she took a couple of deep breaths, got her head straight, and then opened the door.

Radek Heger had been tied down to one half of a set of bifold closet doors. The door and the prisoner had then been balanced on an ottoman Julie Ericsson had brought down from the living room.

Vlcek leaned in and whispered in Megan's ear, "You're going to waterboard the guy?"

She shook her head. "Just watch."

Heger had a hood over his head and couldn't see. When Cooper had reached his crumpled Range Rover he had indeed been wearing his seatbelt, but his air bag had deployed and he had suffered multiple injuries. One of the injuries was a shattered collarbone. Next to the femur, it was one of the most painful bones to break. When the patient was moved, the shards and fragments rubbed together, causing intense flames of pain to shoot throughout the body. Rhodes had decided to use that to their advantage.

With Julie Ericsson silently holding on near Heger's feet so he couldn't flip himself off the ottoman, Rhodes walked up to his head and bent down.

"Mr. Heger," she said slowly. "You have sustained several very serious injuries. In addition to what you can probably gauge from self-assessment, we believe your back has been broken in three places and that you also have internal bleeding."

Vlcek looked at Ericsson, who shook her head. Rhodes had planned to ramp everything up for maximum psychological impact. As the man carried nothing on his person to indicate that he had a wife, children, girlfriend, dog, or anything of any importance to him, she needed to leverage whatever else she could.

"It is important," continued Megan, "that you cooperate with us. The sooner you do, the sooner we will be able to get you to an appropriate trauma facility."

From beneath his hood, Heger rasped. "I'm going to kill you."

Rhodes laughed. "I'll make sure to send you a can of oil for your wheelchair so that you at least have a sporting chance of sneaking up on me."

"I know who you are. All of you. I'm going to hunt you down and kill each of you."

"Really?" said Megan. "That's very interesting. Who are we?"

Heger didn't answer.

"Yeah, I thought so," she said to him. "You have no idea who we are and you have no idea where we're from. But I'm going to assume you know what we want."

"You're Americans," he rasped. "I know American accents."

"To you, I sound American. To another, German," she replied, changing her accent as she went. "To yet another I am Danish, Dutch, or South African. You see, who I am is unimportant, Mr. Heger. All that matters is what I want.

"We killed a lot of your men tonight. I want you to keep that at the forefront of your mind. The only reason you are alive is that I have let you live.

"We're not very different, the two of us. You're a businessman and I'm a businesswoman. I'm proposing a deal. You give me what I want and I will let you live."

Under his hood, Heger laughed. "Of course you will. I can trust you."

"Radek," said Rhodes. "I am going to warn you once and only once. Do not play with me. I don't like it."

This made the man laugh even harder. It was nothing more than bluster, pure bravado. "The materials that were inside the bunker in Zbiroh. Where are they?" she asked.

"Go to hell," the man hissed.

Megan looked at Julie Ericsson and said, "Okay, let him have it."

CHAPTER 35

Radek Heger screamed in pain as the weight of his body crushed down on his shattered collarbone. So far, Megan Rhodes had been true to her bet with Vlcek. Technically, she had not laid a hand on her prisoner.

Squatting so she could speak directly into his ear and be heard, Rhodes said, "They say the pain you are feeling is akin to being crucified, just upside down."

Heger tried to choke back his screams.

"I can make it stop. Just tell me what I want to know."

When Heger refused to answer, Rhodes took her thumb, jammed it down into his shoulder and dug it around. It didn't take her long to find what she was looking for as the Czech's body went rigid and he practically levitated off the board.

He screamed bloody murder as his head snapped to the side and he tried to bite Rhodes through his hood.

After a few more seconds of imposed agony,

Megan nodded and Ericsson tilted him back up so he was lying flat.

Heger's breathing came in rapid, short gasps. Rhodes allowed him a minute to catch his breath. She didn't need to remove his hood to know that his face was wet with tears. She took no pleasure in aggravating the man's pain, but he held the keys to his own deliverance.

"Radek," she said when she thought he had calmed down enough to listen to her. "We're going to keep doing this until you cooperate."

"You are dead," he mumbled from beneath his hood. "All of you will die."

"Listen to me, Radek. Remember when I told you about the damage done to your back? Remember what I said about internal bleeding? What do you think happens to those injuries every time we tip you upside down like that?"

Heger didn't respond.

"Sooner or later, you are going to tell me what I want to know. The only question is whether you decide it's worth allowing yourself to become paralyzed, or worse, in the process."

She gave him a moment to think about what she was offering. "It's up to you, Radek. Why don't you just tell me what I want to know?"

"Go to hell," he spat again.

Rhodes signaled for Ericsson to tip him over again and she did, *hard.* The board bounced against the floor, his head bounced against the board, and he cried out again in agony.

She asked him once more what had happened to the contents of the bunker and when he refused to answer, she dug her thumb back into his pulverized collarbone and watched his body tense and then begin writhing as white-hot bolts of pain shot up and down his spine.

Several times, she offered him a chance to make it all stop, but he told her what she could do with her offers. Radek Heger was one tough SOB.

Looking up, Rhodes caught John Vlcek's eye. Feigning boredom, he looked at his watch and then pretended to yawn.

She smiled at him in response. Heger would break. It was only a matter of time.

She had Ericsson tip him back up and then she allowed him a moment to catch his breath. His clothes were dripping with sweat.

Then, without warning, without giving him a chance to answer her question, Rhodes signaled for Ericsson to tip the board back over.

As it began to tip back, Heger yelled, "No! Stop."

Rhodes signaled for Ericsson to keep going as she said, "I'm sorry, Radek. We can't stop."

The board slammed onto the floor. "Oh, my God. Stop," he yelled. "Please stop. I will tell you."

"Tell me what?" asked Rhodes, bending down close to him again.

"Anything," he stammered. "Everything."

Megan pressed gently against his broken collarbone with her thumb.

"We never met the purchaser! We only met his attorney. His name is Branko. Branko Kojic. I sold everything in the bunker to him."

CHAPTER 36

The pilot of the aging Beechcraft King Air 100 made sure everyone was buckled in as he circled the dusty landing strip one last time. As alums of the U.S. Army's former clandestine unit out of Honduras, codenamed Seaspray, he and his copilot had made so many jungle landings they could do them in their sleep.

Conducting their final pass, they kept their eyes peeled for any goats, chickens, or locals that might need to be scared off. They also assessed the integrity of the landing strip itself. The last thing they needed was an inopportunely placed rock or a gaping hole to snap off a piece of their landing gear, or worse. They had very precious cargo onboard and they knew what would happen to them if anything bad befell their VIP passengers.

Leslie Paxton looked at Jack Walsh and smiled. She'd never seen him out of his uniform before. He looked good in civilian clothes, though she didn't think anyone would suspect him of being a missionary. His bearing, his haircut, that gaze that could cut right through steel, it all just screamed military.

If the truth be told, there wasn't much if anything about their team that looked missionary. Even the explosives expert Jack had brought along, a retired naval EOD tech by the name of Tracy Hastings, looked military. While she was an attractive girl, she had the body of an amateur weightlifter. The woman must have worked out at least eight hours a day. There also seemed to be a question about her health, as Jack had asked her a couple of times about headaches, to which Tracy responded that she was feeling fine.

It seemed to Leslie that the two had an interesting father-daughter type of relationship. Jack said that he had worked with Tracy before an accident had forced her out of the Navy. She was one of the best EOD, or Explosive Ordnance Disposal techs, he had ever seen. She was also one of only a few women in the entire Navy ever to hold the job.

But despite Tracy's significant skills, Jack confided in Leslie privately, a bomb that she had been disarming had gone off. As a result, she suffered severe facial lacerations and had lost an eye.

Paxton was not only hard-pressed to notice any scarring, which apparently many rounds of plastic surgery had helped mask, but the surgeons had done such a good job matching her existing pale blue eye that she never would have known that Tracy had lost the other had Jack not said anything.

In addition to Tracy, Jack had brought along four operators for security. This was a highly irregular assignment. In fact, Red Cooney, the chairman of the Joint Chiefs, had wanted him to bring more security, but Jack had talked him out of it. They already had too big a footprint in his opinion. When you included the man they were meeting at the airfield, their party would number eight people total.

Jack's argument to the chairman was that the operation stopped being covert the minute they doubled their numbers and added the security detail. Cooney, though, didn't care. He wasn't about to hand al Qaeda, Hamas, or whoever else was floating around in these jungles such a huge PR coup without a fight. Cooney didn't even want to think of the hay the terrorists could make if they captured not only one of the Pentagon's top intelligence people, but also the director of the top military research agency.

The security men were polite, but kept to themselves. They spent most of the flight sleeping. Of average height, but exceptional build, they were Special Forces soldiers from Seventh Group, formerly stationed in Panama, and now stationed at Elgin Air Force Base in Florida. Though Seventh Group had seen a lot of action as part of Task Force 373 in Afghanistan, the men all spoke fluent Spanish and had extensive experience in the jungles of South America. They were honored to have been handpicked for this assignment and were glad to be getting back to the jungle.

The airplane bounced on the dusty runway and taxied over to a small building a step above a hut that functioned as the terminal, control tower, refueling depot, and bar.

Sitting on a stool chatting with the airport's sole employee and bartender was Ryan Naylor.

As the bush plane taxied over toward them, Naylor thanked the bartender, paid for his Diet Coke, and walked out into the sun. Once the pilot had shut down the engines, he approached the aircraft and waited for the door to be opened and the air stairs lowered.

Jack Walsh came down right behind the SF personnel.

"Admiral Walsh," said the young doctor cum spy. "It's a pleasure to meet you, sir."

"I've read a lot of your reporting," replied Walsh. "The pleasure is all mine. You've been doing great work down here."

"Thank you, sir."

Walsh turned to help Leslie Paxton and Tracy Hastings as they came down the stairs. Then, he made all of the introductions.

Naylor helped unload their gear. Parked next to the "terminal" were two beefy-looking Toyota Land Cruisers with brush guards, rows of halogen lights, engine snorkels, and extra-large off-road tires. Secured to their roof racks were spare gas cans and expedition equipment.

Pointing at a door behind the bar, Naylor said, "This will be your last chance at indoor plumbing for a while, so if anyone is interested, now's the time."

The ladies excused themselves, and while Walsh tried to decide what gear he wanted in which Land Cruiser, Naylor got to know the SF men.

He gave them a rundown about terrorist activity in the area as well as what the RUMINT was. They discussed who'd go in which vehicles, who would lead, and then one of the SF men issued Naylor a radio.

By the time they had their logistics sorted out, the ladies had returned.

"Not exactly the Plaza," said Paxton, referring to the facilities.

"Javier is going to upgrade the bathroom right after the free wi-fi goes in," said Naylor.

"You're joking, right?"

"No, ma'am," he replied, drawing her attention to a satellite dish on the roof. "He also makes a mean margarita."

"I'm definitely a margarita girl," said Tracy.

Naylor smiled. *Was she flirting with him?* "When we come back," he said, "I'll buy us all the first round. How's that?"

"Deal."

They continued to make small talk until the SF men had loaded the last of the gear and then Walsh said, "Time to saddle up."

It was decided that they would ride four per vehicle, Walsh, Paxton, and two of the SF men in one Land Cruiser, Naylor, Hastings, and the remaining two SF operators in the other. As Naylor was the most familiar with the area, his was designated the lead vehicle.

"What can you tell me about the canister?" Tracy asked as the truck bounced along the rutted jungle road.

"Not much, I'm afraid," said Naylor. "I'm not a bomb guy."

"How do you think it got to where you found it?"

"I think one of the terrorist groups training in the area put it there. It could be AQ, Hamas, anybody."

"Why would they just leave it out in the middle of the jungle?"

Naylor shrugged. "I know. It doesn't make any sense."

"There were dead bodies near it as well?"

"Bodies, vehicles. There's a ton of weird stuff."

"Do you think it caused the death of the people you found?" she asked.

"You mean is it some sort of chem/bio weapon? I don't think so. What happened to these people is like nothing I've ever seen."

"So what's this all about?"

Naylor adjusted the air conditioning and looked into the rearview mirror at Tracy. "I assume that's what you're here to help figure out."

CHAPTER 37

They drove as far into the jungle as they could and then stopped. Naylor had wanted to hire some Guaranis to act as porters but Walsh had been against it. He wanted their visit kept quiet—the fewer people who knew, the better. This, of course, meant that they were going to have to carry all of their own gear.

They removed everything from the vehicles and loaded it into their packs. Weapons were then distributed to everyone with military training, which meant everyone but Leslie Paxton. Jack told her he'd give her a weapon if she wanted one, but Leslie politely declined. "I'm not a soldier," she said. "I'm a scientist."

After camouflaging the vehicles, they struck off into the jungle on foot. It had rained earlier and the ground was muddy. It made for slow going.

The SF men took turns scouting forward and circling back to make sure they weren't being followed. They were intense professionals who took their job very seriously. As far as they were con-

cerned, this was hostile territory and they expected
to be attacked. It was easy to hope for the best as
long as you were prepared for the worst.

Two hours later, they came to the beginning of
the old, abandoned road. Naylor showed them the
pavers and explained that they were getting close.

They followed the winding path down into the
wide gully. Leslie had her Flipcam out and was taking high-definition video of everything.

When they reached the enormous stones, the
team stopped so that she could investigate them.

After shrugging off his pack, Naylor walked over
and joined her. "Pretty impressive, aren't they?"

"Incredible," she responded.

"Look at these," he said, leading her over to the
strange symbols he had seen carved into the stones
on his first visit. "What do you make of them?"

"They're runes."

"As in Viking letters?"

"Kind of," said Paxton as she zoomed her camera
in for a close-up. "What you see here are symbols
used in Germanic languages before the adoption of
the Latin alphabet. The Scandinavians used something different called futhark. This isn't futhark.
This is definitely Germanic."

"How'd they get here?"

"I don't know for sure," she said.

It was obvious she had some sort of an idea, but
if she wasn't going to offer up her hypothesis, Naylor was enough of a professional not to press her
for it.

"Do you want to see the rest?" he asked her.

"Absolutely," said Paxton as she finished filming
and followed him over to where they had set down
their packs.

They took a few minutes to hydrate and rest before moving on. When they were ready, they reshouldered their gear and headed down into the valley.

Naylor had nicknamed it the "valley of death." It was dark, cold, and there wasn't a single living thing in it. Not only could you not see much sunlight filtering through the thick canopy of trees high above, but just like last time, there wasn't a single bird, monkey, or any other kind of animal making any sound. It was abnormal. Jungles were usually teeming with life. Here, there was just dead silence, dead bodies, and something that looked very much like a bomb.

The valley floor spread out before them. It was choked and overgrown with vegetation. Up ahead, he could see the hulks of the overturned vehicles. "Two o'clock," he said to the rest of the team. "That's the first truck from my report."

"Where's the canister?" asked Tracy.

"About 250 yards farther."

Tracy looked at Jack Walsh. "I want to see it before we look at anything else."

The Pentagon man nodded and Naylor led the way. Fifty yards in, he stopped and pointed. "It's over there," he said. As Tracy started to walk toward it, he put a hand on her arm, "So are the bodies."

"I'm a big girl," she replied. "I can handle it."

Naylor doubted it. Even he had been repulsed by what he had seen, and he was a doctor. He let her go.

The SF men fanned out to form a perimeter as Tracy closed the distance with the canister.

The call from Jack Walsh had come out of the

blue. Tracy hadn't spoken with him in almost a year. When he told her what he needed, she thought he was pulling her leg. He wanted her to travel to South America with him to check out a possible bomb. Only Jack Walsh could call someone out of the blue and make that kind of request.

He said it was hard to get to; that they would have to hike in and carry all of their equipment on their backs. It was then that Tracy knew why he had asked her. Jack Walsh's assignment sounded very much like a suicide operation. And Tracy Hastings was the perfect candidate.

Yes, she had no doubt that Walsh respected her for her abilities. She was a fantastic EOD tech, but he'd be hard-pressed to find someone on such short notice willing to go in with everything but a protective bomb suit. At sixty to seventy pounds, no one was going to be able to carry all the tools they needed *and* a bomb suit. It just wasn't going to happen. The other factor, the fact that this assignment could very well end up killing her, was something she found almost appealing. It wasn't necessarily the danger she was drawn to, but rather the potential that this could end everything.

After her accident and medical discharge from the Navy, Tracy had spent a lot of time getting her life back together and learning to live with her disfigurement. Then she had met someone. He was handsome, exciting, kind, and very funny. He was also former Navy, just like her. His name was Scot Harvath, and they had been perfect for each other.

He had just moved into a new house, a former Anglican church near Mount Vernon, overlooking the Potomac. They hadn't been dating long, and on a whim, he had called her in New York to come down to see it. She booked a seat on the last shuttle of the night and picked up Italian on the way back from the airport.

They ate picnic-style in front of the rectory's old fireplace. The next morning, she let him sleep in. With a cup of coffee in her hand, she had stepped outside to pick some of the flowers growing wild near the front door. It was a warm summer morning. Someone had left a package. She bent down and that was the last thing she remembered before being shot.

The gunman was carrying out a vendetta; preying on the people closest to Scot. She had been in the wrong place at the wrong time, but at least she had survived. That was the bright side friends insisted on emphasizing with her. They had no idea how piercing the headaches that she suffered almost daily were. The only relief was when she was heavily medicated. It was no way to go through life. No way at all.

It had taken a while, but she had finally managed to convince Scot that he was better off without her. He wanted a family; children. Those things were just not in the picture for her. In fact, she really couldn't see anything in her picture, which was precisely why she had said *yes* to Walsh.

Approaching the bomb, she removed her backpack and propped it up against a large rock. She could see the torn and misshapen bodies in the near distance and couldn't tear her eyes away. *What the hell had happened here?* Her mind couldn't make sense of it. Even Jack Walsh's attempts to prepare her hadn't come close to getting her ready for what she was looking at.

She realized she was standing there with her mouth agape, studying the horror in front of her. Finally, her eyes fell back down to the canister. That was why she was here. She needed to focus on that, not the bodies. She was here for what might be a bomb, and what might be her destiny.

CHAPTER 38

As Tracy removed the equipment from her pack, she glanced at the bodies. She wondered if the bomb had something to do with what had happened to them. She felt her heart pick up speed as her mind asked if she was in store for the same fate.

Don't think about it, she told herself. *Focus.*

Tracy studied the object in front of her as she assembled a portable Terahertz Radiation, or T-ray, scanner. The object sure looked like a bomb, but not some jihadist's improvised explosive device. It looked military. Naylor had been smart not to touch it.

It was roughly the size and shape of a fire hydrant and was lying on its side. Made out of some sort of metal, it had been painted olive drab. Numbers or letters once stenciled upon it had been all but sanded away. Just seeing pictures of it, Tracy had sensed what Jack Walsh's fear was and she had agreed with him. The device looked like the kind that could contain a small tactical nuke. But by the same token, so could a wheely bag at the airport. It wasn't the housing that ultimately mattered, it was what was inside.

Firing up the T-ray scanner, she marveled at what a great piece of equipment it was. It allowed EOD techs something called "stand off" capability, meaning you could study a potential bomb from several meters away, often gathering helpful information before having to really get up close and personal. That information could save your life.

According to the scanner's display screen, there was no radiation. That didn't mean the device didn't contain a nuke of some sort, it simply meant that at this distance, it didn't appear to be leaking.

Tracy approached the device and did a slow 360 around it. At about 160 degrees in, the scanner alerted her to the presence of a substance known as PBX-9501. *Not good.*

PBX, or polymer-bonded explosive, was a highly explosive material used in several nuclear warhead configurations.

After finishing her turn around the device, she set the scanner down and ran her list of render-safe procedures through her mind.

She began her work by studying the device for any antihandling devices—a fancy term for boobytrap. While she wasn't afraid to die, she wasn't going to walk knowingly into a trap.

As she got down to business, she noticed how much cooler it was here than in the rest of the jungle. That was a good thing, as she tended to sweat pretty hard dismantling a weapon. The fact that this appeared to be a lot more than just your average explosive device was definitely upping the perspiration factor.

There were no wires protruding from the housing and as far as she could tell, there was nothing that had been placed beneath it. In fact, it looked like it had simply just landed there.

Taking a deep breath, she began the disassembly. It was a slow, very deliberate, very precise process. More than once, Tracy stopped, backed up, and second-guessed what she was doing, convinced she had forgotten something. *Once bombed, twice shy,* she joked to herself.

After twenty minutes, she was able to get the cover off, and she laid it carefully on the ground. Picking her scanner back up, she turned it on and swept the open mouth of the device. It hit for PBX, but not for radiation.

Tracy looked inside. Instead of a code-decoder unit attached to a firing unit and then a warhead, as she had expected, she discovered a long aluminum tube wrapped in copper wire. Attached to the end of it was some sort of transformer. There were several other exotic components she didn't recognize.

She carefully removed the items and laid them out on a plastic drop cloth. Once she had finished, she told Walsh and the others that it was safe to come over. She also told herself that she could now really look at the bodies. The team joined her.

Though the sight was incredibly grotesque, Paxton studied each body with the cold detachment of a clinician, a scientist. Once her first examination was complete, she captured each corpse on video.

"What happened here?" Tracy asked.

"We don't know," Leslie replied.

She stared at the mangled corpses and body parts sticking out of the sheer rock. "Does this have something to do with what I just disassembled?"

"We're just as much in the dark on this as you are."

Tracy didn't know whether to believe that or not. "Really?" she said. "I saw the way you looked at those bodies. If I didn't know any better, I'd swear you'd seen all this before."

Tracy was nice enough, and Jack seemed to like her a lot, but she wasn't authorized to be read in on what was going on here. Pointing at Naylor, Paxton said, "It was all in his report. He included photographs."

There was something about the way she defended herself that Tracy found less than convincing. Before she could respond, though, Walsh motioned for her to come join him at the bomb.

"So what do we have?" he asked as she walked over and stood beside him.

Tracy looked down at the various parts. "At first, I thought we were looking at something along the lines of a tactical nuke, but now I'm not so sure. I've never seen anything like this."

"If it was a nuke, where's the warhead?"

Tracy shrugged. "That's just it. There is none. In fact, I couldn't find any explosives in it at all, just trace amounts picked up by the scanner."

"Any indication of country of origin or who this might have belonged to?"

"I couldn't find any discernible markings."

"May I?" asked Leslie Paxton, who had tucked away her camera and was now looking at the bomb components.

"Be my guest," said Tracy.

"So you thought this might be some kind of tactical nuke, just like I did," stated Naylor.

"Yes," she replied, putting her fingers up in the air to make quotation marks, "but there's no 'nuke' to this device. It's something else."

"It certainly is," said Leslie as she picked up the long aluminum tube wrapped in copper wire. "This piece here is called a flux compression generator."

"What is it?"

"It creates something that has the potential to be more horrifying than the Black Death, more costly in lives than any war we've ever fought, and so financially devastating it could make Hurricane Katrina look like a handful of change lost under a couch cushion."

With the rest of the team staring at her, she clarified her remarks. "You're looking at a crude electromagnetic pulse weapon."

CHAPTER 39

"B asically," said Paxton, "electromagnetic pulse, or EMP, is an electromagnetic shockwave."

"It completely fries things that are electronic, right?" asked Naylor.

"That's right," replied Leslie. "We got our first real taste of what an EMP could do after we ignited several hydrogen bombs over the Pacific in 1958.

"The resultant hurricane of electrons traveled hundreds of miles and blew out street lamps in Hawaii, while disrupting radio transmissions in Australia for over eighteen hours. We decided then and there that if we could harness this destructive force, it would make one heck of a weapon."

"And I'm assuming we did," said Tracy.

Jack Walsh nodded. "Much of it's classified, but suffice it to say that we have a lot of EMP weapons in development and in our arsenal."

"As do our enemies," added Paxton. "Electromagnetic warfare has been one of the military's greatest concerns. Successfully employed, an EMP weapon could send us back to the Dark Ages. We wouldn't be able to heat or cool homes, pump water, remove sewage, dispatch police or firefighters, process or deliver food and medicine. It would be absolute chaos. Millions upon millions of people would die."

Naylor looked at the device they were standing over. "From one small bomb like this?" he asked.

Walsh shook his head. "This kind of device is not going to take down the entire United States power grid. For a one-shot, one-kill like that, you'd need to actually detonate a nuke high above the center of the country.

"What's dangerous about an e-bomb like this is that they are very inexpensive to fabricate. Any nation or terrorist group with 1940s level scientific technology could build one.

"For less than the cost of a new car, you could build twenty of these devices and plunge the island of Manhattan into darkness for months. With our dependence upon electricity for just about everything in our lives, New York City would become a dead zone, virtually uninhabitable. On top of that, anything stored on computer would be evaporated—banking records, stock transactions, medical records. Also, anything with electronic circuitry would be, as you said, *fried*. The economic impact would be incalculable. Add to that the loss of human life that would occur and you would have a terrorist attack that would easily dwarf 9/11.

"Give a terrorist organization one hundred thousand dollars and they could do this in ten cities; with a million dollars they could do it in one hundred, and so on. There'd be nothing we could do to stop it."

"So how did this bomb get here?" asked Tracy.

Paxton held up the aluminum tube and pointed inside it. "This tube is normally filled with a high explosive like PBX. That's the *boom* part of the bomb. The fact that this device was rendered inert suggests that it is probably being used in a training exercise of some sort."

Naylor nodded. "We've got plenty of terrorist organizations to choose from down here. We can start with just about any of them."

"Hold it," said Tracy. "What does an EMP device have to do with what happened to these bodies? Is there another aspect of EMP detonations that we don't know about?"

"Apparently, there's a lot going on that we don't know about," replied Leslie. "Are we concerned that some sort of weapon did this to these people? Yes. That's part of the reason we're here. What I think we should do now is scour the site and see what other evidence we can gather."

With the SF men maintaining a perimeter, Paxton suggested they split into teams. She sent Ryan and Tracy in one direction and then led Jack in the other.

Once they were well out of earshot, she said, "I think that bomb is from Pakistan."

"Pakistan? What makes you think that?"

"Because the Indian military intercepted several similar devices a year ago en route to Bangalore, their version of Silicon Valley. They believe it was a plot funded by Pakistani intelligence."

"I remember something about that," said Walsh. "But wouldn't that give more credence to the notion that this bomb didn't materialize out of thin air, but is here because terrorists were training with it?"

Paxton shook her head. "I don't think a terrorist group is going to go to all that trouble to smuggle a bomb into Paraguay, just to leave it in the middle of the jungle."

"So you think it came through the device?"

"Don't you? Should we go back and look at the bodies again? You know what caused that carnage and why they were melded to those rocks."

She was right. "Okay," he agreed. "Let's say all of it did come through the device. Why here? Why Paraguay?"

Leslie swept out her arms. "The World War II–era trucks. The old road. *This* was a receiving point."

"Receiving point for what?"

"Gold. People. Equipment. Stolen artwork. You name it. This would have been humming like a Nazi Greyhound bus station."

"But when I think of Nazis fleeing Europe for South America," said Walsh, "I normally think of Argentina or Brazil. Those were the real hotspots. Why not set the receiving point there?"

"I had the same question until I saw the runes carved in those old stones," replied Paxton. "Nueva Germania."

"*Nueva* what?"

"Nueva Germania. *New* Germany," she replied as she walked over to him. "In the late 1800s, Friedrich Nietzsche's sister and her husband traveled to Paraguay to establish a colony in the jungle that would demonstrate German superiority and the superiority of the Aryan race to the entire world. It's where Josef Mengele fled after the war."

Walsh stared out at the thick, overgrown jungle. "This was Neuva Germania?"

Paxton shook her head. "I think this was the site of the original colony. It thrived for a while, but they were under constant assault from the indigenous Guaranis, who eventually chased them off. The colonists moved on and built a more conventional style town, closer to civilization, but the original colony always maintained a mystical, almost cultlike aura for them."

Walsh thought about that as Leslie continued. "Maybe we weren't the only ones to know about what Kammler was up to, but we were the only ones to successfully get our hands on the research and the majority of the scientists at the end of the war."

"But we haven't made significant progress with it, have we?"

"Remember what Einstein said: *If we knew what we were doing, we wouldn't call it research,*" Leslie replied without really answering his question.

"Einstein also said that what we were doing with quantum teleportation was *spooky.*"

"And I would agree with him. In a sense, it is spooky, but let's get back to my hypothesis about what happened here."

Walsh was uncomfortable with hypotheses. He preferred facts. That was the difference between science and the intelligence field. Scientists came up with an answer and used it to find facts while intelligence operatives came up with facts and used them to find an answer. Nevertheless, they were dealing with someone that straddled her world and his. To get to the answer, they were going to have to work together. "Okay, so tell me what happened," he said.

"So we had a monopoly on the Kammler personnel and the Kammler technology, but at some point that changed. And we know someone picked the bunker clean in Zbiroh.

"Let's assume that at the very least they have been able to rebuild the device."

"I'd say that's a fair assumption," replied Walsh.

"Are you going to leap right into big experiments? Or are you going to start small?"

"Small, of course."

"Is pushing people through or pushing a bomb through big or small?"

Walsh looked at her. "It's big. *Very* big."

"And what does that tell us? It tells us that they probably already completed their lower-range experiments. It tells us they, whoever *they* are, felt ready to move to the next level."

Walsh had a bad feeling he knew what she was thinking. "Are you saying that whoever this is, they're only a few steps away from us with this technology?"

Leslie thought about her answer for a moment. "I think what happened here is an anomaly. I think they started with safety pins, pencils, or tennis balls, probably inorganic items that were even smaller. I think they were able to specifically direct those items to a designated receiving point somewhere."

"But why did this stuff end up here?" asked Walsh.

"That's a good question," she replied. "We had something similar happen during our research. The scientists back then called it an echo. After multiple successful transmissions, we decided to adjust and send things to a new location. Inanimate objects worked fine, but the minute something with a certain amount of electricity or electromagnetism was sent through the device, it began randomly defaulting to the old location. It also ended up scrambling whatever was sent through."

"So you think that's what's happening?" asked Walsh. "You think their equipment is defaulting to here?"

Paxton nodded. "I do. I think they managed to reconstruct the Kammler Device from Zbiroh and this was its original receiving point."

"How long before they get it straightened out?"

"I don't think it matters," replied Paxton.

"Why not?"

"Because the bomb they sent through didn't end up scrambled. It might have been only a test run, but the bomb itself was perfect. Sooner or later, they're going to figure that out. Sooner or later they'll also realize that every third or fourth bomb isn't going to make it through. At that point, they'll simply chalk up the bombs they can't account for to the cost of doing business."

Walsh wanted to argue with her, but once again she was right. He also had a very bad feeling about who the bombers' ultimate target was going to be unless they were stopped.

CHAPTER 40

The stunning glass and steel structure had been built by a world-renowned engineering and design firm. From its internal internet hub and proprietary server farm to its cutting-edge security system, it was considered one of the most sophisticated and most secure buildings in Eastern Europe.

It occupied a prominent position on the left bank of the Sava River in the Serbian capital's bustling business center known as New Belgrade. Its tenants were prestigious multinationals and leading Serbian businesses. A mixed-use development, it offered not only commercial and retail space, but also luxurious residences to those who could afford them. Attorney Branko Kojic was one of those people.

The Athena Team had flown from Prague to Belgrade via private jet and took rooms at a hip,

four-star hotel. They left Vlcek in charge of their
two prisoners while Hutton decided what would
be done with them. On their way out, Megan had
given Vlcek a playful kiss on the cheek, and even
though they debated who had lost their bet, he still
offered to take her to dinner.

After catching what little sleep they could on the
short plane ride in from Prague, they had grabbed
a few more hours at the hotel and then had gotten
to work.

No one knew very much about Branko Kojic.
That wasn't necessarily a surprise. Many people
had reinvented themselves after the Yugoslav wars.

Some had returned years later with new names,
new identities, and passports from new countries
of citizenship, while others had found ways to
emerge from expensive cocoons reborn, with shiny
new personas, unmarred by the violence that had
so scarred the region. Branko Kojic was believed to
be one of these "Serbian butterflies," as they were
known. The Athena operatives were instructed to
use the utmost caution when dealing with him.
They were on his turf, and they took the directive
very seriously.

To conduct good surveillance you needed one
thing in abundance—time. But time was something they didn't have. From what little they had
been able to learn from Megan's interrogation of
Heger, Kojic lived and worked in the same building. He rarely went out. When he did, it was in an
armored vehicle accompanied by a follow car and
multiple private security specialists.

They entered and exited the building via its
highly fortified garage, which, like the building's
lobby, had a strong security presence of round-the-

clock guards. It was next to impossible to plan to take him en route, because they had no idea where he would be going, or when.

Casey had come up with the idea of posing as an American attorney whose client was looking to open an office in Belgrade. She hoped to get him to dinner, or to at least get a face-to-face meeting with him in his office. When she called that morning, the woman who answered his phone told her that Kojic was not accepting new clients at this time. That was it. Though Gretchen pushed for a referral, something most professionals were usually happy to provide, the woman said she could not be of any help and hung up.

This put them in a very difficult position. Not only did Kojic not leave the building that often, he also didn't take meetings, at least not with anyone new. That left them with two choices. Either they could force him out, or they could force their way in. For a moment or two, they explored the idea of setting the building on fire, but then decided against it.

Without weeks to surveil him and watch for any pattern or weakness, they had no other option than to go into the building after him.

While Hutton and the team back at Fort Bragg assembled satellite imagery of the building and began gathering as much information about it as they could, Casey, Rhodes, Cooper, and Ericsson did the footwork.

Using one of the false-front consulting companies the DoD had established for intelligence operations, Cooper and Ericsson were able to set up meetings with three businesses in the building to compile as much of an idea as possible of the security on the commercial side. Casey and Rhodes arranged to tour multiple units in the residential portion of the tower that were for sale.

As they had been trained, the women took in everything while not appearing to be very interested in anything. They were also alert to opportunity, and Cooper was able to steal a building ID badge from an employee in one of the offices they were visiting.

At the end of their first day of intelligence gathering in Belgrade, they met back at the hotel to debrief. The consensus wasn't good. Though Cooper had done a great job grabbing an ID badge that also functioned as an access card, it was tied to its owner's biometrics. They would have to find another way.

Casey ran down what she and Rhodes had learned via their walkthroughs of several high-end condo units with one of the building's sales agents. The man had been incredibly forthcoming, even to the point of admitting that he was telling them things he shouldn't. All of the women laughed at this remark, as they knew it was part of the raison d'être for the Athena Project.

The man's candidness had given Casey an idea. It was dangerous, but it was a scenario they had trained for. "And if we do it just right," she said, "I think we may be able to pull it off."

CHAPTER 41

Gretchen's plan was in fact extremely dangerous and Rob Hutton wasn't exactly quick to endorse it. "Let's see if we can get the other pieces in place," he had said.

Casey knew he'd come through for them. That was what a commander did. He made sure his team had everything they needed to get their mission completed successfully. If Hutton came up with a better idea for pulling this off, Casey and her teammates would be all ears, but until that happened, they were preparing to go with Plan A.

And, with nothing better to do than sit around and wait, Casey decided they should go out and get something to eat for dinner.

They picked a Serbian restaurant not far from their hotel in the old part of the city known as the Bohemian Quarter. Even Cooper, who leaned a bit more to the vegetarian side, found something to enjoy on the menu.

Casey didn't need to warn her team about their alcohol intake. They were all adults. They were also all entitled to a little R&R. They had been going ninety miles an hour with their hair on fire since Venice. A couple of drinks would probably do them some good.

Casey held up her wine glass. "To the toughest, smartest, and best-looking bunch of women I know," she said.

The rest of the team voiced their agreement and clinked glasses. While they could handle any operation thrown at them, by definition the Athena Team members weren't marathoners. They were sprinters. Get in, get it done, get out, get home. That's what they did. And even though not a single one of them had complained or would complain, they were overdue for something like this.

They laughed and told stories. There was a lot of good-natured ribbing as well. Being highly competitive and fiercely loyal to each other meant that there were no subjects that were off-limits.

Casey was in the middle of pressing Ericsson on whether Vlcek ever cooked breakfast for her the morning after or if Rhodes should just plan to be gone before he woke up, when the secure Qualcom CDMA phone she'd been given for the assignment began vibrating.

There was only one person who had the number. "Casey," she said, holding the phone up to her ear.

The restaurant was crowded and there was a strolling band of Serbian minstrels that was nearing their table. "Hold on," she stated. "I can't hear you. I'm going to step outside."

Mouthing the name Hutton to her teammates, she stood up and indicated that she was going to finish the call outside. When she exited the restaurant and stepped onto the sidewalk, she raised the phone back up to her ear.

"Sorry about that," she said.

"Where are you?" asked Hutton.

"Some restaurant. Having a glass of wine and getting something to eat. Don't worry, I'll make sure to save the receipts."

"You're going to need to get the check," he replied.

"As soon as we're done eating."

"Get it to go. You're going in tonight."

"Tonight?" repeated Casey.

"Yes," said Hutton. "We've been able to breach part of their security network. According to what our folks discovered, they do server maintenance tonight. They hand off different operations in shifts to a backup system. Our people are looking at whether they can penetrate the network while this is going on. If they can, they think they'll be able to control the elevators, door sensors, and video feeds before you attempt to enter the building."

"They *think,* or they know?"

"You know how this works, Gretchen."

Yes, she did know, but that didn't mean that she had to like it. "What about the gear?" she asked.

"Everything will be waiting at the airport. Tell the ladies I'm sorry I ruined dinner."

"They won't believe me, but I'll tell them."

"Listen," he said, sensing her concern. "Your safety comes before everything else. You know I wouldn't ask all of you to do this if I didn't think it would work."

"I know," said Casey, wanting to get back inside and at least grab one hot bite of food before they had to take off running again.

"There's something else I want you to know," he added. "I heard from Walsh. He's personally seen one of the bombs these people have transmitted. You need to get to this Branko Kojic and find out who he is working for and where all the equipment from Zbiroh went. And you need to do it fast. He doesn't care what it takes."

"I understand," said Casey, and she meant it. It was one thing to be upset about not getting enough downtime. It was something else entirely when your commanding officer told you that the director for intelligence for the Joint Chiefs needed a bomber run to ground ASAP. This wasn't about her and what she wanted. This was about the job and what needed to be done. It was a job Gretchen Casey was 100 percent committed to.

"I'll talk with you as soon as we're ready to launch," she said, ending their call. She then walked back into the restaurant, placed several bills on the table, and stated, "We may have just caught a break. Rob has okayed our plan. He wants us to move. Now."

CHAPTER 42

Thomas Sanders looked at his boss. With a thick gray beard and abundance of poised self-confidence he appeared Zeuslike. "I don't understand how you can be so relaxed."

They were sitting on the stone stairs in front of the compound's main building waiting for Viktor Mikhailov to arrive. Abressian held a snifter of B&B in his hand and was smoking a Gurkha Black Dragon from the hand-carved camel bone chest in his office. "Patience, Thomas, is the art of caring slowly."

It was a warm, breezeless night. Stars punctured the dark curtain of sky above. The only clouds came from the leathery smoke of Abressian's eleven-hundred-dollar cigar.

"I have a bet with our security chief, Marko, about how many cars Viktor will bring," Sanders remarked. "I'm guessing five—a full, flamboyant show of Russian muscle."

Abressian plucked a small piece of tobacco from his tongue and rolled it between his thumb and forefinger before flicking it to the ground. "And how many cars does Marko believe are coming?"

Sanders smiled and shook his head. "He says only one."

"And how much did you bet?"

"Only a hundred dollars."

"Well, you'd better get your money ready," said Abressian as he stood and drained the liquid in his snifter. "Comrade Mikhailov has arrived, and he brought only one vehicle."

Sanders looked toward the gate. Their heavy metal doors were still closed. He tilted his head, but he couldn't hear a thing beyond the normal sounds of the night. Seconds later, men came out of the guardhouse and opened the large doors. It wasn't until he saw the halogen headlights of Viktor's Audi slicing through the darkness of the twisting uphill road that he knew he was close. Only now could he make out the car's engine. Armen's hearing was amazing.

The low-slung black Audi passed through the gates and crunched across the gravel motor court. It came to a stop in front of the stone stairs and the front passenger door opened.

Viktor's lead bodyguard exited the vehicle first, followed by another bodyguard from the backseat. The driver remained with the car.

When the very large bodyguards were content that it was safe for their principal to exit the vehicle, the lead man opened the door and out stepped Viktor Mikhailov.

He was a barrel-chested fireplug of a man. At five-foot-five, his diminutive stature was only highlighted by how enormous his bodyguards were. Mikhailov had a completely shaved head and a neck as thick as a telephone pole. He was about the same age as Armen, but any similarity between the two men ended there. Whereas Abressian was dressed in a linen shirt and linen trousers, and shod in tasteful Italian loafers, Mikhailov looked every inch the mafioso—silk shirt, silk trousers, and several pieces of gold jewelry.

It was an image the Russian had worked hard to cultivate. Abressian had no doubt that everything the man wore, everything the man said, and everything the man did was very well calculated and considered.

"Thank you for coming, Viktor," Armen said as he extended his hand. "I apologize for the circumstances."

Mikhailov's digits looked like a cluster of sausages, but he had an incredibly strong grip. He shook his head as he clasped hands with Abressian. "What has happened is very bad, Armen. *Very* bad. I have given you protection and this is how you repay me?"

"As I said over the phone, we need to talk face-to-face. Why don't you come inside?"

Abressian led the way to his office, where a bottle of vodka sat in an ice bucket on his desk. Mikhailov told his men to wait outside.

"What were you drinking in the snifter outside?" asked the Russian. "B&B?"

Armen nodded.

"Good," replied the former KGB agent. "That's what I'll have, then."

Abressian poured the man's drink and handed it to him as he refreshed his own snifter.

"What are we going to do about this situation, Armen?" asked Mikhailov as he took a seat. "Who the hell do you have working for you, Dr. Mengele?"

The Nazi reference took Abressian by surprise. "What do you mean?"

"What do I mean? You're up here in this compound doing God knows what while one of your scientists is snatching up my girls and killing them. *That's* what I mean."

"And I want to compensate you for your loss. It's the right thing to do."

The Russian shook his head. "After one girl, maybe we could have worked something out. Your professor would have had to have his leg broken along with a couple of ribs, but we could have come to an arrangement. Now, though, four of my girls are gone."

"We can pay you for the four girls."

Mikhailov drained the contents of his glass in one swallow and then wiped his mouth with the back of his hand. He set the glass down and looked at Abressian. "This has nothing to do with paying me for the girls, which you will do, by the way. My other girls are afraid. They don't believe I can protect them, and my competitors see me as weak. Everyone knows those girls are gone and everyone knows who did it. I can't let that go unanswered, Armen. I like you, but this is business."

Abressian nodded and took a sip from his snifter. "Then we have a problem."

Mikhailov hadn't been expecting that kind of response. "Excuse me?" he said.

"Professor Cahill is integral to *my* business. I can't allow anything to happen to him."

"Maybe you misunderstood me," replied the Russian. "I'm not giving you a choice. I want Cahill. *Now.*"

Abressian set down his glass. "That's too bad. I was hoping that I could help you see the light; that we could come to some sort of an arrangement."

The ex-KGB man stared at him in disbelief. "Maybe my English is not so good."

"Your English is fine, Viktor, as is mine. I'm not giving you Cahill. He is too valuable to me."

"Then we have nothing left to discuss."

Abressian stood. "I'm sorry we couldn't come to terms." He offered his hand, but the Russian refused it.

"I will burn you to the ground," said Mikhailov as he turned and walked out.

Not if I burn you first, Abressian said to himself.

The Audi spewed gravel across the motor court as the driver spun its tires and sped off out of the gate.

"I take it he didn't see the light?" asked Sanders as he joined his boss once again on the stairs outside.

"Not yet," replied Abressian as he lifted his cell phone and pressed the button for his head of security. When the man answered, Armen said, "He's all yours, Marko." He then ended the call and slid the phone back into his pocket.

Sanders looked at him. "What are you doing, Armen?"

Abressian pointed toward the horizon and said, "Watch."

For several minutes they stood as Armen drew on his cigar and released peaty trails of blue smoke into the air. Just as Sanders was about to ask what they were waiting for and how much longer it was going to be, there was the sound of automatic weapons fire, lots of it, followed by the distinct sound of a rocket-propelled grenade as it sizzled through the air.

Then came the explosion as the RPG slammed into the Russian's Audi and a billowing fireball lit up the night sky.

Sanders turned to look at his boss, "What just happened?"

"I think Mr. Mikhailov has finally seen the light," replied Abressian as he raised his snifter and toasted in the direction of the explosion. "No hard feelings, Viktor," he said. "It's only business."

Though Armen was smiling, Sanders couldn't help but dread the hell they had certainly just unleashed upon themselves.

CHAPTER 43

Early on, Gretchen Casey had a bad habit of telling Hutton how incredible he was. It probably opened the door for everything else that had followed between them. What she meant to say was that the team of people the Unit had access to was incredible. She learned to be much more careful with her words.

Nevertheless, as she stared at the aircraft sitting on the tarmac of the small airport outside Belgrade, she was tempted to once again credit its appearance, as well as all the gear inside, to how incredible Lieutenant Colonel Robert Hutton was. She was going to have to work on that impulse. It was unhealthy.

Waiting for her and Julie Ericsson were two Icarus Extreme FX 69 parachute rigs. They were compact, highly steerable, and provided for fast flight. The max weight of a jumper loaded down with gear—guns, radio, NVGs, harness, reserve chute, and so on—that the FX 69 could handle was 152 pounds. This meant that few, if any, of the male Delta operators could use them. Many Athena Team members did, and those who did loved them.

Like their fellow team members, they had learned their parachuting skills in the Special Forces HALO program and then picked up their advanced skills in specialized Delta training. On top of that, Gretchen and Julie were recreational jumpers. One of their favorite events was the annual para-ski competition at Snowbird, Utah, where they had to parachute out of an aircraft, hit a target, and then ski the rest of the way down the mountain.

The only real competition Casey and Ericsson ever encountered was each other. Via the military, they trained throughout the year. A good Delta team could land together in a ten-foot circle.

Tonight, though, it wouldn't be a whole team landing. It would just be Gretchen and Julie. But they'd be landing in a very tight area. In fact, the plan was for them to land on Branko Kojic's roof.

Alex and Megan pulled the gear meant for their part of the operation off the plane and tucked it into the trunk of the car they had rented. While they didn't mind jumping, they weren't as gung-ho about it as their teammates and were happy to leave that part of the assignment to Casey and Ericsson.

Once the women had gone over the plan one last time, they said their good-byes. Cooper and Rhodes drove off, and Casey and Ericsson got down to the business of checking and rechecking every piece of equipment that had been sent for them to use.

They didn't need to ask where the plane and all the gear had come from. The Strategic Support Branch, also known as SSB, had been established so that clandestine DoD operatives wouldn't need to depend on the CIA for support.

It was after 11:00 P.M. by the time Megan Rhodes radioed that she and Alex Cooper were in place outside Kojic's building. Their responsibility was to provide visual security and coordinate the exfiltration at the end of the assignment. If things went badly, then they were to get their guns into the fight right away.

They would also be providing atmospheric data for the jumpers. Via a Brunton handheld atmospheric data center, they radioed the humidity, heat index, air density, barometric pressure, temperature, wind speed, and wind direction to Casey and Ericsson. Once that was complete they wished them good luck. Ten minutes later, the Let L-410 Turbojet aircraft was in the air.

Belgrade's elevation was ninety meters, so it had been decided the jump would happen at ten thousand feet AGL, or above ground level. This would give the women plenty of time to fly to Kojic's building in freefall.

When the pilot gave the warning, they put their helmets on, stood up, and approached the door. After checking each other's jumpsuits and equipment, Casey opened the door. She checked the wind deflector and then conducted an outside air safety check.

The pilot announced, "One minute."

Thirty seconds later came the warning, "Thirty seconds."

Casey looked outside once more to make sure everything was clear for their jump. She then leaned back inside the aircraft and flashed Ericsson the thumbs-up. When Ericsson returned the signal, Casey counted to ten and they exited the aircraft together.

The temperature was cold as they raced through the night sky at over 120 miles per hour. Flying in formation, they stayed together until they reached their "open" altitude of two thousand feet.

At that point, Casey waved Ericsson off and they separated. Once a safe distance apart, they deployed their chutes. Gretchen led the way down toward the building with Julie tracking a safe distance behind.

As they descended, Megan continued to feed atmospheric data over the radio.

Using a windsock on a nearby building to help compute her glide angle, Casey placed herself about three hundred feet upwind from the building and corkscrewed down.

Watching as her teammate neared the seventeen-story rooftop, Ericsson did a half-brake of her chute, slowed her descent, and allowed Casey a clear approach.

Despite what the sock said, the wind was tricky and Gretchen hit the roof hard. Even with knees bent, it was a rough landing, but she didn't have time to think about it. She had to collapse her chute before the wind caught it and dragged her over the edge of the building. She also needed to get out of the way because Julie would be coming in right behind her.

Casey gathered up her chute and looked up just in time to see Ericsson coming in to land. There was just one problem. The wind had moved her off-target. She was going to overshoot the roof.

She watched as Julie tried hard to correct, but that only made it worse. "Abort! Abort!" she said over the radio. Ericsson either didn't hear, or didn't want to hear.

When she landed, she landed hard, harder than Casey. She also missed the center of the roof completely and came down at the very edge of the roof. With momentum driving her forward, there was no place for her to go but right over the edge. And as her chute collapsed in a skydiver's nightmare, that's exactly what happened.

CHAPTER 44

Gretchen Casey's breath caught in her throat as she watched it all unfold.

Before she realized what she was doing, she ran for the edge of the roof. As Julie Ericsson's parachute was about to disappear, she leaped for it and missed.

Gretchen scrambled to the edge, half-expecting to hear the sound of Julie hitting the ground, but instead she heard something else: the sound of parachute silk being torn. Ericsson's chute had gotten hung up on a window-washing anchor. Casey could now not only hear, but see the material rapidly giving way. Reaching down, she grabbed two fistfuls of silk and pulled with all her might.

Every muscle fiber in her body felt as if it was being torn, just like the parachute itself. Gretchen ignored the searing pain and pulled even harder as the adrenaline surged through her body.

Leaning backward, she ground her teeth and fought to pull Julie back. "Come on, damn it!" she called out. "Come on!"

Casey summoned everything she had. She went to that dark place inside where she hid the very last burst of speed she had ever used in a race. This was her sister hanging there. A woman she not only loved but was responsible for. She wasn't going to allow her to die.

With one last surge of effort she felt the chute move toward her. She pulled again and it moved again. Hand over hand, inch by painfully slow inch she pulled until she saw the top of Julie's helmet.

Clawing her way down the rigging, Casey reached out for Julie's harness, and planting her feet, pulled her the rest of the way up onto the roof.

She collapsed and lay next to her, panting. Her lungs were on fire, as was the rest of her. It took several minutes for the feeling to return to her fingers.

It was Julie who spoke first. "I think I misjudged that one, just a little bit."

Casey couldn't help herself. It hurt to laugh, but she did anyway, until it turned into a hacking cough, her body still desperate for air.

They continued to lie on the roof for several minutes more until Casey had fully caught her breath.

"Is everyone okay?" Rhodes asked over the radio. "What happened?"

"We're okay," coughed Casey. "Just give us a minute."

"That's all you've got," chimed in Cooper. "They're about to do the first handoff. You need to be at the access door behind you in ninety seconds."

"I'm on it," said Ericsson as she pushed herself up to her feet. Gathering up her chute and clutching it to her chest, she crossed the roof to the access door, where she removed a lockpick gun from her bag.

"Forty-five seconds," said Cooper.

"What about the closed-circuit cameras?" she asked.

"Already taken care of," replied Rhodes.

"Twenty seconds," said Cooper.

Ericsson slipped the tension wrench into the door and then positioned the lockpick gun.

"Ten seconds."

Ericsson applied tension to the wrench and began clicking the trigger. She felt the lock give.

"Now," said Cooper.

Julie pulled back the door and held it open for Casey, who was crossing the roof toward her.

"You've got three minutes until the elevator gets there," said Rhodes. "I suggest you ladies get it in gear."

"Roger that," replied Casey as she stepped into the stairwell and Ericsson gently closed the door behind them.

They stripped out of their harnesses, removed their helmets, and stored everything in a small electrical closet.

Drawing the suppressed Glock 19s they'd been issued, they took a deep breath and headed down the stairs.

One level below the roof, they paused and radioed Rhodes.

"The elevator will be there in fifteen seconds," she said.

Casey kept her ear pressed up against the stairwell door until she heard the chime in the hallway announcing the elevator's arrival. "I'm opening the door," she stated.

Rhodes, who was monitoring the true security camera feeds, as opposed to the falsified loop that the building's guard staff were watching, said, "The hallway is all clear."

Gretchen opened the door slowly and peeked out. Seeing that it was in fact all clear, she signaled Ericsson and the two of them stepped across the hall and into the elevator.

There were no buttons inside. "We're in," said Casey.

"Roger that," replied Rhodes, who activated the elevator.

As it began to descend, Ericsson looked at her teammate and simply said, "Thanks, Gretch."

Casey gave her a smile and nodded. "That could have been a lot of paperwork for me."

Ericsson grinned. "Then I'm glad it worked out the way it did."

"Me too."

"Eighth floor," said Rhodes as the elevator slowed to a stop. "Golf clubs, pool supplies, ladies' lingerie."

Casey was just about to ask her if she could silence the chime, when the doors opened and the noise was conspicuously absent. "I should have silenced it for you upstairs," said Rhodes. "My bad. Hallway all clear. Go get him."

"Go to sterile comms," replied Casey as she stepped off the elevator, her pistol up and ready. Immediately, the entire team fell silent. They would communicate via a language of predetermined clicks.

There were three apartments per floor. Branko Kojic's was at the end of the hall.

"Are you able to do this?" Casey asked. "After

what happened on the roof, if you're not up for it, I understand. We can switch."

"I'm good," said Ericsson as she handed Gretchen her gun, took off her boots, and then unzipped and removed her jumpsuit. She was wearing black lace panties and a matching bra.

Running her fingers through her hair, she asked. "How do I look?"

Casey, who was no slouch in the looks department, couldn't hold a candle to Ericsson's body. "If I was a guy and you turned up on my doorstep looking like that," said Casey. "I'd be buying whatever it was you were selling."

Ericsson rolled her eyes. "Let's just hope he's not gay."

Gretchen smiled as she stepped out of the way. "As long as he opens the door, that's all we care about."

Once Casey stepped off to the side with her boots and jumpsuit, Ericsson adjusted her lingerie, making sure her panties rode high on her hips and her bra put everything on perfect display. Then she rang Kojic's doorbell and stood back just far enough to give him an eyeful.

CHAPTER 45

Branko Kojic answered the door in a short, black silk bathrobe embroidered with a dragon. He had a potbelly, a hairy gray chest, and a receding hairline. The sound of a soccer game came from a TV somewhere inside his unit.

Julie Ericsson didn't give him a chance to speak. "Do you speak English?" she asked, glancing nervously over her shoulder and then back at him. "I'm visiting and I got locked out. I can't go downstairs like this. Can I use your phone?"

By the look on Kojic's face, he definitely wasn't gay. He liked what he saw, a lot. Had she been a man, even a man in his underwear, he would have told him to wait outside in the hall for security, but he wasn't going to do that to this gorgeous woman. No way. Besides, she was in her underwear. She couldn't possibly pose any harm to him. What's more, this was going to be one hell of a story. No one was ever going to believe it. "Yes," he stammered. "I speak English. Would you like to come in? You may use my phone and I'll give you something to put on."

Ericsson stood on her tiptoes, ostensibly to look over his shoulder and into his condo. The provocative move only accentuated the length of her legs and the tautness of her body. "It sounds like you have company," she replied. "Maybe I should ask one of the other neighbors."

"No, no, no," Kojic insisted. "I'm all alone. That's just the television."

"Well, in that case," she said, stepping inside.

The man tried to move out of her way to let her pass and they had an awkward moment as she brushed against him in the doorway.

She stepped back into the hall and said, "After you."

Kojic smiled and retreated into his unit. As he did, Ericsson stepped in front of the door so he couldn't slam it shut. That's when Casey sprang.

"Not a word," she ordered, her Glock leveled at Kojic's head as she burst into his condo. "Down on the floor. Do it now!"

Kojic did as he was told.

Casey produced a set of FlexCuffs and handed Ericsson her weapon. When the Serbian was fully prone, she bound his hands behind his back. "If you make one single sound, I will kill you. Do you understand that?"

Kojic nodded.

"Good."

Julie retrieved her clothes from the hall and stepped back inside. As she locked the door behind her and got dressed, she said over the radio, "We're in."

Casey cleared the expensive condo room by

room to make sure that they were indeed alone.

When she came back to the entry hall, Ericsson asked, "Where do you want to do this?"

From their walkthrough with the realtor that day, they knew that most residents had panic buttons located throughout their units. The last thing they needed was for Kojic to get near one.

Casey looked around as she thought about it. "Let's use the guest bathroom."

Helping him to his feet, they led him down the hall to the bathroom. Pushing the door open with the toe of her boot, Casey turned on the light and then knocked the much larger Kojic to his knees in front of the bidet.

"What do you want from me?" he said. "Who are you?"

"I told you not to talk," said Casey, as she kicked him in the ribs. She didn't necessarily like to get violent, but she could when she had to. Interrogations were a power game, especially between men and women. She could be just as efficient as Megan when it came to interrogating suspects, but she could be a lot more physical, even brutal if the situation called for it. Megan was much more patient.

The thing she had learned early on was to assert her dominance right from the beginning and to answer any challenge to it in the harshest of terms. Some people were slower than others, but once they realized that they were going to get whacked for disobeying or challenging your authority, the challenges stopped pretty quickly. It was only the most hardened subjects who seemed to like it rougher. She didn't want this to get too rough, but if it had to, she was willing to go there.

"Branko," she said as the man looked up at her, "I'm going to ask you a series of questions."

"But I didn't do anything," he offered.

"Shut up."

Kojic closed his mouth.

"I know more about you than you realize. If you lie to me, I will be very upset. Do you understand me?"

Kojic nodded.

"Good. I want to talk to you about a man named Radek Heger."

"I don't know any man named Heger."

Casey looked at Ericsson. "Lift his robe up."

"My robe? Why do you want to—" his voice trailed off as Ericsson bent down and flipped the robe up, exposing his thong underwear.

"Lying makes me angry, Branko," said Casey. "When I get angry, things get worse for you. You just lied to me, so now, as promised, things are going to get worse."

Julie reached over and pulled so hard, she ripped the man's thong off.

"What are you doing?" he implored.

"First, I want to hear you lie to me again. Tell me you don't know Radek Heger."

"I don't. I don't know him."

Ericsson grabbed him by the back of the neck and pressed his cheek against the bidet.

Most stress postures worked across all cultural boundaries. Sexual humiliation, though, was different. It worked very well with more religiously oriented cultures, in particular with Muslim fundamentalists. But Western males weren't turned off or threatened by female sexuality.

What they were doing with Kojic was a hybrid

the Athena Team program had developed. They called it the prison posture. When men were naked and bent over, it had a profound psychological impact on 97 percent of them. It was an incredibly vulnerable position. The key was what the interrogator did next.

The Iraqis under Saddam did unspeakable things to their male victims. There was a definite line Casey would not cross. Instead, she preferred to heighten the subject's fear by going in a completely different and more terrifying direction, something worse than what he thought was coming.

She reached into the bag she was carrying, pulled out a roll-up tool pouch and laid it on the floor. "Do you like the ballet, Mr. Kojic?" she asked as she unrolled the twenty-five-pocket organizer.

The man stared at the hypodermic needles, screwdrivers, medical instruments, and other items arrayed inside.

"The reason I ask," Casey said as she examined her interrogation apparatus, "is that I love the ballet. I mean I really, *really* love it. I have since I was a little girl. Isn't that nice?"

Kojic had no idea if it was nice or not. In fact, he found it a rather bizarre question considering the circumstances. Nevertheless, he didn't want to make her any angrier than she already was. So, he *nodded* that it was nice.

Casey saw him nod and she smiled. "I like that you agree. The ballet is nice."

"Very nice," said Kojic.

"Do you know which ballet is my favorite?"

The man watched as she selected an instrument from one of the pockets of her organizer and shook his head.

"The Nutcracker," Casey replied with a smile as she withdrew a pair of pliers.

Kojic nearly fainted.

Casey pointed at his ankles. "Spread his legs," she ordered Ericsson.

"No. No. No. No. No," the man begged, but Ericsson did what she was told. Letting go of his neck, she reached down, grabbed his ankles, and pulled so hard she almost split him like a wishbone.

With no one keeping his face pressed into the bidet, he immediately rocked back on his knees and raised his head. Casey took care of that, though.

Standing up, she pushed his head back down so that his chin hung over the edge of the bidet. She kept him there with her forearm so she could snap on a pair of latex gloves.

"Please," he begged. "Please don't do this."

Casey opened the pliers and began fishing for what she was looking for.

Kojic frantically twisted his head, first to the left and then to the right. "You don't need to do this. We can make some sort of a deal."

She found his testicles, got hold of one with the pliers, and applied pressure. Kojic's body stiffened.

"Mr. Kojic, I now have one of your you-know-whats in a literal vise. I suggest you tell me everything you know about Radek Heger."

"But, if you will only allow me to—" he began, but Gretchen applied even more pressure and cut him off.

"We're a little *squeezed* for time, Mr. Kojic," she said. "No more games, please."

"I have many clients. I deal with many *people*," he said, but the word *people* came out as a shriek as Casey squeezed even harder.

"Listen to me, Branko. I've got a pair of nice, rusty scissors with me. I'd be happy to cut off your eggs and put them all in one basket for you, if you'd like."

Kojic shook his head back and forth. "No, please, no."

"I'm giving you one last chance," she said. "Tell me what I want to know, or after I get done with the pliers and the scissors, I'm going to get out my scalpel and we'll play chop goes the weasel." She tapped the corresponding piece of his anatomy to make sure the man was suffering from no delusions as to what part of his nether regions she was talking about.

"Radek Heger," he said, as if the name had just come to him. "Of course. Radek Heger the Czech!"

CHAPTER 46

S o what are you offering?" asked Kojic. The ladies had him sitting propped up against the wall of the walk-in shower stall, his hands still bound behind his back.

Ericsson couldn't believe her ears. "This guy has a real set on him, doesn't he?"

"Actually," said Casey, shaking her head, "he doesn't. But that's beside the point."

Kojic, a man who was anything but charming, tried to be. "Ladies, this is a negotiation, so let's *negotiate.*"

"This isn't a negotiation, my friend," said Ericsson as she reached for the pliers. "It's an *interrogation.* You're not in a position to negotiate anything."

Casey took the pliers from her. "My colleague doesn't like lawyers very much."

"Who does?" replied Kojic with a shrug.

"You were going to tell us about Radek Heger," prompted Gretchen.

The man appeared concerned as he chose his words. "I did a transaction with him. Yes."

"When?"

"I'd have to check my files, but within the last year," he said.

Casey studied him closely for any sign that he might be lying. "What did the transaction entail?"

"I was hired to purchase several items we believed were buried on Mr. Heger's property."

"And what were these items?" she asked.

"I don't know," he replied.

Casey looked at him. "Mr. Kojic, you just lied to me."

"No, I didn't. Honestly," he argued.

Casey reached into her tool organizer and removed a syringe and a small vial. Kojic's eyes widened as she began to prepare them.

"Okay," he admitted. "It was equipment."

Casey continued to prep the syringe. She didn't look at him. Instead, she focused on what she was doing. "What kind of equipment?"

"Scientific equipment."

"Be more specific," she ordered.

"I don't know," replied Kojic. "It was leftover junk from World War II. My job was to offer him enough money to dig it up and let us truck it out of there."

"How much money?"

"Twenty million, U.S.," he said.

"That sounds like a lot of money for scientific junk left over from the war, don't you think?"

The man shrugged once more. "I have learned not to ask questions."

"Let's hope you've learned how to answer them," replied Casey. "Who hired you to approach Heger?"

"I had never met him before."

"That's not what I asked. I asked who hired you."

Kojic shook his head. "Now, you and I are back to our negotiation."

"Give me the pliers," said Ericsson.

Casey held up her hand. "Mr. Kojic, you are going to tell me. How much pain you endure before then is up to you."

"I need protection."

"From who? The man who hired you?"

"Yes," he said. "You are Americans, correct? You can give me protection in America."

"Maybe," said Casey. "But it would depend on how much you cooperate."

"He's going to want immunity too, aren't you?"

The man looked at her. "I don't know what you're talking about."

With his hands behind his back, he was unable to adjust his robe, which was falling off one of his shoulders.

"See his tattoo?" Ericsson asked.

Casey nodded.

"Arkan's Tigers. They were a Serbian paramilitary group. One of the most violent in Kosovo."

Kojic stared at her, and the look of pure hatred in his eyes confirmed her suspicions. "I'll bet the war crimes prosecutors would love to have a chat with you, wouldn't they?" Ericsson said.

"So maybe we do have something to negotiate after all," stated Casey. "Who hired you?"

"What about protection?" he asked, before looking at Ericsson, then adding, "*And* immunity."

"You tell me what I want to know and we'll discuss it."

"No deal," said Kojic.

Casey grabbed a fistful of his chest hair and

pulled his face to hers. "You tell me who hired you or I'm going to cut your balls off and leave you here to bleed to death. Better yet," she said, letting go of him, "I'll call some people we know with the Kosovo Liberation Army. I'm sure *they* wouldn't let you bleed to death; at least not right away."

The woman had been correct from the beginning, she did have him in a vise. "His name is Thomas Sanders," he said, "but he is not an easy man to track."

"You know where he is, though, right?"

Kojic shook his head.

"Where did you have the equipment delivered to?"

"I didn't arrange for that. Sanders sent his own people to pick it up."

"Then you really don't have anything of value for us, Mr. Kojic. I think we'll see how much the KLA wants you."

The man shook his head again, much more vigorously this time. "I do have something of value," he insisted. "I know how Sanders does his banking; how he moves his money around. I also know a little about his email traffic and how he set up the electronic dead drops we used."

Casey didn't trust him. "I don't buy it," she said. "I want to see the information first. If it's legitimate, then we'll discuss what we can do for you. Where is it?"

"On my laptop. In the study."

"Fine," said Casey. "I assume it's password protected. Give it to me."

Kojic leaned over until his fingers protruded from behind his back and then wiggled one. "It's biometric."

"Of course. Just like everything else in here," she said as she picked up the syringe.

"Wait," replied Kojic. "I'm cooperating. What is that for?"

"To make sure you *continue* to cooperate."

Ericsson pulled back the robe and restrained him as Casey injected him with several milligrams of Valium. They hadn't given him enough to knock him out, just enough to make him happily compliant.

Their plan was to change into the evening wear they had brought, call down to the garage valet as a giggling girlfriend, and request his car be brought around, then steer him into the elevator, down to the garage, and out of the building in his own car.

Before they did that, though, Casey wanted to make sure Kojic was telling them the truth. "Let's get him over to his computer before he gets too goofy," she said.

With each of the women helping lift from under his arms, they got him to his feet and walked him out of the bathroom. His legs were already a bit wobbly. Casey was concerned that she might have given him too much. A man his size should have been able to better handle the dose she had administered.

"How much did you give him?" asked Ericsson, as she felt herself having to support more and more of his body weight.

"The usual adult dose," she replied as they half-carried him into his study. On the TV mounted in the bookcase, the soccer game was still playing.

"Where should we put him?" asked Ericsson. "At his desk?"

Casey shook her head. "Let's put him on the couch."

They navigated around a large glass coffee table and dropped him. His fat ass landed perfectly in the dented cushion. Put his feet up, the remote in one hand and a beer in the other and this was probably what it looked like every night at Château Kojic.

Casey walked around to the desk and scanned it before opening any drawers. Right above where his legs would have been she found a panic button. It was a good thing they hadn't sat him there.

In the center drawer, she found and removed his laptop. Opening it, she saw that it did in fact have a fingerprint scanner. Pressing the power button, she picked it up and carried it over to him.

Kojic's head was lolling on the back of the couch and looked like an orange on a jack-in-the-box spring. Valium was a tricky drug. You could estimate how much you thought someone would need, but then be completely surprised. Its effectiveness was not related to a subject's size.

When the computer prompt popped up on the screen requesting Kojic to swipe his finger on the print reader, they leaned him over to get at his bound hands. With Ericsson balancing the laptop, Casey grabbed his right index finer and tried to swipe it. Nothing happened. She tried again. Nothing.

Fingerprint readers were often problematic even when a person was trying to swipe his own finger. Throw a huge, drugged-up Serb with his hands tied behind his back into the mix and it was no surprise they were having trouble.

Casey removed her folding knife, snapped the blade into position, and cut away Kojic's restraints.

Jerking his right arm out in front of him, she

dropped his hand onto his thigh and then grabbed his index finger. She scanned it across the reader and his fingerprint was accepted.

But while Casey and Ericsson were busy with his right hand, they had not been paying attention to what his left hand was doing.

Kojic brought a lamp crashing into the side of Casey's head just as he used his other hand to slap the laptop up into Ericsson's jaw.

Reaching next to the couch, he hit a secondary panic alarm and struggled to stand.

"A panic button has just been activated," said Rhodes over the radio. "What's going on in there?"

"Deactivate it," said Casey as Ericsson tried to grab Kojic.

"I can't," she replied.

Casey was about to tell her to at least shut down the elevators when Branko lunged at her.

She was still stunned from being struck with the lamp and that impaired her reaction time. The best she could do was lash out with a quick kick to his knee.

The strike caused him to lose his balance and stumble to the side. Before either Casey or Ericsson could catch him, he went face-first into the glass coffee table.

It all seemed to happen in slow motion as the glass erupted in thousands of gleaming shards.

"Damn it," Casey yelled. "Damn it, damn it, damn it!"

Ericsson bent down to feel for a pulse, but there was none. Kojic had struck his head on one of the table's wrought-iron legs. His open, lifeless eyes stared off underneath the couch while a pool of blood began to form on the carpet underneath him.

"Security is on its way up," said Rhodes. "You need to get out of there. Now."

It took Casey a moment to snap to.

"Gretch, we've got to go," said Ericsson.

Casey nodded. "Get the laptop," she replied as she left the room. "I'll get the tool case so I can get his finger."

As their elevator raced toward the top floor, Megan Rhodes read out atmospheric data for them. Their exit was going to be even more dangerous than their entrance.

Hitting the access stairs, they burst through the door and ran up two flights. Retrieving their harnesses, they prepped as quickly as possible. Tightening their helmets, they gave their reserve chutes one last check and then gave each other the thumbs-up.

"Security just arrived," said Megan. "They are one floor below you headed your way."

Casey and Ericsson ran out onto the roof and went in two different directions. They ran as fast as their legs would propel them, and when they reached the edge of the roof, they leaped out and off into the night.

CHAPTER 47

Ben Matthews checked to make sure no one was eavesdropping on their conversation and said, "She's got someone following me? Since when?"

Dean Pence tore the top off another pack of sugar and dumped the contents into his coffee. "Since she gave you the phones to plant."

Ben couldn't believe it. He hadn't seen anyone. But if Pence said he was being followed, then he was definitely being followed. "So now we know she's not operating alone."

"I told you she'd screw up."

"How many people does she have on me?" asked Matthews.

"At least two that I've been able to ID so far."

"Damn it. I should have seen them."

Pence motioned for him to relax. "I almost didn't pick up on them either. These guys are good; real good."

"So, this operation against the airport is much bigger than we thought."

"That's what it looks like."

Ben leaned forward. "Dean, we've got to go back to Mumford right now. We've got to tell her what we've learned."

"Already done," said Pence.

"What?"

"I already spoke with her."

"Without talking to me first? Are you nuts?" demanded Ben. "We haven't even gotten our stories straight yet."

"Well, we're going to get them straight now," replied Pence.

"How much did you tell her?"

"What am I, new? How much do you *think* I told her?"

Ben massaged his eyes with the heels of his hands. "Shit," he said. "It's all over, isn't it?"

"Like hell it is," replied Pence. "I'm not about to sink one of the biggest espionage cases of the decade. I told you, this is going to *make* our careers, not end them."

"So, you lied to Mumford is what you're telling me."

"I don't like the word lie."

Matthews chuckled.

"I was selective with the truth," said Pence. "Listen, I told her what she wanted to hear. You know how she is. This is all about her career. Now that she realizes what she stands to gain from all of this, she's behind it."

"Now you're lying to me. There's no way you could have explained this to her in such a way that she would have completely gone along with it. No way."

Pence nodded. "There's going to be some disciplinary action, yes, but—"

Ben leaned back in the restaurant booth. "Now the truth comes out."

"But we're still on the case. She's allocating extra resources now and everything. We can have anything we need."

"Including our choice of lethal injection or firing squad."

"You're speaking metaphorically, I hope," said Pence.

Matthews reached for his coffee. "I'm speaking about our careers, Dean. We're done."

"Ben, we're not done. Our careers are more than intact. Stop worrying. As far as anyone is concerned, we haven't broken any laws. Mumford doesn't know anything about the warrantless eavesdropping."

"How about me falsifying my employment application to TSA?"

Pence sucked some air in between his teeth and nodded. "Yeah, she knows about that."

Ben threw his hands up in the air. "Fabulous. Did you take responsibility for anything?"

"Actually, I did. I told her that this was my idea and that I put the entire thing together. And that whatever you had done, you did because I told you it was the right thing to do.

"Then I explained that while we might have bent a few regulations here and there—"

"Dean, we did more than bend a few regulations."

"She doesn't know that," said Pence, "and she's not going to. I copped to the stuff that we couldn't cover up. The rest of it never happened."

"So what's our story?"

"If you give me five minutes, I'll explain."

They actually spent the next forty-five minutes discussing what Pence had told their boss and how the SAC had decided she wanted them to proceed.

When Pence was through, he looked at Ben and said, "So you're supposed to assume that you're under complete surveillance, got it?"

Ben nodded. "I understand."

"That means you don't stop by the office, you don't call in, you don't email. You're to remain completely in character; completely undercover. Okay?"

"I got it, Dean. I know what not breaking cover means."

Pence held his hands up in mock surrender. "I'm just trying to help."

"You've helped plenty."

The elder FBI man looked at his partner. "We did the right thing, you know."

"No we didn't, Dean. We're the good guys. We're supposed to play by the rules."

Pence shrugged. "Fine. Beat yourself up all you want. I'm glad we're going to stick it to those Russian bastards."

Ben looked at him. "If we're going to stick it to them; if we're going to load Suffolk's listening devices up with phony conversations and data, why do I have to even bother with this charade? Who cares how deep I go into the bowels of that airport? Why can't I just sit my ass in the TSA's crappy little break room and lie to her?"

Dean Pence returned his partner's gaze. "Because you're not exactly a good liar. That's why."

"What are you talking about?"

The elder FBI agent took a deep breath. "I know you've been sleeping with her, Ben."

His immediate instinct was to deny the accusation, but Matthews was tired of lying. Instead, he remained silent.

"You're not the first guy in the Bureau to have slept with a foreign intelligence agent, so don't feel bad."

"I don't."

This time, it was Pence who chuckled. "It's written all over your face, Ben. You're a good man, and good men make lousy liars. Listen, Mumford doesn't want to risk tipping Suffolk off. For all we know, she's got a way of monitoring the movement of the devices. Suffolk needs to believe, without the slightest hint of doubt, that you did what she asked. It's the only way she and the Russians will believe the information that we'll plant on those phones."

"And who's going to do that?"

Pence shrugged. "NSA? CIA? I have no idea. All I know is that this'll be over soon and we can lock that crazy chick up and all will be well with the world."

As the waitress came by and topped off their coffee, Ben Matthews hoped his partner was right, but the same voice that told him he never should have slept with Victoria Suffolk was now telling him that he was in a lot more danger than he possibly could have realized.

CHAPTER 48

B en exited the tiny canyon coffee shop and walked across the parking lot. Most of the vehicles were the same ones that had been there when he had pulled in.

Trying not to appear obvious, Ben observed his surroundings. Even though Pence told him he hadn't been followed to their meeting, his situational awareness had kicked into overdrive.

Before hopping into his truck, he took one last glance around the lot. If Vicki Suffolk or another operative working with her was out there, he couldn't tell. But even if someone had been watching him, he'd already taken the precaution of explaining away his meeting with Pence in advance.

He'd told Suffolk he was getting together with a biking colleague who was hoping to recruit Ben to his racing team for next year. There was nothing clandestine or unusual about having coffee.

He powered up his truck's big diesel engine, pulled out of the parking lot, and navigated his way out onto the highway.

Settling into the middle lane, Ben set the cruise control and studied the cars around him. Somewhat satisfied that he wasn't being followed, he allowed himself to relax a little.

The movies made undercover life seem glamorous, but it was anything but. It was stressful, and now that he knew he was being watched it was even more stressful. He'd have to be on his guard and keep his wits about him 24/7. He couldn't trust anyone. The only unguarded moments Ben Matthews was going to get were moments like these when he was alone in his truck.

After making sure his iPod was connected, he turned the stereo on. Gripping the steering wheel, he was hoping to forget who he was and what he had done for a little while. He didn't want to be an FBI agent who had betrayed his ethical and professional codes of conduct; he didn't want to be an adult screw-up. He just wanted to be an American killing a few hours before his shift started like everybody else.

Matthews was nearing the employee lot at Denver International when his cell phone rang. He answered the call through his truck's Bluetooth system, half-expecting it to be Dean Pence with an unnecessary, last-minute pep talk.

"This is Ben," he said into the truck's microphone.

"You never called. How'd coffee go?"

It was Vicki.

"It was okay, I guess."

"What's that mean?"

"The guy's kind of an asshole. That's all. I'm just not in the best of moods."

"I'm sorry to hear that," said Suffolk. "So you're not going to ride for him next year?"

"I don't know," replied Matthews. "Maybe. We'll see."

Vicki was quiet for a moment and he wondered if one of their cells had dropped the call. Just when he was ready to ask her if she was still there she said, "Ben, is everything okay?"

"Sure, why?"

"It's not like you not to call me. You don't seem yourself."

"I've got a lot on my mind," he said. "I'll be all right. I'm just a bit nervous about going into the belly of the beast."

"You're going to do great," she said. "I'll be waiting for you when you get home and I've got a surprise for you."

"Really?" he replied. "What is it?"

"I'm going to be naked. *Completely* naked."

"Promises, promises," he said, snapping out of his funk for a moment.

"Ooh, baby," she purred. "I've got the hottest lingerie you've ever seen, my high heels, and the air-conditioning is turned all the way up at my place. You'd better hightail it over here after work. If someone else beats you to my bedroom, you'll only have yourself to blame."

The woman was an incredible tease. "I'll text you later," said Ben.

There was silence on the other end.

"I've got to go," he said as he pulled into the lot. "I'm running late."

"I'll see you tonight," she tried to say, but he had already ended the call.

* * *

"Will he plant the devices where you told him to?" asked Peter as he grabbed Vicki Suffolk around her tiny waist and pulled her back into bed.

"Peter," she cooed to her handler as she tossed the phone to the side. "If you're not careful, I may lock you up and never let you leave. Maybe I'll make you my slave for life."

He buried his mouth in the nape of her neck and gave her a little bite. "Before we drift off into fantasy land," he said, "let's deal with our business in the here and now. Today Ben Matthews starts his new position. He now has much greater access at Denver International. Will he do what we've asked him to?"

"You mean will he do what *I've* asked him to?" she stressed, running her hands up the inside of his thighs.

"If I didn't know better," said Marcus as he leaned back and surrendered himself to her, "I'd say you were trying to seduce me."

"Would you like me to seduce you?" she asked as she looked up from between his legs and licked her lips.

"I have to send in my report," he said, trying to untangle himself from her.

"Am I in it?" she asked, narrowing her eyes as she pinched him.

"Maybe," he replied, grabbing her and kissing her beautiful face.

His answer made her laugh. "Really? Will you begin by talking about how much you love the front of me, or the back of me, which leads to how you both love and hate to see me walk away, right?"

Marcus pulled her on top of him and pressed

his lips to her mouth. "I'm not going to tell them a thing about our physical relationship," he said. "If word gets out about how incredible I am in bed, widows and divorcees from around the world will flock to me."

"Peter!" she exclaimed, slapping his chest. "You are so vain."

"What about Matthews?" he asked, changing the subject. "Is he going to get the coordinates we need to strike that underground facility, or not?"

"I don't think you have anything to worry about," she replied. "I've yet to meet a man who wouldn't do exactly what I wanted. Present company included."

Marcus laughed, but his expression softened as he looked up at her. "You were made for this business, you know that?"

Vicki was thrown off-balance by his sudden tenderness. "I don't know how I'm supposed to answer that," she said looking down at him.

"How about, *I wouldn't be where I am without you, Peter*?"

She smiled and kissed his nose. "You've been very good to me," she replied.

The man looked off out the window. He could see planes taking off and landing in the distance. He knew that with their attack, the world was about to change. Things were going to be dramatically different.

Suffolk laid her head on his chest. "What are you thinking about?"

"The two of us taking a nice long vacation when all of this is over."

"I've got a better idea," she said. "Let's buy some land; better yet, an island. Let's pick one way out in the middle of the ocean where no one will ever find us."

Marcus caressed the side of her face. It was interesting that she had suggested buying an island, as he'd already picked one out. The world was about to be reborn and for some, it was going to be very, very bad. He wanted to be as far away from "civilization" as possible when it happened. He'd already made up his mind about taking Victoria with him, but first they needed to finish their assignment.

"I have big plans, my dear, but before we discuss those, let's go through why we're here one last time," he said. "I want to be certain that none of the evidence ties back to either of us."

CHAPTER 49

Gretchen Casey had conducted numerous base jumps in her time, but never off the top of an office building in the middle of the night with people shooting at her.

Both she and Julie Ericsson had packed Vonblon steerable chutes as reserves and they had worked perfectly, though they never should have had to use them. The women should have been able to drive right out of Kojic's building, in Kojic's car, with Kojic drugged up in the backseat. But as any operative knew, Mr. Murphy, of Murphy's Law fame, had a way of insinuating himself into even the best-laid plans.

When the women touched down from their jump, Cooper and Rhodes were waiting for them. Gathering up their gear, they leaped into the car and made their escape. Examining her chute, Casey realized how close the shooters on the roof had come to hitting her. Several rounds had pierced her canopy. She had been very lucky.

The drive to Tuzla took three hours. Just as during most of their drive from the Slovenian coast up to Zbiroh a few days ago, it was dark and boring. Nobody spoke much. Casey and Ericsson were both disappointed at having lost Kojic. He had been their prisoner and their responsibility. It was an unfortunate accident, but the accident had happened because of carelessness on their part. It was a hard lesson to learn, and one neither of them would soon forget.

Camp Eagle was a black site the United States used to move and interrogate ghost detainees in the war on terror who were being kept off the books. It had a history of covert operatives moving in and out, and therefore the staff knew not to ask a lot of questions.

Casey and her team got something to eat at the Longhorn Café on base and then Gretchen told the girls to get some sleep. They didn't all need to help her upload the contents of Kojic's computer back to Bragg. She could do that on her own.

Hutton had arranged for her to have everything she needed, including a private office with high-speed internet and access to a secure telephone. The telephone was unnecessary. She didn't want to talk to Hutton, not now at least. She just wanted to upload the contents of Kojic's computer, write up her report, and go to bed, which was exactly what she did. She and her teammates slept like rocks for over eight solid hours. It felt better than any trip to any spa.

Once they had showered and changed clothes, they went back to the Longhorn Café for another meal.

Summer had hung around longer in this part of the world, but as the afternoon wore on, a cool breeze had picked up, suggesting fall was on its way.

It made Casey think about home and what autumn would mean for her. The leaves would be changing colors. There'd be football games, and before you knew it Thanksgiving, and then Christmas.

The holidays were about the last thing she wanted to think about. They always reminded her of the mistakes she had made in her life, particularly when it came to her relationships.

After lunch there was talk of going to work out and even checking into flights home, as Tuzla had direct flights to the United States. They were hopeful Hutton was about to cut them loose.

Gretchen was wondering what she would do once she got back when her cell phone rang. *Speak of the devil,* she thought to herself. "Casey," she said as she activated the call.

"You and your team did a good job," stated Hutton. "We'll be going through the stuff on Kojic's hard drive for a long time."

"I'm glad," she replied.

"I read your report. How seriously are you and Julie injured? It reads to me like you downplayed things, as usual."

Casey smiled. He knew her too well sometimes. "I got a little cut," she said, touching the wound on her scalp. "It probably could have used a stitch or two, but Coop closed it up with Krazy Glue."

"And Julie?"

"She was slapped in the face with Kojic's laptop. She's got a bit of a bruise, but she'll be fine too. We're all fine."

"Everybody's fine but Kojic."

"Listen," Gretchen began, "about that—"

Hutton stopped her. "The guy did it to himself. Okay? Don't give it another thought. It wasn't your fault."

Casey decided to let it go. She didn't want to talk about it and she wasn't in the mood for a pep talk from Hutton. "Did you find out anything more about the man who financed Kojic's purchase of all the Kammler equipment from the Zbiroh bunker?"

"Thomas Sanders," said Hutton, repeating the name Kojic had given them back in Belgrade, shortly before he had died. "We're compiling a jacket on him now. There isn't much out there. What is interesting, though, is that Sanders didn't want Kojic knowing who he was either. He tried to remain in the shadows, but Kojic tracked an IP address he used one time, and that became a jumping-off point for building a jacket of his own on him."

"What was in it? Anything good?"

Hutton flipped through the printouts that covered his desk back at Bragg. "There's mention of someone else we're trying to run down, named Abressian. Armen Abressian. Don't know who or what he is. The rest of it is pretty much banking information, but that's where it gets interesting."

"How so?" asked Casey.

"It's like Russian nesting dolls, trying to pick apart all of the shell companies and phony accounts these guys use, but it appears Thomas Sanders has recently done business with your swim partner from Venice."

"Nino Bianchi, the arms dealer?"

"Yup."

"The bomb discovered in South America, do

you think Bianchi might have had something to do with that?" asked Casey.

"That's what I want you to find out," said Hutton.

"How am I supposed to find that out?"

"You're going to ask Bianchi yourself."

"All right," she replied. "I'll get the team ready."

"No. You don't need the team. Just you. I'm going to send a car to get you. Where are you?"

"I'll walk back over to the Longhorn Café. The car can get me there," said Casey. "Can I grab a bag at least?"

"You won't need one," replied Hutton. "The car will be there in five minutes." And with that, he disconnected the call.

CHAPTER 50

A Humvee showed up four minutes later and Gretchen Casey climbed in. Like everyone else she had met at Tuzla, the driver was polite, professional, and didn't ask a lot of questions.

He drove her out toward the airfield. "Do I have a plane waiting for me?" she asked.

"No, ma'am," her driver replied as he kept going.

The kid had obviously been told to pick her up and not make conversation, so she decided to leave him alone. From what she could tell, they weren't driving off the base, which meant she'd find out what this was all about soon enough.

At the far end of the airfield was a cluster of pre-fabricated buildings. Just beyond the cluster was a building surrounded by a high cyclone fence. When Casey saw who was standing at the gate, twirling a key on his finger, she began to understand what this was all about.

"Where is he?" Casey said as she climbed out of the Humvee.

"We haven't seen each other in days and that's

your first question? No, 'Hi, Scot, How's it been?' "
replied Scot Harvath.

"Hi, Scot. You look like crap."

"Actually, I haven't been sleeping very well.
Which is probably because I haven't been letting
Bianchi sleep very well. He's a real tough nut to
crack."

Casey looked at him askance. "Is that some sort
of macho, male anatomy joke?"

Harvath put his hands up. "No hostile work en-
vironment here, boss. I don't want to get written
up."

"Relax. I'm just pulling your leg. Where is he?"

"He's downstairs in the play place having a
happy meal."

"Can I see him?"

Harvath stepped back and swung open the gate.
"I was told to give you full access. By the way, he's
probably not going to be very excited to see you."

"I wouldn't expect him to be."

"When you tossed him out the window, did you
know he couldn't swim?"

Casey shook her head. "I had no idea. He sure
picked an interesting city to live in then, didn't he?"

They walked across the packed, brown earth to
the building. "My only request is that you don't tell
him where he is."

"No problem," replied Casey as they reached
the building's main door and Harvath slid his key
in and unlocked it. "Where's Riley?"

"She went to hide her clothes. She's afraid you're
going to borrow something again like you did on
the yacht."

"C'mon, seriously."

"I am serious," replied Harvath with a grin.

He walked them over to a steel door with an electronic card next to it. Removing a card from his pocket, Harvath swiped it through the reader. There was a buzz followed by a click as the lock released and he pulled back the heavy security door.

He led Casey down a flight of metal stairs to the basement level. They had not seen anyone else and she figured that was on purpose. The fewer people who knew Scot Harvath and Nino Bianchi were here, the better.

They passed several doors until they reached one marked 5. Harvath slid his card through another reader, the lock released, and he held the door open for her.

It was a long room, and sitting in the center was the play place, as it was known, an enormous cell, constructed out of heavy, modular concrete panels that could be broken down and moved. It had its own heating and air-conditioning unit that could create wild temperature swings inside if an interrogator so chose.

Casey had seen enough of them to know what the interior looked like. It would be monitored by video and be outfitted with strobe lights and Dolby surround-sound speakers. There would be an eye hook in the center of the floor to restrain the prisoner in stress positions. Not only would the prisoner have no idea where he was, but the play place was completely soundproof. Access was via yet another heavy security door and card reader. On the outside, someone had taped a picture of an evil Ronald McDonald.

There were two desks and a bank of closed-circuit monitors to watch what was happening inside the cell. Right now, Nino Bianchi was eating.

He looked worse than Harvath. His clothes were soiled and his hair was unkempt. He probably hadn't bathed or shaved since Casey and her team had handed him over.

"Well," said Scot. "He's all yours. Do you want me to go in with you?"

Casey shook her head. "I'd rather go in alone."

"Understood."

"And no video, okay? I'm not here and this never happened. Are we good?"

"We're good," replied Harvath as he walked over to the cell door and swiped his card.

When the lock released, he pulled it back so Casey could walk in. Once she had entered, he closed the door behind her and waited for the lock to reengage before walking over to one of the monitors to watch her interrogation unfold.

"Hello, Nino," Casey said as Bianchi looked up from his food.

If he was unhappy to see her, she couldn't tell. The man had a drawn expression. Gone was the arrogance of only a few nights ago. He looked broken, but broken didn't mean he wasn't dangerous. Despite his being shackled to the eye ring in the middle of the floor, she still made sure not to get too close. Caged animals were just as dangerous as those roaming freely in the wild.

"Have you come back to throw me out another window?" he asked.

"No," she replied as she pulled a chair from the corner and straddled it. "I want to talk about weapons."

"I sell computer parts. I don't know anything about weapons."

"What did they give you to eat?" she asked, trying to figure out what he was scooping up from his plate with a piece of bread.

Bianchi made a face and set the plate aside. "For an Italian, this is *true* torture."

"I think the chef has a bottle of Dom Perignon White Gold outside. Would you like me to check?"

"Considering that it may be a very long time before I taste champagne again, I made a good choice," he replied, a bit of a smile forming on his mouth.

"Have you been cooperating?"

"Are you the good cop, then? The other man who has been in here with me certainly isn't."

Casey had seen Harvath in action before. He had issues. He most definitely wasn't the good cop. In answer to the man's question, she said, "That depends."

Bianchi sighed. "Of course it does. It always does."

"You understand that because of your involvement in the bus bombing in Rome—"

"I wasn't involved," the Italian insisted.

"You sold the explosives to the terrorists," stated Casey. "That's involvement enough. More than twenty Americans died. At your trial, the United States will push for the death penalty."

She expected some fervent defense, felt certain that he would stand up for himself and justify what he had done, but instead he just hung his head. She had no idea what Harvath had done to him. There wasn't a mark on the man, at least not that she could see, but it was as if someone had gone to work on him with a hammer. There was no resistance, no fight in him.

"I'll give up the people involved. I'll make a deal. Is that what you want?" he asked.

Casey needed to be careful and not screw up whatever Harvath was trying to achieve with Bianchi. "That's not why I am here, Nino. That's for you to discuss with the other man."

"The bad cop," he said dejectedly.

"Yes," she replied. "The *bad* cop. I need to talk to you about something else."

He looked up and said, "You have come to talk to me about Thomas Sanders."

CHAPTER 51

"B ecause," said Bianchi, "for however long I have been down here, I have been waiting for bad cop to ask me about it. But he hasn't. Instead he has asked me about all of my other business dealings. He has asked me about Hamas, Hezbollah, al Qaeda, the Taliban, ELN, FARC, Abu Sayyaf, and on and on and over and over."

"You sold computers to all of those organizations?" asked Casey. "You must be a very good salesman."

He smiled. "I can get anything people want."

"So what did Thomas Sanders want?"

"Let's talk first about what *I* want," demanded Bianchi.

"And what would that be?"

"I want to walk out of here, wherever this is, a free man."

Casey started to speak, but he raised the index finger of his shackled right hand and continued. "I also want a guarantee that no one will come after me. That I will be safe."

"Nino, you are directly involved in the murder of more than twenty Americans in Rome alone. I can't even begin to imagine how many U.S. soldiers and Marines have been killed because of the people you have helped equip. You just expect us to let you go free? After all that you have done?"

"If you don't make a deal with me, millions of people in your country are going to die. I can help you stop that from happening."

"How?"

"First things first," he said. "You are here because of Mr. Sanders, aren't you? Everything else was to soften me up, to make me more cooperative."

Casey didn't care what the guy thought, as long as it kept him talking. She nodded.

"I knew it," said Bianchi. "How did you find out? About Sanders and what he has planned?"

"Listen, Nino," stated Casey, "I'm the one who will ask the questions. Now, as to Mr. Sanders. What is it you know that might be of value to us?"

"I want some sort of a guarantee. In writing."

Casey patted her pockets before saying, "I must have left my pen on the subway. You'll have to take my word for it."

The Italian shook his head. "No. I want something from your president. Something signed."

Casey laughed. "You've been watching too much television, Nino. Our president doesn't do that sort of thing. Even if he did, we would need to know exactly what you were offering."

Bianchi thought about that for a moment. "Mr. Sanders wanted bombs from me. A very special, very specific type of bomb."

"What kind?"

The Italian shook his head again. "A man has to have some secrets."

"You know what I think, Nino?" said Casey as she stood up. "I think we overestimated your usefulness. I'm sorry I wasted your time."

Casey walked over to the door. Just as she was about to rap on it to be released, Bianchi said, "EMP bombs. Electromagnetic pulse. Are you familiar with those?"

Gretchen turned around and leaned her back against the door. "I've heard of them."

"Well, that's what Sanders wanted."

"And that's what you got for him?"

Bianchi nodded.

"How many?" asked Casey.

"He wanted three at first."

"At *first*?"

"Yes. Then he contacted me and said he needed more. That he wanted them quickly. He told me he would purchase whatever I could get my hands on."

"And you being you," said Casey. "You had no problem finding more of these things."

He smiled. "There are a few countries that see EMP devices as the weapons of the future. They are producing certain EMP devices in quantity. In most of these countries, the scientists and members of the military are poorly paid. They are easy to come by. The hardest part is getting the bombs to their destination."

"Which in the case of Mr. Sanders was where?"

Bianchi shook his head. "As the good cop, you can appreciate that I must have my guarantee."

Casey wanted to go over and slap the smug bastard across the face, but she kept her emotions in check. "Nino, this is still not enough for me to take to my superiors and request special treatment on your behalf. It's all words, smoke. We can't prove if any of what you say is true."

"You are toying with me," said Bianchi, a bit of the spark back in his eyes.

"No," replied Casey, "you're toying with me and I'm done having my time wasted." She pounded on the cell door to be let out. As she waited for the door to be opened she added, "I'll tell your friend outside that you're done with your lunch and that you're ready to pick back up wherever you two left off."

Casey didn't even bother looking at him as the door opened and Harvath stood back so she could exit.

As the door began to close, Bianchi yelled, "Wait!"

CHAPTER 52

Jack Walsh hadn't had a full night's sleep in two days. The trip to Paraguay had only heightened his anxiety. His sixth sense was telling him that there was going to be an attack of some kind. He could feel it.

He had called his counterpart at the CIA, Phil Farnsworth, to try to get some assistance, but it wasn't going well.

"A friend of mine at the FBI," said Walsh, "tells me that they've never heard of Armen Abressian before."

Farnsworth sounded distracted, as if maybe he was checking his email while on the phone. "I'm not surprised," replied the CIA man.

"Why not?"

"Who knows?"

"Phil, am I interrupting something?" asked Walsh.

"I'm sorry, we've just got a lot going on here."

"You were saying about Abressian?"

"What was I saying?"

Walsh gripped the phone a little tighter. "That you weren't surprised that he's stayed off the FBI's radar."

"He's probably a smart guy."

"Wait a second. We went from you not being surprised that he's stayed off the FBI's radar to you saying he's *probably* a smart guy? What's going on over there?"

"It's sensitive, Jack."

"That's why we all have top-secret clearances," replied Walsh. "C'mon, what do you know about this guy?"

There was a pause on the other end as Farnsworth's attention was diverted once again. Finally, he said, "What's your interest in Abressian?"

Walsh had assumed he'd ask, so he had his story prepared. "We've got some unconfirmed intel that he might have provided a couple of Taliban factions with material support in southern Afghanistan."

"Hmmm," replied Farnsworth distractedly. "Why don't you write up what you've got and send it over? I'll have our guys take a look at it and see what they can come up with for you."

"I was hoping you could do a little more than that for me, Phil."

Suddenly, the CIA man was interested in the conversation. "I find it heartwarming that you finally want to work with us."

Walsh shook his head. "Let's not do this."

"Hey, you're the guys with all the money who are out there running around hiring away our best people."

"You've got plenty of excellent people at Langley."

"But when the best of them retire and get into contract work, they've all been signing up at your shop," stated Farnsworth.

Walsh really didn't want to get into this with him. "You're talking to the wrong guy, Phil. I'm just a cog in the wheel, trying to make it to Friday. You know that."

Farnsworth laughed out loud. "That's priceless. It's a total load of BS, but it's definitely priceless."

"Are you going to share what you've got with me or not?"

"I told you to write it up—" began Farnsworth.

"And send it over," replied Walsh, finishing the man's sentence for him. "Yeah, I got that. And I'm asking *you*, not your people, to help me out right now."

"What do you know about an Italian arms dealer named Bianchi who was ghosted in Venice a couple of days ago?"

Walsh leaned forward in his chair and lied. "Nothing. Why? Are they connected?"

"Maybe," said Farnsworth. "Listen, I shouldn't be going into this with you."

"You haven't gone into anything. Come on, Phil. What do you have? Please."

"Hold on a second."

Walsh heard Farnsworth get up from his desk and shut his door.

"You still there?" he asked when he returned.

"I'm still here."

Farnsworth took a deep breath. "The arms dealer out of Venice was named Nino Bianchi. Anything, anywhere, anytime was his reputation; and he was *that* good."

"Who grabbed him?"

"We don't know. All we've heard was that it was an all-female team. We think it might have been the Russians."

"Any idea why they would have wanted him?" asked Walsh.

"This guy Bianchi double-crossed a lot of people," replied Farnsworth. "We're still trying to figure it out."

"You said there was a connection between Bianchi and Abressian?"

The CIA man took in a deep breath and exhaled. "This is not for dissemination and you didn't get this from me, okay?"

"Understood," said Walsh.

"We believe Abressian has built a sophisticated shadow intelligence network. From what we can tell, it's filled with former and even current spooks and special operations types. Kind of like the stuff you're running."

Walsh let the remark slide.

"Anyway," continued Farnsworth. "Abressian began by contracting his merry band out to wealthy individuals and corporations. Then he moved on to small countries with limited intelligence agencies that needed to improve their capabilities and their reach. He provided training and his people even helped plan and conduct operations.

"Right out of the box, that was bad enough. Then, we started hearing they were taking jobs for larger countries that didn't want their fingerprints on certain, let's say sensitive, undertakings like assassinations, kidnappings, terrorist attacks, and other various ops that would draw international condemnation. Abressian's group guarantees complete anonymity, which brings us back to Nino Bianchi.

"We began taking a serious interest in Bianchi when a source of ours in Pakistan told us he was looking to buy whatever he could get his hands on there. He was particularly interested in nukes and EMP devices. He bought two shipments of the latter, allegedly for Armen Abressian.

"Now, Abressian wasn't mentioned by name. He normally uses cutouts to do his business. The name of the person Bianchi was buying these EMP devices for was some character named Sanders. Thomas Sanders."

"You're sure about all of this?" asked Walsh.

"As sure as we can be," replied Farnsworth. "But it gets more troubling. From another source, completely unrelated and outside of Pakistan, we heard that Abressian's group was looking to help facilitate some sort of spectacular attack on the United States with those same EMP devices."

Walsh's worst fears had just been confirmed. "Do you know who Abressian's group was supposed to be helping?"

"No, we don't," said Farnsworth.

"Do you know what the targets were?"

"We had hoped Bianchi might lead us to those, or at the very least Sanders and Abressian. We were in the process of trying to put something together with the Italians when Bianchi got taken."

Walsh didn't know what to say. "That's it? You don't have any other leads?"

"We're chasing down a rumor right now about a hit that happened yesterday in Croatia."

"Croatia?"

"Yeah," replied Farnsworth. "A former KGB official and his three-man bodyguard detail were ambushed. Lots of AK47s and an RPG were used.

The hitters appear to have been imported for the job."

"What's this got to do with Bianchi?"

"It doesn't. This is about Abressian. Supposedly, he and this deceased KGB man, a Viktor Mikhailov, had some sort of falling out."

"Over what?" asked Walsh.

"We don't know. Like I said, this just happened yesterday. I'm getting it all out of a source in Moscow. We'll probably have more in a week or two."

"Do you think Abressian was behind it?"

"I don't know," replied Farnsworth. "Mikhailov was no choir boy. I'm sure he's made more than his share of enemies."

"Interesting."

"Yup," said the CIA man, wrapping up the call. "Listen, don't forget to get me anything you've got on Abressian and the Taliban. The more I hear about him, the more I don't like him."

"Me too," replied Walsh. "We'll get something over to you as soon as we can." With that, the two men said their good-byes and hung up.

Jack Walsh then immediately dialed Rob Hutton at Fort Bragg.

CHAPTER 53

Armen Abressian had planned his ambush of Viktor Mikhailov down to the very last detail. He had kept it all a secret, even from Thomas. The only person who knew the full scope of what was going to happen was his head of security, Marko.

Both Armen and Marko knew that Viktor would leave word with his men that if anything happened to him, they should assume Abressian had done it. That was why Marko arranged to have a team of contract killers brought in from the Ukraine.

After the Ukrainians successfully ambushed Viktor's Audi and killed all of its occupants, Marko and his men killed the Ukranians. Two of the hired killers then had cell phones planted in their pockets that showed calls back and forth with several members of another organized crime network very hostile to Viktor's. As corrupt as the local police were, they weren't stupid.

It wouldn't take long for this information to get to Viktor's men. With their boss dead, they would follow the carefully laid trail of money transfers Armen had put together. There were a couple of other clues he had buried so deep that no one would probably ever find them, but if someone did, they would never suspect anyone had gone to that much trouble. It was the kind of orchestration that Abressian was very talented at.

When Sanders was brought in on the plot, he was quite relieved. He had no problem with the Bratva going to war, as long as it wasn't with them. His boss never ceased to amaze him. The man always seemed to be one step ahead of everyone else. He assumed it was the result of exceptional analysis and thorough planning, but figured there had to be just a bit of good luck thrown in as well. Somewhere at some point in his past, Abressian must have done something right to have stored up such a trove of good fortune.

That was the thought that came back to Sanders's mind when he was combing the email accounts he used as electronic dead drops and found a note left in one of the draft folders. This was the modern version of how spies used to leave messages hidden for each other in parks or under bridges, except now it was a much simpler process. An email account was created and two parties had the user name and password. Instead of sending messages across the internet to each other that could be intercepted or traced, they simply read and erased messages left in the account's draft folder.

It was in just such a folder that Sanders found a

wonderful piece of news. Getting up from his desk, he walked into Abressian's office. "I have good news, Armen."

Abressian turned from where he had been looking out the window. Despite the hour, he already had a drink in his hand. "What is it?"

"The shipment has arrived."

"What shipment?"

"*The* shipment," said Sanders. "From Bianchi. I just heard from the man in Ljubljana. As soon as the money transfer is confirmed, they'll make the shipment available. He wants to know is if we want it packaged the same as last time."

Abressian wasn't sure how to react.

Sanders studied his employer. "You don't seem pleased."

"I don't like it. Bianchi was taken four days ago."

"You think this might be a trap?" asked Sanders.

Abressian bowed his head in thought.

"This isn't any different from the way the deal unfolded last time," continued Sanders. "Think about it. We gave Bianchi a substantial down payment just like before. The process was probably in the works before he was grabbed. Just because the railroad boss gets hit by a train doesn't mean all the trains stop running."

"Perhaps. But I'm still concerned."

"So what should I do? Tell the guy we don't want them? Tell him that he should just keep our deposit?"

Abressian held up his hand. "I'm trying to think."

Sanders knew not to press his boss. Laying his hands on another shipment of EMP devices was all Abressian had been thinking about. He was under a tremendous amount of stress over it, as evidenced by the cocktail he currently held in his hand.

Abressian looked out the window for a long time. Finally, he said, "We'll do it, but I want you to double our security precautions. I don't care how much it costs. I want to make it impossible to follow this shipment."

CHAPTER 54

In the eastern warehouse district of Ljubljana known as Smartinska, Gretchen Casey, Alex Cooper, Julie Ericsson, and Megan Rhodes sat in a nondescript vehicle watching a steel garage door a half block away.

"Nino Bianchi knows we're coming back and taking him for another swim if this is BS, right?" asked Cooper.

Casey smiled. "If he's lying, I'll drown him myself."

"You girls are so dang violent," stated Rhodes from the backseat. "It's no wonder neither of you can ever hang on to a man."

"Please," replied Casey. "I have no problem hanging on to men."

"Handcuffs don't count, Gretch," offered Ericsson.

Cooper pointed at Casey. "I knew it. It's always the quiet ones. The freak runs deep in them."

"You're looking at the wrong sister, sister," stated Casey, pointing over her shoulder at Megan and Julie. "You want to talk freak, talk to them. They run the Freaky Town Rotary Club."

"It's always the dog without the bone who barks," teased Rhodes.

A chorus of *oohs* rose inside the car over that response.

"Thank you," said Rhodes. "I'm here all week. Try the veal."

"By the way," replied Ericsson. "If I had known we were going to be spending so much time in Eastern Europe, I would have stopped shaving my legs and threaded my eyebrows together."

"Some women will do anything to get laid," said Cooper.

The car erupted again.

"You're really coming into your own on this trip, sweet stuff," said Rhodes.

"Jules, I was only kidding," offered Cooper, afraid that maybe she had hurt her teammate's feelings.

Ericsson laughed. "It's cool, Coop. We all give as good as we get."

"Speaking of which," said Casey. "Let's all get ready. The door's going up."

Down the block, the faded metal garage door rolled up and the first truck pulled out of the warehouse.

"There's number one," said Cooper.

They watched as the semi trailer exited the warehouse and headed west.

"And here comes number two," replied Ericsson,

as the second truck exited and headed in the opposite direction.

Suddenly, the unexpected happened. "Wait a second," said Casey. "Number three?"

Rhodes looked behind it and said, "And four?"

"I thought Bianchi said this guy Abressian only used two trucks before; the real deal and a decoy."

"I guess we're seeing how serious they are," stated Casey.

Cooper looked at her and then down at her cell phone. "Why is that not ringing?"

"It'll ring."

"Gretch, there's four trucks. There's no way we can follow them all," said Rhodes.

"Everybody calm down," said Casey. "It's going to be okay. Just be calm."

Seconds later, Casey's cell phone rang. "Yes?" she said. "Thank you."

Hanging up, she put the car in gear and said, "Truck number three," and pulled out into the street after it.

"I still think we ought to drown the guy just on principle," said Rhodes, referring to Bianchi.

"So far, so good," cautioned Gretchen. "He said his warehouse manager would alert us to which truck and that's exactly what he did. I think Bianchi is a scumbag and I'm going to be first in line to sign up for his firing squad, but the verdict is out of my hands."

"I'm getting real tired of all your law and order lip, missy," Rhodes joked from the backseat.

"Your mom and I," said Ericsson as she indicated she was speaking about Rhodes, "are very disappointed in you. Aren't we, dear?"

Megan nodded. "Absolutely. I didn't raise any

daughter of mine to be such a softie. Do you want us to take your Glock away? Is that what you want? Because we'll do it."

"What I want," said Casey, calling for some decorum, "is for everyone to pay attention. We're on the clock."

The team didn't need to be told twice. They all focused on the truck that was several car lengths in front of them.

Casey decided to fall back a little farther. The semi was a big, easy target that wouldn't be hard to follow.

It led them through stop-and-go traffic across the Slovenian capital. Though Casey had requested professionalism when the pursuit had first started, Ericsson and Rhodes couldn't help themselves, and eventually a stream of jokes poured from the backseat. It broke the tedium and a couple were actually funny, so Casey allowed them.

When the semi slowed down and pulled into another warehouse, she didn't need to ask her team to look sharp. They were already with her.

Casey kept driving, turned around two blocks down, and then came back and found a parking spot where they could monitor the building without being observed.

This was now the part that was completely out of their hands. Whereas they had Bianchi's warehouse manager inside from the first location, here they had nobody. This location had been of Abressian's choosing. The Athena Team could only imagine that the three other trucks were pulling into similar warehouses at different points around the city.

"Did anyone get a look at our driver or the man riding shotgun?" asked Rhodes.

"I saw a little bit of a face in the passenger mirror," replied Cooper, "but not enough to make a positive ID."

"Then we'd better hope we don't screw this up," said Ericsson.

The women waited in silence, their eyes glued to another rolling garage door.

After about four minutes, Rhodes said, "So, Gretch. What was it like seeing Scot Harvath again?"

"Yeah," added Ericsson. "Has he dumped Riley yet?"

Casey didn't bother turning around to look at either of them. She just took two fingers, pointed at her eyes, and then turned the fingers and pointed out the windshield toward the warehouse. They got the message and the car fell silent once again.

Ten minutes later, the garage door rolled up.

"Whoa," said Cooper as four trucks poured out and went in different directions. "This guy Abressian is taking no chances at all, is he?"

"No, he's not," replied Casey as they watched the trucks exit and the garage door roll down.

Minutes passed and Casey could sense anxiety out of the backseat. Before the peanut gallery could say anything, she said, "Wait for it."

It was the longest twenty minutes of their lives, but sure enough the garage door rolled back up and out drove a silver G Class Mercedes SUV. Bianchi had been telling them the truth. He'd also been right that they would very likely run the same scam they had the first time they'd accepted a shipment from his Ljubljana warehouse.

"Those sneaky bastards," said Rhodes.

"What a shell game," admitted Cooper, a little

awe in her voice. "Load the bombs in the SUV and load the SUV in the back of one of the semis and then keep people guessing."

Casey waited until the Mercedes had passed them and put their car in gear. "Now let's see where they take us."

CHAPTER 55

As they neared the outskirts of the Croatian town of Pula, Rob Hutton told the team to back off.

"We've got them via satellite," he said. "Unless they drive into a submarine, we're going to know exactly where they are transporting their cargo."

It had taken less than three hours to drive from Slovenia to Croatia's Dalmatian coast, also known as the new European Riviera. It was a stunning mosaic of stone buildings and whitewashed houses with red-tiled roofs.

"So now what do we do?" asked Cooper.

"According to Hutton," said Casey, "we sit tight here while they decide what our next move will be."

"Where's *here*?"

Rhodes was already pulling up information on her iPhone. "Pula, Croatia," she stated, "known for its winemaking, fishing, shipbuilding, and tourism."

"What's it say about men with full sets of teeth?" asked Ericsson as she leaned in.

"It says Pula attracts large numbers of German, Scandinavian, Italian, and other tourists through early fall," she replied. "This could be very good for you."

Julie laughed. "The hell with me. I'm thinking about Coop."

"Oh, yes," agreed Megan. "Pula is all about Coopah!"

Cooper threw up her hands. "All I want is a hot shower and an ice bucket full of beer. Maybe some pizza if we can find it."

"We'll find it," said Casey. "I don't think the powers that be back home are going to have this thing spun up for at least another twenty-four to forty-eight hours."

The other women nodded in agreement.

"Megs, can you pick out a hotel for us?"

"Already done," she replied. "Tonight, Uncle Sugar will be putting us up at the Hotel Histria."

Casey shook her head. "No way. Remember that fleabag we stayed at in Thailand, the Fallopian?"

"That's not what it was called. It was the Phillipian."

"And this one sounds dangerously like the Hotel *Hysterectomy*. Pick another."

"Remind me again, country girl, who the snobs are in this crowd?" asked Rhodes.

"The Histria looks like a nice hotel," stated Ericsson.

"Actually, it looks like a *very* nice hotel," added Cooper as Rhodes showed her a picture of it.

"All right, all right," Casey conceded. "The Hotel Hysterectomy it is. It better be good, Megs."

"Frommer's gives it five rusted Yugos," replied Rhodes. "With that kind of endorsement, it's gotta be good."

The girls laughed and navigated their way to the hotel. At the front desk, they pushed Cooper into charming the manager into an upgrade, and she actually succeeded in doing it. They were given a stunning two-bedroom suite overlooking the ocean.

"This beats the hell out of Tuzla," commented Megan when they were shown inside.

Cooper wasted no time calling down for beer and Casey drew a bath. Ericsson, ever the news junkie, flipped on the TV and found an English-language cable news station.

Rhodes stepped out onto the balcony and called back inside to Casey, "They've got plenty of boat slips here. You should have Scot sail up. I see a nice place near the beach with shallow water and a bunch of sharp rocks where you can drown Riley if you'd like."

Casey walked over, slid the sliding glass door shut, and locked Megan on the balcony.

She caught Ericsson looking at her. "You want some?" she threatened with a smile.

Ericsson shrugged. "That's okay," she said. "I never liked her much anyway."

"Good," replied Casey as she walked into the bathroom and closed the door.

Ericsson went ahead and let Megan back in.

"Some people," said Rhodes as she stepped back inside.

Cooper lay down on the couch and was asleep before her beer even got there. Rhodes, who never seemed to run out of energy, went downstairs to

look around while Ericsson stayed in the room and
held the fort.

When Megan came back, Cooper had awakened
from her nap and Casey was done with her bath.
They each pulled a beer from the bucket and shared
a toast.

Gretchen was on her second sip when Hutton
called. "So much for downtime," she said as she
reached over and picked up her phone from the
coffee table.

"The bombs were delivered to a walled compound about twelve kilometers south of you,"
said Hutton. "We believe it belongs to Armen
Abressian."

"Do you think the equipment from the Kammler facility could be there too?" she asked.

"That's what we need you to find out."

"How's his security?"

Hutton paused before replying. "Just the little
bit we've been able to pick up from the satellites,
it's pretty sophisticated—cameras, laser motion
detectors, even a dog team working the perimeter. Overall, we estimate that the compound has
a twenty- to thirty-man security force that's heavily
armed, probably with paramilitary training."

"Is that all?" Casey asked. "What happened? Was
the moat-diggers union on strike the day they in-
stalled their security?"

"Gretchen, listen," said Hutton. "We figure we
could help you get around some of the intrusion
measures, but not all of them. Not without more
time. But based on all of the activity we're seeing, we think they're getting ready to launch those
bombs. We need to move on them right away.
Tonight."

"You want us to hit a walled compound with twenty to thirty heavily armed men, dogs, and electronic sensors and do it tonight?" she replied.

"Yes."

"Even if we had weeks to surveil the place and piece together how we were getting in, we'd still need to come up with one hell of a diversion."

"Tell your team to get ready," replied Hutton. "I think we may be able to get you your diversion."

CHAPTER 56

When Casey and Rhodes arrived at the run-down apartment building, they saw several high-end luxury vehicles already parked in front.

"There's nothing better than blending in, is there?" asked Megan.

Gretchen shook her head. "Russian mafia. What do you expect?"

Two large men in cheap suits with fake Rolexes took entirely too much time patting the ladies down. "You know, I normally get dinner first," quipped Rhodes.

Casey had had enough as well. Turning, she gave the man behind her a surprisingly good shove, forcing him back on his heels. "Party's over. Where's your boss?"

The men got the message.

Casey and Rhodes stood on the cracked tiles of the foul-smelling lobby as one of the Russians spoke into his radio. When a response came back, he looked at Casey and said, "You upstairs now."

The women walked up to the fourth floor where two more men, cradling shotguns, were sitting outside an apartment door.

As the ladies approached, the men stood up, walked over to them, and indicated that they would be frisked again.

"Too bad Cooper didn't come," Megan whispered. "This is more action than she's seen all year."

Gretchen was starting to get angry. *"Nyet,"* she said, holding up her hand. "This is business. Go get Luka. *Now.*"

Whether the men understood English didn't matter. They definitely understood her tone. One of the Russians stepped back and knocked on the apartment door. There was a grunt from the other side and it was opened. The Russian then stepped back and gestured for the women to enter.

The interior was just as decrepit as the rest of the building. Paint was peeling from the walls and a sour odor pervaded the entire apartment. Neither Casey nor Cooper could tell if it was coming from something that had overstayed its welcome in the fridge or from the twenty-five Russian men crammed into the tiny flat.

The Russians were in various states of undress. Some wore undershirts, some no shirts at all. Many had tattoos, and they were all in exceptional shape. Weapons of all sizes and calibers were scattered around the apartment. There were several metallic briefcases along the wall, which were probably crammed full of cash. Sitting at a table in the kitchen, the ladies were introduced to the man they had come to see, Luka Mikhailov—heir to his uncle Viktor Mikhailov's crime syndicate.

They shook hands and Mikhailov barked at two of his men to get up from the table so that Casey and Rhodes could sit down.

"We're sorry for your loss," said Casey.

Luka was younger than they had expected; somewhere in his late twenties. He appeared more polished than his colleagues and came off as more management than mobster.

"Thank you," he replied, as he studied his guests. Leaning back in his chair he flipped open the refrigerator door. "Would you like something to drink?"

"No thank you," said Casey.

Mikhailov allowed the door to swing shut and brought his chair legs back to the floor. "Apparently, we both have powerful people we answer to," he said.

Gretchen understood what he meant. According to Hutton, Jack Walsh had quietly reached out to some of his colleagues in the Russian intelligence world. Through some subtle pressure, Luka Mikhailov had been persuaded to agree to this meeting.

"We also have a common enemy," replied Casey. "Armen Abressian."

The name obviously meant something to the Russian, as the expression on his face instantly changed. It was only a flash, but Casey had caught it.

"Why would you think that Armen Abression is my enemy?" he asked.

"Because if he had killed my uncle, that's exactly what he would be to me."

"How do you know he killed Viktor? Do you have proof?"

Now came the hard part. Everything would depend on how badly Luka Mikhailov wanted to believe the story she was about to tell him. "Shortly before your uncle was killed, the Central Intelligence Agency intercepted a phone call between the men responsible for his murder and a man named Thomas Sanders."

There was another flash of recognition on the Russian's face.

"I take it you know this man?" asked Casey.

Luka nodded.

"The CIA also intercepted an earlier call from Armen Abressian to Sanders, during which he authorized the murder of your uncle."

She could see the Russian's anger building.

"I would like to hear this phone call," he said.

Casey shook her head. "I'm sorry. The call has been classified by my government."

"Why?"

"We're pursuing Abressian on another matter that I'm not free to discuss." As she let that sink in, she said, "Our Treasury Department is also now tracing a large sum of money we believe Abressian moved in order to pay your uncle's killers."

Luka Mikhailov remained silent.

"We also believe the AK47s and the RPG used in the attack were provided by a known arms dealer connected to Abressian, named Nino Bianchi."

Casey felt no remorse in lying to the man. He was a scumbag underworld figure who had probably brought more misery to more people than she would ever know. If he could be manipulated into doing something useful, then so be it. With the water sufficiently chummed, she then sat back, kept her mouth shut, and watched to see if he'd bite.

Another man, who appeared to be a consigliere of sorts, bent over and whispered in Mikhailov's ear.

Luka listened and, after several moments of reflection, looked at Casey and said, "Tell me what you would like us to do."

CHAPTER 57

Rob Hutton had made sure the women had all the equipment they needed. He had also chosen quite an interesting delivery method. All they had needed to pick it up was a boat, which Luka Mikhailov had been more than happy to provide.

They piloted the vessel several miles out into the sea, where Casey used a flashlight to signal the aircraft Hutton had sent in. The gear was then thrown out the plane's door and dropped into the water a quarter of a mile away. The women fished the big, floating bag out of the sea and headed back to port.

Back in the hotel room, they sorted through the equipment and went over the details of the operation one final time.

According to the satellite imagery, the compound consisted of nine buildings. Neither Luka nor any of his men had ever been inside, so they couldn't provide any additional insight. The team would have to move fast.

Hutton had made their rules of engagement perfectly clear. Any and all persons encountered at the compound were to be considered hostile and the team was authorized to deal with them accordingly.

Their objective was also made perfectly clear. If the Kammler Device was anywhere in the compound, the United States wanted it. They also wanted any documentation, research, data, or personnel associated with it. If possible, they were to take the men known as Thomas Sanders and Armen Abressian alive. Finally, they were to secure the EMP bombs.

It was a tall order, not the kind of clear-cut, get-in-and-get-out assignments they liked to be given, but Athena was part of Delta, and this was the type of mission Delta was often given. If it was easy, the saying went, there'd be no need to give it to Delta.

Standing by, the team had two F-16 fighters from Aviano Air Base aloft over the Adriatic to lend support. As a last resort, Casey and Company were authorized to call in airstrikes to level the entire compound. Only the United States would be allowed to leave with the Kammler technology. Should the F-16s have to violate Croatian airspace and engage targets on Croatian soil, the Defense Department would figure out a way to pick up the diplomatic pieces later.

At 3:00 A.M., the Athena Team left their hotel and drove toward the tip of the Istrian peninsula.

In a copse of trees, just south of the compound, they hid the car and unpacked their gear.

It was a clear night with a bright moon. The women used camouflage paint sticks, or combat Maybelline, as they liked to call it, to mute their faces.

When they were all suited up and had checked

their radios and weapons, Casey gave the command for them to move out.

The team crept silently through the darkness and approached the compound from the southwest. It was perched on a high hill and they had picked the most difficult spot for their breach. The southern edge of the former monastery sat on a craggy, almost sheer rock face sixty feet high.

Because this side of the compound was so inaccessible, Hutton and the team back at Bragg believed that it would have the fewest security resources devoted to it. Because of its dramatic view, it was also where the monastery's church had been built. From the huge generators arrayed outside to the amount of activity they saw coming and going, it appeared to be the nexus of everything that was happening at the compound.

Cooper was the best climber on the team, so she was in charge of picking out the course they'd take up to the top. After identifying the easiest and fastest routes, she immediately discounted them. Had she been in charge of security for the compound, that's exactly where she would have planted intrusion sensors, or worse, antipersonnel devices.

Selecting her first handhold, she grasped a small outcropping of rock, dug her boot into a narrow fissure, and led her team toward their objective.

The women moved like demons in some medieval nightmare scaling a castle wall. Hand over hand they climbed, never slipping, never slowing down. While things often went bad in operations, sometimes they went well, and this was one of those times. It was as if they had climbed this piece of rock a thousand times before.

Though none of them was foolish enough to

jinx the operation by saying so, they all felt that it was a good indicator of how their assignment was going to go. That was until they had almost reached the top and they heard the explosion.

Luka Mikhailov and his men had jumped the gun.

CHAPTER 58

Dean Pence put his hand on his partner's shoulder. "Okay," he said. "Are you ready for this?"

Ben nodded. "Yeah, I'm ready."

"I'll see you up there, then."

Ben looked down at the map Vicki had drawn for him. He'd only been to Arapaho National Forrest a handful of times and definitely never to the area where she was leading him.

Shouldering his pack, he began walking. The fact that he wasn't looking forward to what was about to happen probably had a lot to do with his slower-than-normal pace.

He'd made the biggest mistake of his career, but now he was going to try to make it right. Once the arrest happened, he knew that what he had done might be used as a way to embarrass the FBI, but those chips would have to fall wherever they fell. He had an opportunity to do the right thing, the professional thing, and that was what he was going to do.

Focusing on the trail, Matthews kept climbing. He had resolved to get his act together once this case was over. Despite his mistakes, he saw himself as a decent person who deserved a shot at happiness in life. He just needed to find the right woman.

The idea of finding the right woman, though, made him think of Vicki Suffolk, and he forced the image from his head. Picturing her naked was not a good idea, not with what he was about to do.

He covered the rest of the distance by focusing on his graduation ceremony and how proud his parents had been when he had joined the FBI. When he saw the dilapidated cabin up ahead through the trees, he stepped off the trail, took a breath, and got himself ready.

This is it, he said as he adjusted his pack. He didn't want it to have come to this, but he knew there was nothing he could do about it. He was already committed.

Walking across the open space, over the carpet of pine needles, he arrived at the threshold of the cabin and pushed open the door. Vicki Suffolk was waiting for him.

She was sitting on a blanket in the middle of the room with a picnic laid out. The minute he saw her, he knew there was no turning back and his heart began to beat that much faster.

"You found me," she exclaimed, a smile spreading across her face.

"You led me right to you," he replied.

She looked at him as he held up the map.

Vicki laughed. "I'm glad to see you have no problem following directions. Did you bring back the listening devices?"

Ben pulled the three phones from the outer pocket of his backpack and walked them over to her. His assignment was almost complete.

"Are you hungry?" she asked.

"I'm sorry, Vicki. I didn't come for a picnic."

"Well, what did you come for then?" she asked, leaning back seductively on the blanket.

"Not that either," he replied. "I'm here to arrest you for espionage."

"Arrest me?" Victoria Suffolk said. "Ben, what are you talking about?"

"It's over, Vicki," he said, showing her his FBI credentials. "Get up."

"Ben, let's talk about this."

Matthews pulled out his Glock and pointed it at her. "Victoria Suffolk, you're under arrest."

The young FBI agent moved in to subdue her, and when he did, he was shot twice through the window with a suppressed weapon.

Vicki screamed as Matthews fell backward, both rounds having hit him square in the chest.

"You were supposed to kill him," said her handler as he stepped through the window into the cabin. "Not sleep with him once more for old times' sake."

"What are you doing here?" Vicki demanded.

"I knew you wouldn't be able to go through with it," he replied as he kicked Ben's gun to the side.

"You didn't even give me a chance."

"I saw all I needed to see," he said, gesturing to her picnic.

"Peter," she replied. "You're jealous."

"Shut up and help me drag him outside."

"I would think a big, strong Russian like you could handle something like this all by yourself."

He looked at her with contempt. "I'm not Russian, you idiot."

"But you told me—" she stammered.

"I told you what I needed to tell you to recruit you."

"So we're not working for the Russians?"

The man laughed. "No, we're not. Now help me carry him outside."

"Not until you tell me what this is all about," she insisted.

He shook his head. "We're working for a man named Armen Abressian."

"Who the hell is Armen Abressian?"

"He's the man who paid us to pinpoint something very special beneath Denver International Airport."

Suffolk fixed him with an icy glare. "Is your name even Peter Marcus?"

"No, it's not," said Ben as he suddenly rolled over and raised a second Glock that had been hidden beneath his shirt. "His name is Dean Pence."

The elder FBI agent had his pistol in his hand, but he didn't point it at Matthews. "Let me guess," he said. "You had a bulletproof vest in your backpack."

Ben tapped his chest and nodded. "And on top of everything else, you just added attempted murder of a federal officer."

Pence laughed. "Probably the least of my problems. How'd you know? How'd you figure it all out?"

"I didn't know anything," said Matthews. "At least not until I went to Mumford. That's when I learned that she had no idea what we were doing. You never spoke with her or anyone else at the Bureau."

His partner shook his head. "You're weak, Ben. You couldn't live with it, could you? You had to unburden yourself and admit your indiscretions."

"I had to do the right thing."

"Anybody else would have just enjoyed the sex and kept his mouth shut," said Pence. "You're a fool."

"Drop your weapon, Dean," Ben ordered.

"And then what? We rot in cells for the rest of our lives? Nobody's going to conduct an exchange for us. That's not how the people we work for operate. In fact, we'll probably be dead before any trial even starts."

"Don't be stupid, Dean. Drop your weapon," Matthews repeated.

"I'm sorry, Ben."

There was a flash of movement to Ben's left as Vicki Suffolk dove for her weapon. As she drew it, Matthews was left with no choice. He pulled his trigger twice and watched as she slumped over.

When he spun to re-engage Pence, the elder FBI agent had already reached the cabin door.

Ben heard Carole Mumford yell from outside for him to drop his weapon and then watched, with a twinge of regret, as Pence charged the heavily armed FBI team that was waiting for him and their bullets began to fly.

CHAPTER 59

G o, go, go," Casey ordered her teammates as the Russian mobsters began their attack on the front of the compound. All of the alarms and sensors were going off at this point. The hope was that the attack on the front of the compound was so intense that it would hold the focus of Abressian's men while the women carried out their assignment.

They climbed the rest of the rock and positioned themselves on an almost nonexistent piece of ledge.

"Megan, you're up," Casey said.

Rhodes removed a grappling hook and a length of rope from her pack. When she was ready, she swung the rope up and over the wall at a point where she believed it would catch. Pulling on it to make sure the hook had a good grab, she began to climb.

Once she was at the top of the wall, she looked

out over the pandemonium raging in the compound. Abressian's security team, dressed in military-style fatigues, were engaged in a heavy firefight with the Russians. Now was their chance.

Megan unslung the new LaRue OBR rifle she had been issued and signaled the others to come up. She kept each of them covered until they had climbed over the wall and down the other side. Once they were all inside the compound, it was time to move.

They hugged the wall and ran for cover. The sound of the gun battle raged, punctuated by the frequent detonation of grenades fired from launchers beneath the weapons of Mikhailov's as well as Abressian's men.

Following Casey, they broke for the church in a single-file stack. Casey watched for anything in front. Cooper and Ericsson handled their exposed left side, and Rhodes kept their backs, or their "six" as it was referred to, clear of any danger.

They pulled up short just before the church and pressed themselves against the wall. There were three guards crouched nearby. Casey signaled for Cooper and Ericsson to take them out. Alex and Julie broke off, their suppressed MP7 submachine guns up and at the ready.

Cooper took out the man nearest them while Ericsson quietly took out the other two. Once that was done, they rejoined the others.

The cords leading from the large generators into the church told them they were exactly where they needed to be.

"Everyone ready?" Casey whispered as they neared the doors. Rhodes, Ericsson, and Cooper all nodded.

"On three," said Gretchen. "One, two, three!"

She pulled open the doors and the team swept inside. They found themselves in the nave and immediately spread out and took cover.

At the very end of the building, where the altar should have been, was what looked like an enormous representation of the Greek symbol for Omega, Ω. It was at least twenty feet high and covered with runic symbols. It was humming and seemed to be pulsating.

"We need to shut that thing off," said Cooper. "Now."

Casey agreed. "You and Julie disable those generators, fast. Megan and I will handle this. Go."

Cooper and Ericsson snuck back outside, while Casey and Rhodes crept forward. They used the desks, computers, and other pieces of equipment as best they could for cover.

As they got closer, they could see three people frantically up to something at the front of the room. There was a man in his sixties with gray hair and a beard, flanked by two others—a man in a sport coat and another wearing blue jeans and a T-shirt. Next to them were stacked the EMP bombs from Bianchi's warehouse in Ljubljana. Casey and Rhodes knew they were looking at the Kammler Device and that the men in front of them were arming the EMP bombs to shove through. It was decision time.

Casey signaled to Megan to start shooting. Coming up from behind one of the desks, Casey got the man with the beard in her sights and was about to pull the trigger when the computer next to her exploded in a burst of gunfire.

She spun just as Megan Rhodes fired two shots

in quick succession. She couldn't tell where the shot at her had come from until she saw a head pop back up along with a weapon.

She got her MP7 up first and pulled the trigger, hitting the man with a three-round burst to the head. As he went down, she scanned for any other threats, but less than halfway through sweeping the room everything went dark. Cooper and Ericsson had made it to the generators and had cut the power.

Outside, the firefight continued to rage.

"I got two," said Rhodes. "The guy in the sport coat and the guy with the T-shirt."

"What about the guy with the beard?"

"I lost him when the lights went out."

Casey signaled for her to sweep up toward the altar area from the right side, while she took the left.

They moved slowly. The interior lights had been so bright, it was tough getting adjusted to the darkness. Shouts, gunfire, and the occasional explosion of a grenade continued from outside.

"They've seen us," Cooper said over the radio. "A bunch of security personnel have broken away from the front and we're starting to take heavy fire."

"Hold them off," Casey ordered, "and make sure no one leaves this building except us."

"Roger that," Cooper replied.

As the fighting intensified outside, Casey and Rhodes converged on the Kammler Device. Sure enough, just as Megan had said, she had nailed both the man in the T-shirt and the man in the sport coat. There was no sign of the man with the beard, though. Casey signaled to keep looking.

From behind the altar area she heard a sound

and quickly spun with her weapon. She thought she saw a flash of motion, but then it was gone.

Moving over to where it had been, she found that the wall behind the altar space was covered with wood paneling. She called Rhodes over to stand guard as she pushed against all of the panels. After a few moments of searching, she found one that gave beneath the pressure of her hand.

Popping it open, she discovered a stairwell and heard noises receding below. Transitioning to her pistol, Casey slung her MP7 and pulled out her flashlight. Rhodes did the same and followed right behind her.

The stone stairs curved down to the left. They seemed to go on forever.

Without warning, the stairs suddenly emptied into a small chamber. Even though the beam of Casey's light was focused downward, it still gave them away. The walls and ceiling sparked as bullets popped and zinged all around them. They retreated up several steps and then, pointing their weapons around the wall and into the chamber, began firing.

When they crept back down they found the body of another of Abressian's security personnel.

The chamber had a door at the end that had been left open. It led to a low tunnel and beyond that, the outdoors. They could see moonlight and thought they could hear the sea. There was also something else, the sound of a car being started. Casey and Rhodes both burst through the doorway and ran through the tunnel. Outside, they spotted a car quickly pulling away.

They emptied their pistol magazines and transitioned back to their primary weapons. Gretchen put a couple of rounds through the trunk and

Megan managed to take out the back window, but the vehicle kept moving. They were certain that the bearded man was in the car and that he had to be Armen Abressian.

Casey knew that Hutton and the team back at Bragg were watching the entire scenario unfold in real time via satellite. "We've got a vehicle at the bottom of the hill, southwest corner, fleeing the facility and heading east," said Casey.

"We see it," replied a voice over Casey's headset.

"Take it out," she ordered.

"Roger that. Engaging target," the voice radioed back.

Moments later there was a flash of light from out over the Adriatic as one of the F-16s from Aviano Air Force Base locked on the vehicle and fired.

No sooner had the car erupted than Casey and Rhodes were headed back toward the tunnel.

"We're coming back your way," Casey said over the radio to Cooper and Ericsson.

"Hurry up," Ericsson replied. "They've got a lot of firepower up here."

"We're on our way."

Casey and Rhodes ran down the tunnel and through the door into the chamber. As they ran up the stairs, they reloaded their weapons.

Bursting back into the church, they heard Cooper over the radio yell, "Grenade!" as the nave exploded.

Casey and Rhodes took cover behind the Kammler Device, narrowly escaping the force of the blast that tore through the church.

Even before the dust had settled, Gretchen tried to raise her colleagues, but they didn't answer. She and Rhodes ignored the gunfire pouring into the building and raced forward. They found Cooper and Ericsson behind an overturned desk.

Before any of the women could say anything, another grenade was loosed. This time it was Rhodes who yelled out the warning as she and Casey dove to cover their two teammates.

The grenade exploded with a deafening blast and tore a huge chunk from the facade only feet from where they lay.

"Let's get out of here," said Casey.

"There's too many of them," replied Ericsson.

"We're not going that way," said Rhodes as she helped Cooper to her feet.

Half-carrying their teammates, Casey and Rhodes moved as fast as they could to the back of the church. Bullets flew all around them.

They were only partway down the stairs when they heard the distant thump of another grenade detonating somewhere back outside in the compound.

The team made it to the chamber below, then through the tunnel and out into the countryside. As they retreated away from the facility, Casey pulled a flare from her vest and launched it high above the compound. It was the signal she and Luka Mikhailov had agreed upon. She hoped he saw it, because he and his men wouldn't have much time before fire fell from the sky.

Getting back on the radio, she informed Hutton and the rest of the team back at Bragg that they had found the EMP bombs and the Kammler Device. She then informed them that the compound was crawling with Abressian's people and requested a strafing run by the F-16s with their 20 mm Gatling-style cannons. "Rain it down," she said. "Smoke anything that moves. Blanket the entire compound."

CHAPTER 60

Thanks to Luka Mikhailov, it took the local authorities in Premantura two entire days to respond to complaints of an enormous gun battle at Armen Abressian's compound. When they arrived, they didn't find much.

There were bullet-scarred walls, signs of explosions, and even a few small fires still smoldering, but that was it. There wasn't a single corpse anywhere. In fact, there wasn't much of anything. It was as if the entire place had been cleaned out, which was exactly what had happened.

After the F-16s made two strafing runs, Casey and her team returned to the compound. While Mikhailov and his men secured the entrance, the women swept through, searching for any survivors. They found several, all scientists who had been working on the project and who had hidden themselves beneath their beds in the dormitory when the shooting and explosions had begun.

One of the scientists helped identify the bodies in the church as those of Thomas Sanders and the project's lead scientist, George Cahill. Casey put Cooper and Rhodes in charge of guarding the EMP bombs and the Kammler Device. They were now property of the United States government and no one was to be allowed anywhere near them.

The scientists, aware of how much trouble they were in, cooperated and helped Casey and Ericsson locate all of the remaining data and documentation on the Kammler project. They admitted to having been hired by Sanders and knowing who Abressian was, but knew very little beyond that. None of them had any clue who Abressian might have been working for or who had funded the entire project.

From his office in D.C., Jack Walsh had coordinated a convoy of civilian trucks at the Bosnian border in the hope that the Kammler Device might indeed be inside the compound. Once he received confirmation, he gave the order for them to roll. They arrived three hours later. A military team in civilian clothes photographed and videotaped everything. Then they dismantled and loaded all of it, including the Kammler Device, into the trucks.

They took the scientists as well, and a final truck even collected the bodies of Abressian's security detail. There had likely been some wounded security personnel at some point, but between the F-16s and Mikhailov's revenge-fueled men, who had swept back into the compound, none of them would have stood a chance.

As quickly and as efficiently as the trucks and their teams had arrived, they departed. Casey,

Cooper, Ericsson, and Rhodes slipped off into the night and disappeared as well.

The Department of Defense launched a full investigation into two U.S. F-16s on a training mission that had accidentally strayed into Croatian airspace and launched a single Hellfire missile. They apologized and promised that both flight crews would be punished severely.

In a small office back at Aviano, the crews of the F-16s were ordered to sign a series of top-secret nondisclosure documents and were all quietly promoted.

The CIA continued its investigation into Armen Abressian. Jack Walsh, though, received a surprising phone call from his colleague at the FBI, the same man who only days before had admitted to never having heard the name Armen Abressian before.

He informed Walsh about Ben Matthews, Dean Pence, and a woman named Victoria Suffolk. Pence, who had claimed to be working for Abressian, had been shot and killed by FBI agents as he raised his weapon to fire at them. Suffolk had also been shot, but she was expected to recover. The Bureau had already begun questioning her, but it appeared she knew nothing about Abressian. She believed she had been spying for the Russians.

Walsh had thanked his colleague and had asked him to keep him up to speed on whatever else the FBI learned. He also asked if Leslie Paxton and DARPA could have a look at the devices Suffolk wanted Ben Matthews to plant beneath Denver International. The FBI man agreed and said, "Are you going to tell me what the hell is going on beneath that airport, Jack?"

Walsh chuckled and told him that he had no idea, that it was too far above his pay grade. The FBI man doubted that, but he didn't press for further details.

Once the Kammler Device had been secured, Leslie Paxton assembled a team and flew to Tuzla to examine it and debrief the scientists who had been apprehended. They seemed to have no idea of the scope of the research and development projects going on beneath Denver International Airport. All they knew was that based on his research, Professor Cahill believed that once he was able to get the Kammler Device functional, the United States had a device at DIA that could track and neutralize it. Therefore, they had intended to strike first.

Jack Walsh realized how lucky they had been. Had Pence and Suffolk been able to deliver targeting coordinates to Abressian, and had he managed to transmit even one of those EMP devices into the facility beneath Denver International Airport, it would have had immeasurable consequences for America's high-tech weapons program. What's more, there was no reason to believe that Abressian would have stopped there. It very likely would have been only the beginning. Those bombs and others would have begun appearing and detonating all across the United States.

Walsh hoped that with the strike on Abressian's car in Croatia, his organization would be severely diminished, if not completely decapitated. The two questions he was unfortunately not going to get answered, with Abressian dead, were who he and his people had been working for, and how they had discovered the location of the Kammler facility in the first place.

While Jack didn't know if it would produce any further intelligence, he had okayed Tracy Hastings to remain in Paraguay with Ryan Naylor. Naylor wanted to visit the present-day Nueva Germania colony to see what he could learn, and Tracy would be posing as his wife. The hope was that the colony women might be more comfortable chatting with another woman.

Rob Hutton discussed all of this information with his team over dinner at McKellar's Lodge at Fort Bragg.

"What happened to Bianchi?" asked Ericsson as she cut another piece of steak. "We didn't really make a deal with him, did we?"

"He's still being debriefed."

"It's *debriefed* now, not *interrogated*?" commented Rhodes. "So we have made a deal with him."

"Like I said, he's still being debriefed."

Cooper picked up the bottle of wine and topped off their wineglasses. "Which probably means Harvath has handed him over to someone else."

Megan winked at Casey and then asked Hutton. "Yeah, where is Harvath now?"

"Well, that's another thing we need to talk about. Something else has come up. There's this island we've been hearing about near Burma—"

Gretchen raised her hand and put it almost right in Hutton's face. "No way, Rob. No way," she said. "The ghost of Armen Abressian could walk through that door right now and the only thing I'd want to know is what's for dessert. So whatever you have, save it. My team and I are off the clock for a little while."

"Amen," said Rhodes, raising her glass.

"I'll second that," replied Ericsson.

"Me too," threw in Cooper as she lifted her glass.

Casey joined them and said, "To the smartest, best-looking, hardest-working warriors I know."

They all clinked glasses.

Casey then looked at their commanding officer and added, "And also to Rob."

"And also to Rob," they all agreed.

A silence fell over the table as they drank. Hutton was the first to break it. "You know there is one thing I need to ask," he said.

They all looked at him. "Why has John Vlcek been calling me and leaving me six messages a day asking about Megan?"

The women laughed.

"Are you making fun of my man?" Rhodes joked. "'Cause we can take it outside right now, Rob. You say they word and it's go time."

Rob smiled. "You all did a really good job. I'm very proud of you."

They smiled in return and thanked him for the compliment.

"That said," he continued, "I really want to talk to you about Burma."

"Why, Rob? What's so important about Burma?" asked Casey.

Hutton set down his wineglass. "We think we have a lead on a group called the Amalgam. We think that might be who Abressian was working for."

Casey took the wine bottle from Cooper and filled Hutton's glass right to the rim.

"Are you trying to get me drunk?" he asked.

Gretchen smiled, "If that's what it'll take to get you to give my girls a rest, then you'd better hand over your car keys now."

Hutton relented. "All right, we don't have to talk about this tonight. We can discuss it tomorrow."

"Not too early, though," replied Rhodes as she jabbed Ericsson and pointed at the bar.

"Why not?" asked Rob.

"Because Cooper may have a very late night tonight," stated Ericsson.

Alex looked up at one of the men who had entered.

"Let me guess," said Hutton. "Mr. Right has just walked in."

Cooper took a big sip of wine and stood. "I don't know about Mr. Right, but he definitely looks like he could be Mr. Right Now."

Hutton shook his head and the ladies cheered for Alex as she squared her shoulders, put a smile on her face, and made a beeline for the bar.

AUTHOR'S NOTE

As a thriller author, I try to stay three steps ahead of the headlines. To do this, I strive to base my plots on cutting-edge technology, weapons, tactics, and real-world events. There is a certain amount of reading tea leaves that goes into planning the novels, as well as my gut instinct as to where I think the world is headed. Often, topics just resonate with me.

I have wanted to write a novel involving quantum teleportation ever since I first read about scientists in Vienna successfully transporting photons across the Danube River. As global military interest in quantum teleportation began to pick up, I felt that the thriller world was ready for this kind of novel. I also had a sense that this amazing technology was about to take a huge leap forward.

Within weeks of *The Athena Project*'s publication, that's exactly what happened. *Science* magazine dubbed the first ever "quantum machine," the scientific "Breakthrough of the Year." So significant was the development that it beat out groundbreaking advancements in molecular dynamics, RNA programming, and next-generation genomics.

As we all know, truth can be stranger than fiction, but the difference between fiction and reality (as Mark Twain so aptly put it) is that we expect fiction to make sense. I believe quantum teleportation will continue to be one of the most exciting areas of scientific exploration. And while we may not be at the level described within *The Athena Project* yet, based upon how rapidly the field is advancing, I anticipate that we're going to get there a lot sooner than most people think.

ACKNOWLEDGMENTS

I introduced the Athena Team in my thriller *Foreign Influence* and am very happy to have given these incredible women their own book. As with all of my novels, I would not be able to do what I do without the generous support of many people.

I want to thank my good friends **Barrett Moore, Ronald Moore** (no relation to Barrett), **Scott F. Hill, PhD, James Ryan, Rodney Cox, Cynthia Longo, Jeff Chudwin, Mitch Shore, Frank Gallagher, Steven Bronson, Gary Penrith, Chuck Fretwell,** and **Steve Hoffa** for all their help.

I also wish to thank my terrific **readers** and all the wonderful **booksellers** who have helped introduce so many people to my work. My thanks as well go out to the fantastic **moderators** and **members** of the BradThor.com forum.

At Simon & Schuster, there are many extraordinary people to thank: my editor, **Emily Bestler;** my publishers, **Judith Curr, Louise Burke,** and **Carolyn Reidy;** my publicist, **David Brown;** the **Atria/Pocket sales staff, art** and **production** departments; the **audio division;** as well as **Michael Selleck, Kate Cetrulo, Sarah Branham, Irene Lipsky, Cristina Suarez, Mellony Torres,** and **Lisa Keim.**

I also wish to thank my incomparable literary agent, **Heide Lange,** of Sanford J. Greenburger Associates, Inc. as well as the exceptional **Jennifer Linnan** and **Rachael Dillon Fried.**

My thanks as well go to my outstanding attorney and good friend, **Scott Schwimer.**

Last, but not least, I want to thank my beautiful wife, **Trish.** She was not only my inspiration for this book, she is the inspiration for everything else I do. Each of the Athena Team members has a little something special from her. Thank you, honey. I love you.

Atria Books

Proudly Presents

FULL BLACK

The next thrilling novel

by Brad Thor

Available in hardcover

In the clandestine community, the most sensitive classified assignments are referred to as *black operations*.

Few suspect, and even fewer realize, that there is a darker side to black operations. These missions are born in the shadows. They are not classified or recognized. They simply don't exist.

They are Full Black.

CHAPTER 1

His timing had been perfect. Swerving back into the lane at the last possible second, he watched in his rearview mirror as the white Škoda behind him careened off the road and slammed into a large tree.

Applying his brakes, he pulled off the road and stepped out of his vehicle. The air smelled of spruce and spilled gasoline. The woman from the passenger side joined him. They had to move fast.

Half their work had already been done for them. The terrorist in the Škoda's passenger seat had not been wearing his seat belt. He was already dead.

The driver was trying to unbuckle himself when Scot Harvath arrived at his window. He was cursing at him in Arabic from inside. Harvath removed a spark plug, often referred to as a *ghetto glassbreaker*, from his pocket and used it to smash the window.

Grasping the terrorist's head, Harvath gave a sharp twist and broke his neck. Gently, he guided the dead driver's chin down to his chest.

The final passenger was a young Muslim man seated in the back of the car who was screaming. As Riley Turner opened his door she could see he had wet himself. Painting his chest with the integrated laser sight of her Taser, she pulled the trigger.

The compressed nitrogen propulsion system ejected two barbed probes and embedded them in the young man's flesh. The insulated wires leading back to the weapon delivered a crackling pulse of electricity that incapacitated his neuromuscular capability.

Yanking open the opposite door, Harvath carefully avoided the probes as he pulled the man from the vehicle and laid him on the ground. Once the man's hands were FlexCuff'd behind his back, Harvath removed a roll of duct tape and slapped a piece over his mouth. Producing a pair of pliers, he yanked out the probes. The man winced and emitted a cry of pain from behind his gag. As he did, Harvath looked up and saw a familiar pearl-gray Opel minivan approaching.

The van pulled parallel with the crash scene and slowed to a stop. The sliding door opened and a man in his midtwenties, holding a shopping bag, stepped out into a puddle of radiator fluid and broken glass.

The young operative's name was Sean Chase,

and while he wasn't a perfect match, he was the best they had.

Chase was the product of an American father and an Egyptian mother. His features were such that Arabs saw him as Arab and Westerners often took him for one of their own. The question was, would the members of the Uppsala cell accept him?

He was intended to be Harvath's ultimate listening device and was going to switch places with the young Muslim from the backseat of the Škoda, Mansoor Aleem.

Mansoor and the Uppsala cell were the only link the United States had to a string of terrorist attacks that had targeted Americans in Europe and the United States. And as bloody as those attacks had been, they were supposedly nothing compared to what intelligence reported the plotters were about to unleash.

Subbing Chase for Mansoor was the most crucial and the most dangerous part of the assignment. According to their limited intelligence, only two Uppsala cell members had ever met Mansoor before and actually knew what he looked like. The men were friends of his uncle, a terrorist commander by the name of Aazim Aleem.

The men had been dispatched to Arlanda airport in Stockholm to collect Mansoor and return him to the cell's safe house two hours north. Thanks to Harvath, they were now both dead.

The team had had the men under surveillance since they had arrived at the airport. The driver had made only one phone call after they had picked up Mansoor and left the airport. Harvath felt confident the call had been to the cell in Uppsala confirming the pickup.

Harvath now pulled the young Muslim to his feet and pushed him up against the van. Drawing his Glock pistol, he placed it under the man's chin and pulled the tape from over his mouth. "You saw what I did to your friends?"

Mansoor Aleem was trembling. Slowly, he nodded.

While his uncle was a very, very bad guy, as were the two dead men slumped in the Škoda, Mansoor was on the cyber side of the jihad and hadn't experienced violence or dead bodies firsthand. That didn't mean he wasn't just as guilty as jihadis who pulled triggers, planted bombs, or blew themselves up. He was guilty as hell. He was also a potential treasure trove of information, having run a lot of his uncle's cyber operations. Harvath had no doubt the United States would be able to extract a ton from him. But first, he wanted to be as sure as he could be that he wasn't sending Chase into a trap.

"We know all about the Uppsala cell," said Harvath. "We want you to take us to them."

Mansoor stammered, trying to find his words. "I, I can't."

"What do you mean, you can't?" Harvath demanded.

"I don't know them."

Harvath jabbed the muzzle of his weapon further up into the soft tissue under the man's chin. Mansoor's eyes began to water. "Don't bullshit me, Mansoor. We know everything you're up to."

"But I don't know anything," he said emphatically. "Honestly. I was just supposed to get on the plane. That's all. That's why they picked me up at the airport. I don't know where they were taking me."

Harvath studied the man's face. He was looking for microexpressions, *tells* people often radiate when lying or under stress from an act they are about to commit.

As far as Harvath could surmise, the man wasn't lying. "I want a list of all the cell members. Right now."

"I don't know who you're talking about."

Harvath pushed the gun up harder, causing Mansoor more pain.

"I only knew the two men in the car," he said as his eyes drifted toward the wreck.

"You're lying to me," said Harvath.

"I'm *not* lying to you."

"Describe the other cell members to me. Their ages, backgrounds, I want all of it."

"I don't know!" Mansoor insisted. "You keep asking me questions I can't answer! The only two people I know in this entire country are dead! You killed them!"

With so little time, that was as good as Harvath was going to get. Patting Mansoor down, he located his wallet and tossed it to Chase. He then went through his pockets and removed everything else.

Chase already had a U.K. passport with his picture issued in Mansoor's name. He also had a driving permit, ATM card, two credit cards, and a host of other pocket litter that would make him even more believable.

Chase fished through the handful of items Harvath had taken from his prisoner and pocketed a boarding pass, a London Tube card, and Mansoor's house keys.

Opening the Škoda's trunk, the young operator sifted through Mansoor's suitcase and quickly studied the contents as he replaced the clothing with his own. Knowing everything the cyberjihadist had packed would give him more insight into the identity he was about to assume.

When he was done, he zipped up the case, removed it from the trunk, and closed the lid. Looking at Riley Turner, he said, "Let's get this over with."

Turner approached and unrolled a small surgical kit. She was in her midthirties, tall, fit, and very attractive. Her reddish-brown hair was pulled back in a ponytail. She had blue eyes and a wide, full mouth. Removing a syringe, she began to prep an anesthetic.

Chase shook his head. "I appreciate the thought, but I'll pass on the Botox."

"It's your call," she replied, gesturing for him to sit down on the backseat. "This is going to hurt, though."

The young intelligence operative winked at her. "I can take it."

She swept back his dark hair and abraded his forehead with a piece of sandpaper. To his credit, he sat there stoically, but that was the easy part. Next, Turner removed her scalpel. Placing it at his hairline, she dug in and cut a short, craggy line.

Chase sucked air through his clenched teeth as the blood began to flow down his forehead and into his eyes.

Turner handed him a handkerchief.

"God, that hurts," he said.

"I warned you."

Having secured Mansoor in the van, Harvath now rejoined them. Bending down, he gathered up a handful of broken glass and handed it to Turner, who sprinkled pieces into Chase's hair, as well as the folds of his clothing.

Harvath searched the dead men and recovered their cell phones. After cloning their SIM cards, he reassembled the driver's phone and tossed it to Chase, saying, "Showtime."

CHAPTER 2

Mustafa Karami had not been expecting another call, especially one from Waqar. Waqar was supposed to be driving. *Nafees was to send a text message when they got close to Uppsala.* Something must have gone wrong. Karami answered his phone with trepidation.

"Please, you must help me," said a distraught voice.

"Who is this?"

"Mansoor."

"Why are you calling from this number?"

"There's been an accident. I don't know what to do."

Karami was a thin, middle-aged man with a wispy gray beard. He had been extremely sick as a child growing up in Yemen and had almost died. The sickness had affected his physical development. He appeared frail and much older than he actually was.

Despite his physical limitations his mind was incredibly sharp. He was well suited to the role he had been assigned. Nothing escaped his flinty gaze or his keen intellect.

Having been brutally tortured as a young man by the Yemeni government, he had learned the hard way to place operational security above all else. He didn't like speaking on cell phones. "Where are your traveling companions?"

"I think they're both dead."

"*Dead?*" Karami demanded.

"A car swerved and we hit a tree."

"What kind of car?"

"I don't know. Who cares what kind of car? *Waqar and Nafees are dead.*"

The young man was borderline hysterical. Karami tried to calm him down. "Are you injured?" he asked calmly.

"No. I mean, I don't know. I hit my head. There's some blood."

Karami needed to bring him in. "Is the vehicle operable?"

"No," replied the young man.

"Were there any witnesses? Have the police been called?"

"I don't know."

"Where are you?"

"I don't know that either. What am I supposed to do? Are you going to come get me or not?"

Karami forgave the boy his insolence. He was scared and very likely in shock. "Tell me what you see around you, so I can discern where you are."

Chase rattled off a few of the landmarks nearby.

"Okay," Karami replied as he removed a map from his desk. "That's good. I believe I know where you are. I will send two of the brothers to pick you up. There's a village less than three kilometers up the road. As you enter it, you'll see a grocery market on your left. Beyond that is a soccer pitch. Wait there and the brothers will come for you."

"Praise be to Allah," said Chase.

Karami gave him a list of things he wanted him to do and then ended the call.

Turning to two of his men, Karami relayed what had happened and dispatched them to pick up the young computer wizard.

When the men had gone, Karami turned to his most devoted acolyte, Sabah. Sabah was a large, battle-hardened Palestinian. In his previous life, before becoming a mujahideen, he had been a corrupt police officer in the West Bank town of Ramallah.

"I want you to find this accident, Sabah, and I want you to make sure that it was in fact an accident. Do you understand?"

Sabah nodded.

"Good," Karami said in response. "Whatever you learn, you tell no one but me. Understood?"

Once again, Sabah nodded.

"We cannot afford accidents. Not with everything that has happened. We can only trust each other. No one else." With a wave of his hand, Karami ordered him out. "Go."

He was paranoid, but he had cause. So many of their plans had been undone that Mustafa Karami was suspicious of everything and *everyone*.

He hoped that Sabah would be able to get to the bottom of it. It was a small country road, after all, and not very often traveled. Karami had selected the route himself. If the accident scene was undisturbed, Sabah would be able to ascertain what had happened. If the police or bystanders were already there, there would be nothing he could do.

If that was the case, Karami would have to conduct his own investigation. It would begin with Mansoor Aleem himself. Until he was satisfied, he could not risk trusting even the nephew of a great man like Aazim Aleem. Anyone could be corrupted. Anyone could be gotten to.

Fulfilling their final obligation was all that mattered now. Karami had sworn an oath. He would stick to that oath and he would not allow anything or anyone to get in his way.

He was reflecting on whether it was a good idea to bring Mansoor to the actual safe house or find somewhere else for him to remain temporarily when the Skype icon on his laptop bounced.

He had been sent a message from the man whom he served—the Sheikh from Qatar.

Everything is in place? asked the Sheikh.

Everything is in place, typed Karami.

Stay ready, replied the Sheikh. **God willing, you will be called to move soon.** And with that, the Sheikh was gone. Karami refocused his mind on Mansoor. For the time being, he would have to be kept elsewhere, away from the safe house and the rest of the cell. There was too much at stake.

The man who called himself "Sheikh from Qatar" closed his laptop with his liver-spotted hands and looked out the window of his cavernous apartment. He had quite literally a thirty-million-dollar view of the Manhattan skyline. It was stunning. Even at this predawn hour.

He had always made it a policy to be up before the markets. Despite his advancing age, he found he needed less sleep, not more.

As he privately swilled astronomically expensive vitamin cocktails and fed on exotic hormone and stem cell injections, he publicly told people he'd had abundant reserves of energy ever since he was a boy and credited genetics and his impeccable constitution as the source of his vigor.

Such was the Janus-faced character of James Standing. Even his name was a lie.

Born Lev Bronstein to Romanian Jewish parents, he was sent from Europe to live with relatives in Argentina at the outset of World War II. His parents remained behind, tending their business and hoping things would get better. They never made it out of the death camps.

At thirteen, he ran away from his Argentinean relatives, renounced his Judaism, and changed his name to José Belmonte—an amalgamation of the names of two world-famous Spanish bullfighters at the time—José Gomez Ortega and Juan Belmonte Garcia.

The newly minted Belmonte found his way to Buenos Aires, where he took a job as a bellboy in a high-end hotel. Thanks to his drive and proficiency for languages, he started filling in on the switchboard at night, eventually moving into the position full-time. It was at this point that he began to build his fortune.

Belmonte, née Bronstein, listened in on all of the hotel's telephone conversations, especially those of its wealthy guests. At fifteen, he entered the stock market. By eighteen, he was perfecting his English, and at twenty, he had changed his name yet again and moved to America.

Standing had been the name of a handsome American guest with a gorgeous, buxom, blond American wife who visited the hotel in Buenos Aires every winter. To Belmonte, they looked like movie stars and represented everything he felt the world owed him. Using the first name of one of his favorite American writers, James Fenimore Cooper, he adopted the Standing name as his surname and James Standing was born.

He emigrated to America, where he parlayed his substantial savings and penchant for trading on insider information into one of the greatest financial empires the world had ever seen.

Now, from his gilded perch overlooking the capital of world finance, he read all of the papers every morning before most of the city was even awake.

Regardless of his morning ritual, he would have been up early today anyway. In fact, he hadn't been able to sleep very well. He was waiting for an important phone call.

Someone, to put it in vulgar street terminology, had fucked with the wrong guy. That "wrong guy" being James Standing. And the someone who had fucked with the wrong guy was about to be taught a very painful and very *permanent* lesson.

In fact, it would be the ultimate lesson and would stand as a subtle reminder to the rest of his enemies that there were certain people who were not to be crossed. Not that Standing would take credit for what was going to happen. That would be incredibly foolish. Better to simply let people assume. The mystery of whether he'd been involved or not would only add to the aura of his considerable power.

Though he'd gotten to where he was by breaking all of the rules, he still needed to appear to be playing by them—at least for a little while longer.

Soon, though, like an old hotel on the Las Vegas strip, America was going to be brought down in a controlled demolition. And when that happened, the rules would no longer apply to James Standing.